Dr Fred Lockwood is Emeritus Professor of Learning and Teaching, Manchester Metropolitan University, UK. He is also a PADI Master Scuba Diver.

His career in higher education involved consultancies within over 100 universities in more than thirty countries. Fred has travelled extensively and dived in the waters of Central America and Africa, the Middle East and South East Asia, Australasia and the Pacific Islands.

Once a keen runner and squash player he is now an equally keen cyclist, walker and skier. He lives in a small village in Northamptonshire with his wife Beryl.

Author's Note

As you start to read this novel you will immediately notice something is different; the text is "left-aligned" rather than "justified".

The print layout for the majority of novels is justified. This is where the line of text starts precisely at the left hand margin and ends precisely at the right hand margin. Justified text stretches and compresses the normal spacing within and between words so they fit on a line of specific length. You will have noticed this when some lines in a novel are severely compressed and others have words with an odd spacing of letters. There are many who believe that justified text looks professional or neater than left-aligned text. However, research evidence reveals justified text is more difficult to read! This is because as we develop as readers we recognise and read clusters of letters and shapes of words rather than individual letters and words. In this book there are more than 80,000 words – that's a lot of reading.

I am extremely grateful to Pegasus Elliot MacKenzie Publishers Ltd. for agreeing, as an experiment, to adopt a left-aligned format for this book. I do hope you enjoy Total Loss and find it easy to read.

Dr Fred Lockwood

Total Loss

Fred Lockwood

Total Loss

Vanguard Press

VANGUARD PAPERBACK

A CIP catalogue record for this title is
available from the British Library.

ISBN 978 178465 102 2

Total Loss is a work of fiction. The names and characters, organisations and
businesses, places, events and incidents are either the products of the author's
imagination or used in a fictitious manner. Any resemblance to actual persons,
living or dead, or actual events is purely coincidental.

Vanguard Press is an imprint of
Pegasus Elliot MacKenzie Publishers Ltd.
www.pegasuspublishers.com

First Published in 2016

Vanguard Press
Sheraton House Castle Park
Cambridge England

Printed & Bound in Great Britain

Acknowledgements

My thanks to Andy Hillier, PADI Master Instructor, for his help and advice on diving questions. Andy made me a better and safer diver.

Contents

Section 1

Jack Collier: Partner in the
Marine Salvage & Investigation Company

Chapter 1

Situation out of control

What was he going to do?

Jack was sat, slumped on the dirty, oily deck of the barge alongside Sandro, his joint partner and only other employee in their fledgling *Marine Salvage & Investigation Company*. Alongside Sandro were Penny, a junior HM Border Force Officer and next to her was Kev, Jack's former Dive Master and friend. In the hot Kenyan sun, with no shade, Jack was hot, sweaty, bruised, thirsty and miserable – and had a headache. Most likely he was going to get even hotter, sweatier, more bruised, thirstier and even more miserable! The top of his back, near the shoulder, ached where a rifle butt had clubbed him to the ground. Stunned he was unable to cushion his fall and had banged his forehead on the concrete pier. The bleeding had stopped but he could feel the bump. Still, it could be worse; he could have ended up dead like the dive boat crew! He lowered his head onto his knees and tried to think – but the smell of spilt diesel, and the sticky layer he was sat in, was overpowering. It was almost as strong as the stench from the remains of rotting fish on the hot concrete dockside and open sewer that flowed along a crude channel and dropped into the water next to the barge. He tried to concentrate but couldn't. Perhaps he was slightly concussed or dehydrated; he couldn't remember when he last had a drink and it was hot. Like a confused dream his thoughts drifted through unconnected images. Thoughts drifted back to his father, to teaming up with Sandro, setting up their *Marine Salvage & Investigation Company*, and embarking on this wreck inspection.

His father, John, had been a keen scuba diver and had encouraged him to learn to dive as a teenager. He enjoyed it and was good at it. He was better than his dad. He was soon supplementing his pocket money by doing small diving jobs at the local marina. It seemed there was no end to the number of outboard motors being dropped to the bottom of the marina. There were bottom scrapes to photograph and damaged propellers to inspect or to cut free from lengths of rope. It was his first outboard motor retrieval that taught him a lot. The owner of a gleaming fifteen metre sailing boat had moored outside the marina, off a marked buoy, and found the outboard simply too heavy as he lifted it off the rail to transfer it to the zodiac. The outboard motor disappeared over the side with a single "plop"! Jack had agreed to retrieve it, but never asked how much it was worth to do so. He remembered buzzing out to the sailboat on a little inflatable, tying up, and in his wetsuit, tank, fins and mask diving the ten metres to the seabed with a length of rope. Even though the visibility had been poor it was pretty easy to locate the outboard, attach the rope and let them haul it on board. It was after he had stripped off his gear, and as he was manoeuvring the inflatable to the side of the sailboat that the north countryman merely shouted his thanks, never offered to pay him, and started to disengage from the mooring buoy. It was a valuable lesson. From then on he was aware his time and effort was worthy of payment.

Jack's thoughts suddenly switched to the present. "How could I have been so stupid not to have taken precautions," Jack chastised himself. "I was told to be careful." But almost immediately other images and recollections intervened.

Long ago Jack had realised that he was nothing special, that he wasn't particularly talented. However, he would acknowledge that whatever talent he possessed he made the most of it. Jack simply "put the hours in" and worked at it, like diving.

At school he had drifted through most of his school work and was "middle of the road". Occasionally some subject or topic would capture his interest and he would not be satisfied until he had understood or exhausted that particular interest. In truth he knew he was not top stream. In fact when he was about seventeen years old, in the Lower Sixth, it was touch and go whether he would go to university or get a job. His grades in many of the subjects were borderline between pass and fail. However, with a sickening jolt he recalled the month of August 2008 when everything changed and he grew up very quickly. One summer weekend he was a bored teenager, watching daytime TV, putting off the school projects and hoping he'd get a call from the marina to do some diving work. The next, his life was turned upside down as Constable Williams rang the doorbell and told him the devastating news that his mother and father had been killed on the M6 that morning. He felt the same sickness now as he had then.

The policeman had told him that a Romanian truck driver, who had driven non-stop from Bucharest, had apparently fallen asleep at the wheel, driven through the central reservation and straight over his mum and dad's car. It had been instantaneous. He later discovered that the family Ford hatchback had been unrecognisable and it had fallen to Uncle Charlie, John Collier's brother, to identify the remains. It was something that Jack was spared. However, the upheaval over that summer had been profound. It seemed that overnight he had grown up. Whereas he hadn't been particularly interested in what he might do after leaving school, let alone a career, now it was at the forefront of his mind. He'd never thought of where the money for food and the Sky TV subscription came from, nor how much electricity he used or how much the phone cost. His mum had given him a small allowance, which was really spending money, because she either bought his clothes or gave him money to buy them. Suddenly, he recalled, it was scary. How does it all work? Would he have to leave the house?

A faint smile touched his dry, gummy mouth as he thought of Uncle Charlie and Aunt Doreen. The pain in his head was now a dull ache rather than sharp and throbbing.

Uncle Charlie and Aunt Doreen had been good to him. They were supportive and encouraging but not pushy. They had included him in decisions even though he had no real idea of what to do. Together they had organised the church service and later the sale of the house. Charlie and Doreen made their spare room available to him and made it clear there was always a place for him in their home; he was always welcome. Jack was still grateful for this kindness but the experience had a profound effect on him; almost overnight he had been transformed. Jack had suddenly buckled down to his school work with every intention of following in the footsteps of his father and becoming a Marine Engineer. He knew there was no way he could catch up on

22

all the work he had missed or ambled through in the previous school year. He didn't do brilliantly in the exams but just well enough to get a place at the University of Portsmouth on their Marine Engineering degree course.

Even in the first few weeks of the course it was clear he wasn't the brightest in his group. However, he resolved to be the hardest working. As the others headed off in the evening to the town bars, and impromptu parties, he studied. At the weekends, when the others went home, played sport, stayed out all night he was diving with the local diving club or doing diving chores at the local marinas. At the time he hadn't realised, but later he was told, that he became almost invisible to his fellow students but was identified as having potential amongst his tutors and a growing figure in the diving community.

As the heat and stench wafted over him his mind flicked to his graduation day, Charlie and Doreen sitting so proudly in the audience and, somewhat surprisingly, an offer of a place on a Masters Degree in the Department. His mind flicked again to the Dive Club and the much more modest celebrations as he progressed to Technical Diver, PADI Diving Instructor and Dive Master.

Chapter 2

Sandro – A buddy above and below water

Jack stirred, lifted his head and glanced at Sandro who was sat next to him on the barge. Sandro looked as though he was sleeping but the act of moving his head had been at a cost. It caused a sudden, sharp pain behind his forehead. Jack tried to relax and remembered that it was during the first week of the Masters course that he met Sandro, or rather Alexsandro Marcus Calovarlo, for the first time. Jack had slipped into the seminar room unnoticed and was making his way towards the chairs. He and Sandro were attending the first in a series of seminars on Engineering Design leading to the calculation of stresses in hull structures. Sandro was stood chatting to a small group of fellow students but had stood out. He wasn't particularly tall, under six feet, but well proportioned. Jack's first impression was of Michelangelo's David. It was that confident, slightly effeminate stance, plus slightly too long and curly jet black hair and deep olive tan. Almost as soon as Jack had noticed him someone in the group must have mentioned that Jack had arrived. Immediately Sandro had turned around, displayed a big open smile and perfect white teeth, stepped away from the group of students and held out a hand.

Even now Jack could remember what Sandro had said. 'Bon journo, just the man I wanted to meet. They tell me you are the smartest man in the group and the best diver in the university. Will you teach me to dive?'

His openness had been disarming. He just seemed so sincere and genuine. It was the start of a close friendship that included them acting as buddies both underwater and above it.

The headache was no better and he had a raging thirst as the sun continued to beat down. He wondered if he and Sandro would be able to extricate themselves from this nightmare before his thoughts returned to their time at the university.

The post graduate course had flown by. A mixture of lectures and seminars, simulations and projects during the week and diving at the weekends kept them both busy. Jack admitted to himself that Sandro was a natural when it came to diving but he didn't like the cold British water! In record time, but with one to one coaching and the reading of lots of manuals, Sandro became a Technical Diver, an instructor and Dive Master just like Jack. However, on Saturday and Sunday nights, when Jack returned to his dissertation, Sandro was out on the town. Sandro liked girls and the girls liked him. They liked roaring around town and the countryside in his old style red Alfa Romeo Spider. They liked his Italian accent, his flair and that he seemed thrilled to be in their company. He made them feel special.

Jack's memories suddenly switched to a lunch time towards the end of the course when he and Sandro were working on a test case they had been given in preparation for the final exam. The scenario was of a mythical crude oil tanker that had run aground on a sandbank off the Irish coast. Their task was to attempt salvage. He recalled having a marine chart of the area on the table, notes of prevailing currents, and heights of tides, pump rates etc. He was busily calculating the position and size of air bags that might be able to raise the keel sufficiently for it to float off on the high tide – assuming massive orbital pumps could transfer thousands of tonnes of crude oil from the stricken ship to another. He had looked up to see Sandro sat back in his chair with a serious expression on his face. Odd because Sandro was seldom serious. Jack challenged in, 'What's the problem?' as he dropped the pencil onto the pad and sat back. 'Have you got a better idea?'

Sandro had paused and said. 'No, I agree, you are very, how do you say, thorough. If we assume a soft grounding on a level sandbank then the calculations show that the hull should be able to withstand the additional strain, especially if we reduce the load by twenty-five per cent. If we can get the lifting bags in place before the high tide, and have two tugs in assistance I think there is every chance we could refloat her before she settles. I can't see any flaws in your strategy.' Sandro paused again as he formulated his next comment.

'So what's the problem?' Jack repeated, somewhat irritated by the tone and unease he had detected.

After a longer than expected pause Sandro spoke. 'No problem, but I've been thinking. Why don't we set up our own Marine Salvage and Investigation Company instead of working for somebody else?'

Even now, feeling as wretched as he did, Jack felt the same reaction he had then. He had been stunned. He had only just come to terms with the idea of having to apply for jobs and wondering where to start. He had heard that one or two of the others on the course had already secured jobs, assuming they got their Masters Degree. Obviously Sandro had given it some thought and went on to describe how his father and friends were often approached about salvage work and underwater inspections but didn't have the skills. If his father couldn't get the boat out of the water he couldn't do anything. He had reminded Jack of the jobs he did at the marina and the couple of hull inspections he had done as favours. He remembered Sandro warming to his task and going on to describe a niche in the market between amateur divers and the big salvage companies. Jobs that were two big for one or two people but too small for a multinational. He had illustrated this by pulling out a folded newspaper cutting of a car ferry that had run aground en route to Harwich several weeks ago. Sandro had explained how he had phoned his cousin, who worked for the ferry company, and had been told that *NorSalv*, the Norwegian Salvage Company, had told them they would inspect the hull and draw up a salvage plan for a hefty fee. However, the 'ball park' salvage cost was likely to be astronomical and more than the ferry was worth! Sandro's cousin had confided that the ferry company were thinking of calling it a total loss. Sandro had continued saying that the ferry was a much smaller version of the crude oil tanker grounding that they had been working on. Sandro was of the opinion that the inspection and salvage plan they could assemble would be as good as *NorSalv* and they could sub contract a team to undertake the salvage. He had asked Jack to consider it.

For the second time a smile flitted across Jack's face as he recalled abandoning the test case and spending the rest of the afternoon jumping from one point to another as they explored the idea of forming their own company. The back

27

and forth exploration had continued over a curry at a local Indian restaurant and into the evening. Before midnight it was clear to both of them that they had a viable plan. Jack was able to get access to the proceeds of his parents' estate; it had been held in trust until he was twenty-one. Sandro was confident he could match the sum with his own savings and money from his father. They were going to give it a try.

Jack was jolted awake by Sandro falling against him and saying something he couldn't understand. His headache had been replaced by a woozy feeling; he also felt ill and desperately thirsty. He started to prop Sandro upright between himself and Penny. Obviously Sandro was feeling as bad as he was. Jack returned to his slumped position.

He remembered the time, not too long ago, when his dissertation had been submitted and it was merely a case of waiting until the department came to a decision over the combined continuous and final assessment marks on the course. Both Jack and Sandro had been assured, informally, that if students survived to submitting the dissertation it was pretty likely they would be awarded the degree. Jack was suddenly bored and listless; he didn't like waiting but the next step, to actually forming a company, was becoming increasingly daunting. It was at this time that he spotted a buried news item in the *Financial Times.* The abandoned newspaper was on one of the overstuffed leather chairs in the post grad common room. It was not a paper he would normally read but, distractedly, he flicked though and noticed a brief item about the SS *Rockingham Castle*, a UK based container ship that disappeared, believed to have foundered, several days after leaving Charleston, USA. It seems the forecast at the time was that tropical storm *Edith* would swing south west towards the Gulf of Mexico leaving the ship a clear path across to Europe. Unfortunately the tropical storm had rapidly grown into a full-scale hurricane, changed course, and run directly over the track of the vessel. The Automatic Identification System on board the ship, that provided location, direction and speed data to orbiting satellites, which was then relayed to the owners, had failed. These systems were regarded as almost "bomb proof" so it must have been a catastrophic incident to knock it out. Airborne surveillance, and attempts to locate the ship using sonar sweeps had failed to find any trace of it. The ship was considered lost.

A movement on the dockside suddenly disrupted Jack's daydreaming. One of the guards strode to the edge of the dock near the barge, unbuttoned his trousers, and urinated into the sea. He grinned towards them as he did so and made a great show of easing himself back inside his trousers. The guard paused as though wondering how to get a reaction from Penny.

Chapter 3

Hunt for the SS *Rockingham Castle*

Jack ignored the distraction and returned, in a dream-like state, to his memories of the *Rockingham Castle* and his belief that ships of that size don't just disappear. He had carried the newspaper to the IT suite and logged on. It took him a while to discover where they thought the ship had gone down, based on the last communication. He was able to print out a track of the path of the hurricane until it blew itself out mid Atlantic. He was also able to track down a fairly detailed newspaper account from one of the survivors of the ship in a Miami newspaper. Jack recalled walking across to the library with the newspaper and his notes. He had shown his library card and was allowed into the section where maritime charts from all over the world were stored; he picked out the one corresponding to the last known position of the *Rockingham Castle*, placed it on the inspection table and dropped a clear sheet of acetate over it. He had bent over the chart, thinking. From his notes, and with a coloured pen, he marked the last known recorded position of the ship on the acetate, the track of the hurricane, and the estimated position that survivors say it went down. It didn't make sense. The seabed below was relatively clear at that spot, deep, but clear. There is no way that modern aerial detection and sonar sweeps could miss that ship on the bottom. The conclusion was that it wasn't there, it was somewhere else. Jack had moved away from the chart table, sat down on a nearby chair and closed his eyes. He tried to visualise what it would have been like on that container ship in the middle of a hurricane.

He could visualise the scene now. The wind would have been howling at over one hundred mph. At the time it was late afternoon but the hurricane would make it appear dusk, even evening. You wouldn't have been able to stand on deck. The wind and spray would be ripping communication antennae off mountings, hydraulic cranes would be breaking loose. Anything that wasn't bolted down would be torn away. There would be spray everywhere as the ship kicked, wallowed and plunged in violent seas. It would probably seem as if the ship was foundering. Even the most experienced sailor would be scared and maybe seasick. If they lost communications they would be essentially blind and fearing the worst. Jack wondered at what stage they considered abandoning ship. All their training would tell them it would be madness to do this prematurely; the safest place would be on board the ship. However, the longer they waited, the more chance the escape launch and its track could be damaged and they would be bound to the ship. The newspaper statement from the survivor said the ship was taking in water, that pumps had failed and she was going down when they all entered the lifeboat, blew the retaining bolts, and flew down the track and into the ocean. The survivor said that when he looked back he couldn't see the ship; 'We got away just in time.' Thinking about the conditions Jack realised the survivor probably couldn't see anything anyway! The lifeboat would have plunged underwater after leaving the track and would be like a cork. It

31

would be thrown around violently and covered in spray and waves. It would have been as much underwater as above it. The survivors would be concentrating on holding fast and not banging into each other and avoiding broken bones. The lifeboat engine would have been on and propeller turning before they hit the water. It would drive them away from the ship as it was designed to do. So the ship would be roughly behind them not alongside. They didn't see it because they couldn't see it. The report said they were in the escape launch for thirteen hours before they were found and rescued. It was almost six hours later that the first airborne reconnaissance was mounted.

Jack had looked again at the chart. If the *Rockingham Castle* didn't go down there, where might it have gone down? He scanned the seabed along the track of the hurricane and then he saw it. On the seabed was an underwater ridge or reef about one hundred and fifty to two hundred kilometres away from where the ship allegedly went down. What if the ship wasn't foundering at the time they abandoned ship? With a huge rear tower, wheelhouse, galley, accommodation and so on, it would act like a massive sail. What if the wind simply blew the ship along the track of the hurricane? What if it stayed afloat long enough to clear the immediate area and ended up amongst that ridge or reef area? It was certainly worth exploring. Jack packed everything away and took his notes back to the department. He vividly remembered phoning Sandro with his analysis.

After Jack had explained his theory to Sandro about the *Rockingham Castle* Sandro cried off his date with the delightful Sue, begging her forgiveness and promised to make it up to her. He was being sincere, but the prospect of finding the *Rockingham Castle* was too good to miss. Jack and Sandro had a better than average knowledge of salvage rights, but nothing like the detailed understanding of Dr Euan Kendrick; it was his specialty. Jack said he would arrange a meeting with Dr Kendrick as soon as possible.

Assuming the ship was somewhere near the ridge how were they going to find it and obtain proof? Sandro thought he had seen a seminar title advertised earlier in the year by a PhD student from a different department. From what Sandro could remember this guy was working on a detection array that could create a three dimensional image of underwater terrain, or structures, and tell you what it was made of. It was similar to the kit that space probes carry. At the time he wasn't really interested and couldn't even remember the name of the student, but Sandro agreed to trace him.

Assuming this guy's device could search the reef, how could they get him and the device into the middle of the Atlantic? It would cost a fortune. At this Sandro said he would email his father. He knew his father had relatives in Miami, Florida, who were also in the motor cruiser business. It was always possible his father may be able to ask a favour and get them access to a boat. It was worth a try.

For the next few hours they turned over the little evidence they had, re-checked it and tried to find more. They did find further statements from the crew but these merely reinforced the statement they had. They tracked down the group who had insured the ship, Lloyd's of London, but that was all. Jack also checked out the cost of three return tickets to Miami for himself, Sandro and the PhD student and gulped! Was this just a foolish escapade? With his mind still racing they had decided to call it a night and meet up the next day.

Jack recalled that by mid-afternoon the next day they had both good news and bad news. Dr Kendrick had been free and was happy to chat to Jack about salvage rights. 'I didn't know it was so complicated and so varied,' he had confessed as he tried to summarise what he had learnt.

'It seems that there are clearly established principles, but other aspects are open to negotiation. Basically, if the ship is abandoned then whoever finds it, and informs the owners and insurer, has location rights; essentially a fee for telling them where it is. If the ship is too difficult or it is too costly to salvage, then you might get a "thank you and a cup of coffee". If the cargo is valuable and can be recovered economically then this fee can vary enormously. Kendrick gave me some examples of between one to three per cent of the sum salvaged. The person who locates the wreck can also claim salvage rights to the vessel and all the contents. They can then subcontract the actual salvage and agree an allocation of the sum salvaged against the cost of salvage. It seems that it's a hit and miss business. You might find the wreck, but so what, the cost of salvage is too high. It's a case of deciding if the cost of salvage is more than the contents are worth.'

Jack summed up what they had discovered. 'It seems to me we need to find out how much the cargo is worth. If it is worth enough we need to decide if we want to spend money trying to find it. Of course, even if we find it the cargo may be too costly to salvage, so we have wasted our time, effort and money,' he added.

'I've costed three return tickets to Miami at £2,500. Double that for, say, two to three weeks of expenses.

Probably double or triple it again for hiring a cruiser and fuel. That's a LOT of money,' said Jack.

Sandro described how he had checked with the department secretary and traced Robin Brereton, the PhD student; a bright guy, but strange. He was in the Physics Faculty, Computer Imaging Department, or rather buried under a pile of cables, monitors and computing kit in an off-shoot of one of the labs. Robin was only too pleased to talk about his research and what he was doing. The problem was that Sandro understood about every fifth word! It seemed he was trying to modify and develop the space probes used by the European Space Agency for use underwater – but it was a massive task. Obviously water is a much denser medium than air and the devices they use in rarefied environments simply don't work underwater.

'He started telling me how much of the planet was covered in water and how little we know about the seabed. This included the fish and mammals that inhabit it as well as the mineral resources to be found. He went on to tell me how he was attempting to mimic the sound waves that whales and dolphins use to locate and identify their prey. I never realised how sophisticated these locating systems were and that dolphins and whales could locate individual fish, squid and so on, hundreds of metres away and differentiate between them. However, he's really focused on locating mineral deposits. His PhD is sponsored by some multinational mining company and he's essentially employed by them. The bottom line is that he has completed a series of shallow trials of his kit and it looks as though it works. He is almost ready for deep water trials but has work to do on some software, or a data management system, that is at the core of his work. It seems

35

that even if the probes collect a limited amount of data it is possible to extrapolate and generate a computer image of what the spot looks like. The data he collects is also compared to a checklist of deposits in a database and confirms what the deposits are. Basically he reckons he can get a pretty good image and analysis from fragments of the whole thing. Of course the more data the probes collect the better the image and the more confidence you have in specifying what you're looking at.'

'But would he get on a plane and perform his deep water trials off the American coast. And if he did what would it cost?' asked Jack.

'Perhaps we need to find out more about the cargo, whether containers have been recovered from those depths and what it costs before we go any further,' Sandro had suggested.

'Presumably we can get all that information from Lloyd's,' suggested Jack. 'Why don't I contact Lloyd's and see what they can tell us about the *Rockingham Castle* and its cargo?'

By lunch time Jack had spoken to Charles St John Stevens at Lloyd's and set up a meeting in London for the next day. It seems that 'Sinjun' was happy to talk, happy to provide documentation and answer all questions, but would not discuss the *Rockingham Castle* over the phone or supply documents as email attachments. Jack had never met a "St John" but he'd met several public school boys; the language, the tone, and confidence boarding on arrogance was unmistakeable.

Chapter 4

Finding the SS *Rockingham Castle*

Through a kaleidoscope of moving images Jack saw himself walking into Lloyd's of London; it was not what he was expecting. He had been expecting an elegant building façade, probably tucked between equally elegant buildings on a London street. When he had arrived at One Lime Street he was confronted by a modern glass and stainless steel building that looked as though it had been modelled on a mechanical monster. The stainless steel vertebrae of a mechanical spine soared into the air. A modern granite, chrome, glass and leather reception area, with VDUs providing the latest news feeds from around the world, reflected a modern international organisation. A smart and efficient receptionist was expecting him and immediately phoned Charles, or "Sinjun" as Jack now thought of him, to tell him that Jack had arrived. It was when Jack accompanied Charles away from reception that they walked back in time. Old paintings, of even older ships, hung on the dark wooden panels that lined the broad corridor along which they walked. A row of matching chandeliers glistened and gave a soft light as they noiselessly moved over the long and richly coloured oriental carpet covering a highly polished floor. The place simply oozed quality and old fashioned taste; it reflected the institution that was Lloyd's of London.

Charles led the way into a small simply furnished room; a cosy meeting room for a few people. He placed a heavy folder on the side table. On a silver tray, well Jack had guessed it was silver, was bottled water, tea, coffee and biscuits in plastic wrappers. Charles turned, and in a very public school voice asked, 'Can I offer you something to drink? Tea, coffee, perhaps a glass of water. We have still and carbonated.'

'A cup of coffee would be fine,' smiled Jack as he took in the surroundings.

Over the next hour or so Jack changed his opinion of Charles. The initial impression had been superficial. Yes, Charles was the product of a public school and privileged background. His mop of fair hair fell over his forehead and he was brushing it back from time to time. His voice and mannerisms were almost a caricature of upper-crust city types. But Charles was on the ball. He had obviously prepared for the meeting and was ready for every question. What Jack didn't know was how well Charles had prepared. It was his practice to have a small dossier prepared for those he was about to meet and didn't know. Nothing in great detail, just a brief overview and impressions from colleagues and publically available sources. The organisation they dealt with had prepared a brief report on Jack within hours of the request.

Jack was described as average. He was about average height, five foot ten inches and about average weight, about twelve stone and with mid brown hair; average sort of length but with a tendency to curl at the nape of his neck. The photo taken amongst a group of other students showed that he wasn't particularly attractive or handsome in any classic way.

His features were regular; soft brown eyes and a noticeable tan, as though he had just returned from some summer holiday. Of course, his tan only extended to his face and arms. The rest of him that was normally covered in a wetsuit or a dry suit was much paler. He was typical of hundreds of pleasant looking guys that one would pass in the street with hardly a second glance. However, the report went on to say that those who knew him wouldn't focus on these superficial features; they would simply describe him as determined. Not only determined, but to do well at whatever he put his mind to. A tutor at the University of Portsmouth had described him as "having potential", "a hard worker" and "determined".

Charles had started by asking Jack about his interest in the SS *Rockingham Castle* and what he wanted to know. Jack saw no reason to be evasive and explained that he and a colleague had a theory about the loss of the ship and were interested in locating it and, if found, devising a salvage plan. Charles reacted as if this was the most normal thing in the world and asked what he needed to know.

When Jack asked for confirmation of the route of the ship, and confirmed positions, Charles withdraw a small chart from the bulky folder with the track and reported positions marked. The last known position was indicated. When Jack asked about the make-up of the cargo and number of containers, Charles withdrew a summary of the containers on board and their individual, and combined insurance value. Jack was taken aback and tried not to let Charles see his reaction. The SS *Rockingham Castle* was carrying two thousand two hundred containers with an insurance value of £240 million. When he asked about the ship itself, Charles pulled out a small file. It provided several photographs of the

39

ship, a copy of the most recent hull, engine and superstructure inspection, as well as a list of the officers and crew with a summary of their maritime experience.

It was when Jack asked Charles about the attempts to locate the ship that Charles shuffled through the file and pulled out more pages. Charles had scanned the contents and told him that immediately the ship had failed to make a routine report of its position a check on its position had been made. The Automatic Identification System had confirmed that they were still on course and it had been assumed that the hurricane had temporally disrupted communication. However, five hours later the system had failed. Jack knew that these "black boxes" were virtually indestructible so it must have been a catastrophic event to knock it out. A request for satellite confirmation of the position of the ship had been inconclusive due to the adverse weather in the area. A second attempt by the satellite to locate the ship was undertaken several hours later on a subsequent orbit; that too was inconclusive. A third attempt had scanned an area equivalent to where the ship could have sailed, at top speed, from the last known position. There was no sight of the ship. Charles then went on to explain that as soon as the weather had abated airborne surveillance had been commissioned, but it failed to locate any wreckage. Charles had then turned several pages and explained that seventy-two hours after the ship had been abandoned sonar sweeps had commenced and over one thousand five hundred square kilometres of ocean bed had been searched; there was no trace of the ship. Charles gave Jack a chart indicating the area that had been swept; it included the ridge Jack had identified. If the ship had been on that underwater ridge surely they would have seen it he had thought.

Somewhat dispiritedly Jack asked about their salvage policy. Charles was ahead of him. He explained that if Lloyd's were provided with conclusive proof of the position of the SS *Rockingham Castle* they would pay a fee of £240,000. This was irrespective of any salvage undertaken. Almost conspiratorially he added that such a fee would save Lloyds money by avoiding lengthy legal disputes regarding the fate of the ship. He went on to say that depending on the position and state of the wreck, and feasibility of salvaging containers, other fees may be paid to the salvers.

After an hour Jack had gone through all his questions and was thanking Charles for all his help. It was when they were walking back to reception that Charles paused in the long, wood panelled corridor and confided. 'There are some extremely valuable items in those containers. If you can find the ship we would be very keen to encourage a salvage operation. I think you would find that Lloyd's always expresses its thanks to those who have helped us.' With that he handed Jack a business card, escorted him to reception, and wished him good luck.

Jack couldn't remember the trip back to Paddington Railway Station and the fast food outlet inside. He did remember sipping the overpriced, but hot, paper cup of coffee as he waited for the next train back to Portsmouth. He remembered phoning Sandro and giving him a summary of what he had found out, including the fact that sonar sweeps over the area of the reef had failed to locate the ship – if it was there!

41

Sandro had acknowledged the summary but seemed to disregard the bad news. Instead he had told Jack that Robin, the PhD student, had been given permission by his sponsors, *MatCorp*, to make arrangements to undertake the deep water trial and to forward a detailed costing to them. Jack and Sandro agreed to meet up that night and decide what to do next.

Chapter 5

A developing situation

Jack shifted his sitting position. His backside was almost numb but each time he moved the headache returned; he felt wretched. However, reliving the excitement of tracing the *Rockingham Castle* helped him relax and take his mind off what was happening.

With hindsight it had been reckless, but things seemed to simply fall into place. Robin Brereton was enthusiastic about the chance to conduct a trial of his kit in the deep Atlantic water. He admitted that he knew little about the underwater terrain they were interested in, but he would find out. Jack and Sandro had been completely honest with him about trying to locate the SS *Rockingham Castle* and the fee that they would get if they found it. They were stunned when Robin said he was happy to trial the kit, and search for the ship, and if they found it he couldn't accept any part of the fee. He just wanted the recognition that his probes had found it. Neither Jack nor Sandro could understand why anyone would pass up such a bonus. It wasn't until Robin explained, that under the terms of his studentship he couldn't work for anyone else, nor benefit financially from the investment being made in his research. What he did volunteer was a belief that if they did find the ship the value of his probes, and the shares of *MatCorp,* would soar as would his standing in the company.

'If we find that ship I could make more out of it than you,' he said with a smile. 'In fact I can arrange to fund my travel and expenses and cover the cost of the boat to deploy the kit. It's all part of the research plan; it's all agreed and budgeted.'

The implication, of course, was that they would need to be careful not to compromise Robin or themselves by allowing *MatCorp* to fund the exploration. After some discussion they agreed that they would pay half of the hire fee of the survey boat and avoid any hassle with *MatCorp*.

Jack recalled the next few days as a whirl of activity. They checked and rechecked the area to be swept and the depth at which the SS *Rockingham Castle* may lie. A wreck at eleven hundred metres was deep, too deep for a conventional diver but not for submersible robots. What's more there was no shortage of cases where cargo had been retrieved at even greater depths. Indeed, companies like *NorSalv* specialised in such salvage. They were the team that salvaged eighty tons of silver ingots from a World War II freighter that had been torpedoed about two hundred and fifty kilometres off Ireland and was over one kilometre down.

Robin discovered that the ridge was believed to be part of an old volcano or vent. As far as he could determine the area had not been surveyed before and so even more justification for setting up a trial in such a location. He had confirmation from *MatCorp* that he could make arrangements to undertake the deep water trial in the proposed area and forward a detailed estimate of costs for approval. After confirming the details of the search Robin didn't hang around but retreated to the lab to work on the software. He wanted to be sure it would operate as expected. Jack and Sandro had checked the annual weather patterns and long range forecasts; they looked OK for the foreseeable future. It seemed they were all ready to go.

It had been five more weeks before they were ready to leave. It had taken that long for Robin to confirm that the additional programming of the probes was robust and to co-ordinate all the other arrangements. It was just as well that Jack and Sandro wouldn't be carrying any diving gear because Robin's kit took up their entire baggage allowance and more! There were crates and tubes, boxes and grips full of cables all marked "Fragile". The luggage didn't include almost a mile of steel cable and data cable. In addition there was a heavy weight cable drum that was being transported direct to the dockside in America. It took a team of engineers another two days to rig the cable drum to the working platform of the boat and to confirm all the connections were sound.

Matcorp were funding two crew members, a captain and an engineer, to manage the survey boat. They knew the boat well and were both competent and friendly throughout all the dockside preparation. It then took four full days of motoring to reach the sweep zone and prepare for the sweeps. In a rolling sea, handling heavy equipment, wasn't always easy. They had decided that they would sweep a grid that covered just the underwater ridge. If the previous sweeps hadn't located the ship in the surrounding seabed, that was relatively clear, it was unlikely they would locate it.

The GPS tracking system had them sweeping parallel lines two hundred metres apart, hour after hour. The first

45

couple of hours were exciting as they stared at the cluster of monitors spewing out sound traces, line after line of mindless data and changing data codes. Robin explained what the codes represented as they probed the immediate seabed below. Sand, shingle, alluvial deposits, limestone and igneous rock that had spewed out of the volcanic vent.

Though the probes scanned the seabed what emerged on the monitors seemed featureless. However, Robin could read off the codes and say what deposits and rock strata lay beneath. As the sweep continued he confirmed that the ridge had been formed by an ancient volcano; the computer generated picture slowly resolved on one of the other monitors to reveal what it looked like. To their disappointment there was no sight of any ship.

They were almost two-thirds through the horizontal sweep of the reef and immediate surrounding area with no evidence of any ship. Jack remembered his mood at that time; it was becoming increasingly subdued. For the last few hours Jack and Sandro had sat in silence as the boat made its ponderous way up and down the parallel tracks. The diesel engine thumped, the boat rocked and the monitors hummed and the data streamed in. Only Robin seemed to be enjoying himself as he checked the cables, checked the track, and checked the monitors. Occasionally he would make some remark about a changing data code. At first Jack or Sandro would be instantly alert, only to discover the probe had identified some erratic or rock strata that could be mineral bearing. By dusk they had completed the horizontal sweeps.

Over an improvised supper the conversation had been stilted; it was clear that Robin thought the trial was going well. Jack and Sandro were beginning to realise what a long shot it had been. They asked Robin how much more scanning he wanted to do; almost resigned to failure. Jack could recall, almost word for word what Robin had said. 'I suggest we ask the captain to set the auto-pilot to take us round and round in circles and then start the vertical scans at dawn. The ridge is lying roughly on a line NNW – SSE so the legs will be longer and less one hundred and eighty degree turns. We have about twice as much ground to cover so it may take us another couple of days.'

The thought of two more days bouncing around on the ocean, costing them money, wasn't appealing but they were committed to completing the scans. Jack had offered to take the first watch. Even though the boat was decked out like a Christmas tree, with all lights blazing, he had no wish to be run down in the night by some rogue tanker. Before midnight Robin relieved him and they chatted briefly about their plans for the future before Jack drifted off to his bunk.

The beauty of the dawn had not matched his mood as Jack wandered into the galley and helped himself to breakfast. Robin was already checking the kit on the work platform and shouted that they would be ready to start the sweep. The morning started to follow the well worn pattern as they ploughed up and down the track. In truth, Jack had given up; he was resigned to the fact that the expedition was a costly failure. It was mid afternoon when Robin gave him a shout. 'Hey, guys, come and look at this.'

With no great enthusiasm Jack and Sandro strolled to the monitors but nothing had seemed to change.

'You see that band of codes,' said Robin as he put his finger on the monitor. 'That is a band of steel plate that

47

shouldn't be there! Look at the monitor,' as he drew their attention to a green smudge drifting away from the centre of the screen. 'It's difficult to be sure but it looks like an angular mass in the area. On the next sweep we will get closer and it will be clearer. At the moment the probes are more than six hundred metres away from it.'

The mood changed dramatically. Five minutes earlier Jack was depressed, now he was elated and eager for the end of the track so they could return to the spot. The time dragged by until they started to approach the spot Robin had marked. This time they could spot the band of codes and make out the shape of a ship or so they thought. It was tucked against a towering lip of rock.

'Robin, can we suspend the sweep, focus on this spot to confirm what it is, and return to the sweep later? If it is the *Rockingham Castle* down there I'm dying to know,' he said almost breathlessly.

'No problem, We can't simply turn around – not with one thousand metres of cable stretched out under the boat. We can move off the track, turn around and return to it. I'll do multiple sweeps across the area and build up a clearer picture of what's down there and the terrain,' Robin announced with a grin.

Robin typed in new instructions into the automatic pilot and moments later the boat began a slow wide turn before settling on a new return track. In minutes they had completed the track and the boat slowly swung around again retracing its path just a few hundred metres from the spot. Jack and Sandro sat glued to the monitor displaying the computer generated shape on the seabed. It was a ship, a container ship. It seemed to be sat at an angle of about thirty degrees, bow raised as though stuck to the face of the ridge. Why hadn't the professionals and all their fancy kit spotted it – it was big enough to see!

The boat peeled away and slowly turned around, setting itself on a new track. The image forming on the monitor was even clearer. They could see the outline of the superstructure, the shape of the bow, and the rows of containers. Jack leaned across to pick up the plastic wallet he had jammed under some cables. He picked out a large colour photo of the SS *Rockingham Castle*, port side on. His eyes flicked rapidly between the monitor and the photo. They'd found it. The lines were identical, the shape of the huge wheelhouse matched the photo. Jack could see a shape above it. Was the ship wedged under an overhang?

They called Robin over. 'Robin, what's that shape above the ship? It looks like it's stuck to the face of the ridge.'

Robin cancelled the two dimensional moving image and punched in some commands to call up an alternative. It looked like a complicated line drawing, a mesh of lines, but Robin could rotate it in different directions. It was a three dimensional view of the ship. As he partially rotated the image it suddenly became clear. The ship was jammed under an overhang. It looked like a massive version of Wave Rock in Western Australia. He guessed that over hundreds, if not thousands of years, the action of the current had scoured away soft material creating a giant wave of hard rock. By some freak chance the ship had gone down and, somehow, got tucked underneath this fold of rock. They had missed the ship on their first sweep because it was hidden under the overhang. The previous aerial sonar sweep had missed it for the same reason.

49

'Robin, what's the best image you can get from the probes? The one that will provide the most conclusive image that what we've found is in fact the *Rockingham Castle*? Can you make a note of the precise coordinates?' he asked.

'Sure,' answered Robin. 'The programme records the GPS continuously. We know precisely where it is. As to the quality of image, well, it's diminishing returns,' he replied. 'Two or more passes, at different angles and depths is all we need. If we were to make twenty or thirty sweeps the image would be marginally better each time but probably not worth the effort,' he concluded. 'Let's make a few more passes and see what the image looks like.'

Jack and Sandro beamed at each other, they had done it, they had found the *Rockingham Castle*. A £240,000 fee and the prospect of being involved in a multi million pound salvage operation. What a way to start their company. But the elation was short lived. They had to complete the deep trial for Robin and register the find. Jack's joy was suddenly overtaken by the irrational thought of someone else working out where the wreck lay and registering its position. Although he dismissed the idea a nagging doubt remained. They needed to contact Charles and tell him they had found the ship, and sooner rather than later. Within the hour they had drafted a cryptic message to Charles telling him they had located the missing vessel, provided a precise map reference, and would provide details in the near future.

It took another thirty-six hours to complete the trial, to go up and down the parallel tracks, in the featureless ocean. It took another six hours to wind in the steel and data cables and secure the probes. Whereas the outward journey had been full of expectation, and the boat trip had seemed short, the return felt interminable and frustrating. Robin was beside himself with the success of the trial and was happy to sit in the galley and type up his report. The exhilaration experienced upon finding the *Rockingham Castle* had now subsided. At first Jack and Sandro had been keen to start work on a salvage plan but soon realised the scale of the task was way outside their experience or skills. They comforted themselves with the knowledge that Charles had told them the cargo was valuable and so no doubt Lloyd's would be keen to support a salvage plan.

Chapter 6

Before the storm

In his woozy state Jack fondly remembered his return to One Lime Street in London almost a week later with Sandro. This time it wasn't in a small meeting room on the ground floor, but in the grand office of Sir Alistair Murray, Chief Executive Officer, with a magnificent view across the city. Charles had met them in reception and escorted them to an elevator and along corridors to Sir Alistair's office. He was effusive in his praise for them both.

'Do you know how much we spent searching for that ship?' Charles said with a boyish grin. 'We had a satellite reprogrammed to scan the area, planes with underwater detection systems scouring the track and half a dozen boats conducting underwater searches; and you found it!'

He was still congratulating them as they entered Sir Alistair's office. Sir Alistair rose from his desk to greet them. He seemed younger than Jack had imagined and admitted to himself that his image of Lloyd's was of Victorian buildings, even older members and smoke filled rooms; nothing like the location and crisp efficiency and technology he saw all around him. There were more congratulations, cups of tea and then more pointed questions about how Jack and Sandro would salvage the containers off the sunken vessel. On the long journey back from the Atlantic and Miami, Jack and Sandro had thought about the question but more for their professional interest than any preparation for the Lloyd's meeting. Since their return to Portsmouth they had spent every minute searching the internet, wading through specialist magazines and talking to staff in the department. In a few days they had assembled solid evidence of successful salvage operations at the depth of the *Rockingham Castle* and in similar water conditions. What they didn't know was the detail; how to actually do it and the cost. Jack shared their summary with Sir Alistair and Charles.

He explained that the position of the ship was both good news and bad news. Jammed under the towering lip of the ridge the ship was protected from the current but any salvage cables would be dragged to and fro by the current at regular intervals. This would be a problem in raising containers to the surface. Although the vessel may be secure at the moment as soon as containers were removed this could alter the buoyancy of the ship and it could move. Jack went on explaining that he believed the ship had sunk slowly, probably buoyed by the containers. It may have drifted, suspended in mid water, until by fluke it was pulled up against the ridge at the precise time it rested on the seabed.

The image that Robin had obtained showed the ship almost upright but with the bow raised to an angle of twenty-seven degrees. Jack then outlined their salvage plan. It was more in principle than action. He proposed using a Remote Operated underwater Vehicle, ROV, like those used on similar salvage operations. The task would be to place numerous small, directional, explosive charges against the hull; to penetrate the hull and breach water tight compartments. He added that the sequence and timing of the charges would be critical since he would want to ensure the ship was solidly set in its current position. He wanted to secure the ship ready for salvage not move it. He also didn't want to breach any fuel tanks.

Jack explained that moving the first container would be the most difficult. The containers would be shielded from the current but he could not tell how much room for manoeuvre the submersible would have to access the clamping points of the container, stabilise it, and release it. He also wasn't sure if protective plates would have to be fitted to the lip of the ridge to protect both the ridge and the cables when they swung containers free from the boat. Sandro's research had indicated how long it took to raise a forty tonne container from that sort of depth and described how a single salvage vessel, with one set of retrieving cables, would take two years to retrieve all two thousand two hundred containers. Two ships operating in tandem, or with two hoists, would reduce the time but increase the risks of entanglement. Jack ended by saying that depending what was in some of the containers would dictate if they were worth the cost of salvage.

As Jack picked up his tea cup, and now cold tea, he realised that the room was completely silent. He paused with the cup at his lips, his eyes scanning the people in the room. Sandro was smiling, a smile of mutual support or embarrassment? Charles was smiling, but Sir Alistair was beaming as he rose to his feet and moved to his desk. He turned with some papers in his hand.

'This morning I spoke to one of my colleagues and asked how he would salvage two thousand two hundred containers from the *Rockingham Castle.* His strategy was almost the same as yours; congratulations. You've got the right idea but at the moment you don't have the equipment, the back up, the experience and the staff to raise those containers, but I think that sometime soon you will. My advice is to pass on any idea of tendering for a contract to salvage the containers. I guess this will be galling but I think it is good advice.'

Sir Alistair paused as he shuffled the papers in his hand. 'I've taken the liberty of preparing a cheque for £240,000 in grateful thanks for locating the SS *Rockingham Castle*. If the contents of certain containers are salvaged then this sum will be increased. At the present time I cannot say more. However, what I can say is that we are extremely grateful for your help in locating the ship.'

Sir Alistair paused as he handed the cheque to Jack. As Jack took it Sir Alistair remarked, almost in passing, 'We are always grateful to those who have helped us.' He then said, almost apologetically, 'I wanted to hand this cheque to you personally. The finance people weren't happy and insisted I get you to sign for it. I've also asked Charles to keep in touch and let you know of any worthwhile tenders you may wish to bid for.'

More handshakes and a few minutes later they were through the reception area and heading off for the underground station to catch the train from Paddington Station back to Portsmouth.

They talked excitedly on the train journey back to Portsmouth. With almost a quarter of a million pounds in their pocket they could set up their own company and do all the things they wanted to do. However, their previous discussion had revealed how little they knew about setting up a company; where to be based, how to attract business, how to cost the tenders. By the time they arrived in Portsmouth they had a long list of questions to answer.

Over the next week they met each morning at nine a.m. in the department post grad room and worked until early evening. Between the academic terms the university was almost deserted; the department was strangely quiet. Supplied with a box of tea bags, carton of milk and sandwiches from the refectory they brainstormed the questions to which they needed answers, started grouping them together, prioritising them and deciding who could give them sound advice. On reflection, some of the best advice had been from Jeff Watkins, the owner of the marina where Jack had started salvaging outboard motors. He remembered his parting words. 'Don't forget, don't pay yourself too much, keep every receipt, and get a good accountant.'

Six months later the enthusiasm was draining away. They had decided to have their base in Manchester. The city was roughly in the middle of the country and close to one of the biggest ports in the UK - Liverpool. They reckoned that they could drive south to Lands End in six hours and north to John O'Groates in eight. The major container port of Felixstowe, on the east coast, was only four hours away. They judged that wherever the job was they could be there the next day and ready to go. Manchester was ideal, it was a big city, had a busy airport and was much cheaper than London.

Jack had talked to Uncle Charlie and Aunt Doreen about his plans to commit his trust money to buying an apartment in central Manchester and using it as a base for the fledgling *Marine Salvage & Investigation Company*. They couldn't have been more helpful, even offering to make up lists of basics he would need. This ranged from cups and saucers to toilet brush and ironing board. Although a "first time buyer" it only took Jack a few days to discover the going price for apartments in and around the city. From those that looked like futuristic film sets to others that were in need of a lot of renovation! In the end he decided on a recently converted Victorian office block, offering a two bedroom, top storey apartment and a garage in the basement. Just over two years ago it had been the show apartment in the development but the young guy who had bought it, and who was selling it with the same show apartment furniture, had run into financial trouble and was desperate to sell it. It was also within walking distance, well a long walk, of Piccadilly Railway Station; it would be ideal. Before talking to Uncle Charlie and Aunt Doreen he would have paid cash and thus used up all of his trust fund and some of his Lloyd's money. But their advice had been confirmed by his new accountant. He could get tax relief on his mortgage!

Sandro had decided to rent a flat in Salford, just behind Salford University and just over a twenty minute walk to Jack's place.

The easy part of setting up the company, and the most enjoyable part, had been equipping themselves with what they thought they would need to undertake underwater survey and recovery work at modest depths. In the end they went for Inspiration xpd re-breathers, full head masks and associated communication equipment that would take them to one hundred metres and even beyond. They knew that beyond one hundred metres the costs, and the risks, increased dramatically and eventually they would have to invest in a Remote Operated underwater Vehicle or ROV. However, the cost of a ROV would blow the current budget.

They replaced their tired and worn wet and dry suits with custom made ones in fluorescent yellow and dayglo orange. These were no more expensive than top of the range recreational suits. The safety kit and inflatable bags made barely a dent in their working capital. It was like Christmas time, buying "boys toys". However, the extra large industrial-like aluminium travel cases and satellite phone cost almost as much as the rest of their kit!

The fun stuff was balanced with the grind of creating a website and checking the emails daily. Designing flyers, visiting boat yards, placing adverts in yachting and power boat magazines. However, the depressing work was in visiting shipping agents and insurance companies that specialised in marine investigations and salvage. They were all very polite but every one of them explained they already had working arrangements with existing dive companies, contractual links with insurers or merely posted invitations to tender. The website had attracted a few enquiries and they had inspected a couple of sailboats that had either run aground or hit submerged objects. They were keen to take the work but the expenses were almost the same as the fee.

It had been mid morning as Jack sat in a small plain room in his Manchester apartment, staring out over the rooftops towards central Manchester. He had set up the small bedroom as a mini office some months after the pay-off from Lloyd's. He had bought all the office furniture as well as the laptop, scanner and printer inside one hour at a Staples store in the city. He was looking through the various spreadsheets relating to the income and expenditure of the company; not a pretty sight. At this rate they would exhaust all their funds in about twenty-four months. Sandro said he would call in about lunch time, but in reality they didn't know what to do next.

The morning mail normally arrived about ten thirty a.m. and, more like an excuse to walk away from the depressing spreadsheets, he wandered down to the foyer and unlocked his mailbox. There was the usual collection of rubbish, leaflets advertising home delivery pizzas, mail order flyers, charity requests and a thick plain white letter with a Lloyd's of London return address stamped on the front. Jack started to rip it open as he walked back to the lift, and pulled out a document of several pages. There was a letter from Charles and a "Call for Tender". Jack started reading the letter in the lift. Charles was enclosing a "Call for Tender" to undertake a survey, and possible salvage, of a freighter, the *Lee Kwan Fong*, that had sunk off the Kenyan coast. He ended the short letter saying, 'I do hope *Marine Investigation & Salvage Company* will tender. If I can provide any further assistance please do not hesitate to contact me. Lloyd's always expresses its thanks to those who have helped us.'

Jack stopped reading and started thinking. It was that phrase again, the one that "Sinjun" and Sir Alistair had used before. 'Lloyd's always expresses its thanks to those who have helped us.' But this was a public tender, open for anyone to see. Back in his apartment he phoned Sandro.

Chapter 7

Invitation to tender

The phone rang for ages, so long that Jack thought Sandro had already left, but then Sandro picked up the phone. It came out in rush, a babble, that they had an invitation to tender for work on a sunken freighter off the Kenyan coast. It was only when he heard girlish giggles in the background that he realised this was a bad time to phone. He hastily asked Sandro to call him back as soon as he could.

Jack read through the tender document twice. It was all pretty clear. The *Lee Kwan Fong* had been a general purpose freighter built over fifty years ago. At seventy-seven metres long and eleven and a half metres wide she had transported mixed cargo between the Far East, India and Mediterranean for most of her life. About twenty years ago she had been refitted to carry mainly containers and a central hydraulic crane fitted. He glanced at the colour photo of the ship in dry dock at the time of the refit. Pleasing lines, for'ard mast and chunky rear accommodation and bridge tower. The only thing out of keeping was the modern central hydraulic crane. There must be thousands of freighters like this steaming around today. He read on. The ship had apparently hit a submerged reef and was believed to be in forty to fifty metres of water about eighty kilometres off the coast of northern Kenya. The tender was to produce a report on the damage to the vessel, a plan for the salvage of the containers, other cargo and a costing for refloating the vessel for subsequent scrap. Jack immediately guessed that the third clause was more about public relations than economics. The cost of refloating the *Lee Kwan Fong*, even if the fifty-year-old hull could take it, was likely to be more than the scrap value in Taiwan or wherever.

Jack was just starting to make notes against each section of the tender when there was a buzz from the intercom. It was Sandro, he had arrived in record time and was eager to read the letter and see the tender. Their mood had changed completely. In previous weeks they had grudgingly accepted that they had been naïve; that with hindsight they should have joined an existing salvage company and built up their experience and learnt how it all worked. But now they thought they had a chance to enter the market place. They had a month to submit the tender with the knowledge that a decision would be made ten working days after submission. They had no time to lose. The headings and sub headings for the tender document helped, and they realised that experienced companies probably had sections already drafted to slot in place. Their recently acquired Masters Degrees, and background in Marine Engineering would help, but was probably no better than all the other companies tendering. Where the others would have a distinct advantage would be in terms of previous experience and track record. Sandro and Jack were able to assemble reasonable cases under most of the headings and what they thought was a realistic costing. Where they had luck was when Jack contacted Kevin Donnelly his former Dive Master. Jack explained over the phone that they were assembling a tender for a job, their first real job, just off the northern Kenyan coast and needed a dive boat that could carry them and their kit some eighty kilometres off shore. Could Kev find them a boat? Would he be prepared to act as Dive Master for say, two weeks? If they were successful how much would he charge?

Kev had been a Dive Master for twenty years. He had dived all over the world and had lots of contacts. Three days after Jack had asked for help Kev phoned him back; he had found him a boat. Kev explained that a friend of his escaped the UK winter, and freezing Channel water, to run Liveaboards off the Kenyan coast. These were mini floating hotels that took small groups of divers to the more remote dive sites and typically moved on each day. He reckoned that the boat he had found would be ideal. He gave Jack the details.

'I've reserved the MV *Karwe,* I'm told that's Swahili for Manta Ray, for the dates you gave me. It's an eighteen metre steel hulled, purpose built liveaboard with accommodation for ten people. It has got two Gardner 6LXB diesel engines, two Perkins generators and a range of two thousand nautical miles. According to the spec it has a Lowrance Depth Sounder and GPS, Kelvin Hughes Steering Compass, two Navico Marine Radios, Decca Radar and Cetrek Autopilot. It's also got two compressors and can provide all the air and nitrox you want – forget Trimix. Because we are asking for sole use they will give us a preferential rate and a two man crew to accompany the boat. I've made a provisional reservation for two weeks, to be confirmed, in line with the dates you gave me.'

'Oh, another thing,' said Kev. 'The boat is based in Malindi but we can pick it up in a small place called Lammu; it's a couple of hundred miles up the coast and closer to the dive site. My pal says we can rent a pickup in Malindi and it would be quicker and cheaper to drive from Malindi to Lammu than collect the boat in Malindi and motor to the dive site. It seems the weekly package normally sold to tourists is to dive on sites up and down the stretch between Malindi and Lammu. At the end they can then choose a week on the beach or a week trekking and game viewing or head back home.'

Jack was pleased to have secured a boat that would do the job, but was taken aback at the cost. However, he consoled himself with the thought that if they won the tender the cost would be part of it.

Jack and Sandro were systematically working their way through the tender documents, drafting the case and listing the steadily mounting costs. Sandro had assembled all the travel details. He had argued that flying business class wasn't that extravagant because they would each get a massive luggage allowance. An allowance that was enough to cover all their kit. If they went zoo class they would end up paying for all the extra luggage. He had also confirmed that since the *Lee Kwan Fong* was outside Kenyan territorial waters, and even their Contiguous zone, they should have no problems with Kenyan officials, but reckoned they ought to check with "Sinjun". Towards the end of the second week they had assembled the first full draft of the tender and thought it looked good. However, there were still several unknowns and so Jack decided to take up Charles on his offer to answer any questions.

He phoned Charles that morning and asked about the need for business visas and "Letters of Authority" from Lloyd's. 'No problem,' responded Charles after Jack had listed his queries. 'If your tender is successful we will provide a "Letter of Authority" from Lloyd's and also a "Letter of Invitation" from the Kenyan Embassy. We believe the ship is well outside territorial waters and the Contiguous zone but as a courtesy have informed the Kenyan Ambassador of our plans and the nature of the inspection. However, it would be prudent to arrange a business visa not a tourist visa.'

Charles rattled through the rest of the queries and, again, Jack was impressed by how well he was prepared and how knowledgeable. Before the call ended Charles said, 'Oh, just one last thing. You might want to limit the fee to £10,000 per day. Something like four or five days preparation, seven days on site. The weather is pretty good at the moment and likely to stay so for months. A couple of days to wrap it up would be about right. You would have to meet all the other costs of course. Anything else?'

Jack was stunned. He had never expected Charles to give him any pointers to the level of fee, even though he guessed experienced salvage companies would have derived a general figure from tendering over the years. He was also stunned at the mental arithmetic he had performed. The tender would generate a gross of £140,000.

That evening, Jack and Sandro sipped cool Cobra beers in one of the Indian restaurants in the area of Rusholme. This was the home of an amazing strip of Indian shops and restaurants that lined the road just a few minutes drive from central Manchester. It was a blaze of light and busy with late shoppers and early diners. Together they celebrated the mailing of the tender that afternoon. The die was cast. In a couple of weeks they would know if they had been successful or not. What was "unsaid" was how much was riding on the outcome. Despite spending all the effort in advertising the company, and what they had to offer, they hadn't had a single enquiry in the last month. To be fair, they had been so busy assembling the tender, and making a note of the extra gear they would need, that they hadn't trawled the various "Calls to Tender" sites amongst the insurance companies. They decided to start that task the next day.

The hours and days dragged by. There were two or three jobs for which they could tender but there seemed a tacit agreement to wait and see the outcome of the Lloyd's tender. There was nothing in the mail on the day they had expected to hear. Jack felt a gradual growing sense of unease, almost sickness in the pit of his stomach, as though it was growing and he would eventually vomit. He had never felt like this before. The next morning, before ten a.m. both Sandro and Jack were sat in silence waiting for the mail to be delivered. 'I'll go and check at about ten thirty since it's usually arrived by then,' Jack said.

No sooner were the words out of his mouth when the phone rang. Jack was startled and reached across his desk to pick up the phone; it was Charles. 'Congratulations,' said Charles before Jack could say anything. 'Just wanted to let you know that the committee supported your tender, you will get an official letter, courier service, later today along with the various "Letters of Authority" and "Invitation".'

Jack mumbled a reply of thanks but was almost lost for words.

'Oh, just one thing. HM Border Force have asked if one of their officers can accompany the successful inspection team as an observer; one P. Pendleton-Price. They stress that the officer would take no part in the actual inspection; it will be purely an observational role. If you agree you will need to provide them with the details of your flights and itinerary. I'm told they will obtain the plane tickets so the officer can travel with you. You will also need to provide them with an invoice for a proportion of the cost of boat hire, any accommodation, subsistence etc. I know it's a chore, but in the long term it wouldn't do you any harm to forge a good working relationship with HM Border Force. All the details are in the package that's been mailed to you. Anything else?'

There was nothing else. Jack had mixed emotions. He was elated at the news of the successful tender. In a stroke it put *Marine Salvage & Investigation Company* on the map and ensured their existence for another couple of years. However, he felt resentful that someone else was intruding on their domain, even if it was HM Border Force.

As Sandro and Jack discussed it Jack became less concerned. 'Let's look on the good side,' Sandro said. 'The main costs have just been cut by twenty-five per cent,' he added with a smile.

Chapter 8

Heading for the *Lee Kwan Fong*

The next few weeks were a blur. They had read and reread the Tender Terms & Conditions, assembled all the paperwork, passports, visas and vaccinations. They had confirmed the rental of the boat, booked the tickets; it seemed to go on and on. The most enjoyable bit, and somehow confirming that it was all going to happen, was packing the large aluminium gear crates.

It was a hassle finding luggage trolleys at Manchester International A rport on an overcast, chilly November morning, as light rain started to get heavier. However, negotiating the business class check in was much easier and they were through in minutes despite the oversize luggage and running the gauntlet of the duty free stores. Kev decided to find a bottle of single malt, saying he would join them in the business lounge later. Jack and Sandro weaved their way through the travellers until they found the business class lounge.

Jack had phoned the HM Border Force contact number and eventually had been transferred to the right section. P. Pendleton–Price wasn't around but the section administrator knew all about the trip, confirmed tickets had been issued and that the officer would be in the business lounge in plenty of time for the flight. Jack arranged to meet up there.

Sandro and Jack walked up to the reception desk in the lounge and showed their tickets and passport. Sandro said he was off to get a drink and some food and would join him in few minutes. He was happy to let Jack have the job of making the acquaintance of the Border Force officer. As Sandro walked on Jack asked the receptionist if a fellow passenger on his flight, P. Pendleton-Price, had arrived since they had planned to meet here in the lounge prior to the flight but they had never actually met. The receptionist looked down at her list, smiled and said, 'Yes, your friend is in the lounge. If you would like to follow me.'

With that the receptionist turned to lead Jack into the lounge and through the array of tables, chairs and "carry-on" luggage. She stopped next to a low table and large easy chairs filled with passengers and turned to Jack. As she started to move her arm, as though presenting the officer to Jack, he took in the picture of the young guy leaning back in the armchair, holding a newspaper in one hand and a cup in the other. Designer stubble on his chin and head, pink open necked shirt and dark fleece. Jack held out his hand, smiled and was in the process of saying hello, when the receptionist said, 'Oh no, sorry, it is not this gentleman but this lady!'

Slightly embarrassed for Jack the receptionist made a quick exit. The contrast couldn't have been more stark and the jolt more pronounced. He had been expecting some tired and slightly worn Border Force man. He couldn't say why, probably a subconscious caricature. At first he thought the woman was in uniform but that was just because she was dressed in a navy blue skirt and jacket with some sort of white shirt. Her blonde hair was drawn back in a ponytail. The single string of pearls and earrings she wore gave the impression of a young businesswoman off to some meeting. The large black leather pilot-type briefcase all added to the impression. As the seconds of surprise passed he also noticed how pale she looked. Perhaps it was the fluorescent light in the lounge but her skin looked porcelain white and without a blemish. It wasn't sickly, just uniformly pale. An awkward smile crossed her face and she rose directly out of the chair. Jack laughed, 'Sorry about that,' he said as he took her hand only to discover it wasn't going to be a gripping encounter but rather like a gentle dip of fingers into a pool of water which was then withdrawn. 'All I had was a name, and I couldn't see you from behind the receptionist.'

Jack smiled at the guy next to her, who had resumed reading the paper and sipping his drink. 'Let me introduce you to Sandro, he's off getting a drink and a snack. Err . . . it looks like there are free chairs down there. We can bring you up to date with the plan,' said Jack as he eased away from the cluster of chairs towards a table near the refreshment counter.

They intercepted Sandro as he returned balancing a cup and saucer in one hand and side plate piled with sandwiches, biscuits and topped by a chocolate muffin in the other. As he caught sight of Jack and the young woman next to him his face broke into a glowing smile, eyes twinkling. 'Signorina, I would kiss your hand, but both my hands are full,' said Sandro in an exaggerated Italian accent and delivered with a small bow. 'Please take a seat, can I get you something to drink? Something to eat?' he added as he carefully placed the food and drink on the table.

'No, I'm fine thank you,' replied P. Pendleton-Price, 'but call me Penny,' she added.

Sandro couldn't help himself. Meeting any woman for the first time he seemed to click into automatic pilot; or rather smooth control rather than cruise control. Jack had seen it a hundred times and decided to leave Sandro to it, to raid the food and drink counter and to check on the flight times.

When he returned to the table Sandro brought Jack up to date. 'Guess what, Jack, Penny has a First Class Honours Degree in Economics from Bristol and is on this . . . errr . . . express route to become the boss at Border Force.'

Penny gave another awkward smile and with a gentle shake of her head corrected Sandro. 'No, not the boss. I'm on a one year rapid promotion course to become a Senior Border Force Officer. I've just been attached to the Marine Investigation Unit and this is all part of the training.'

Oh great, thought Jack. Here we are on our first major job and playing nursemaid to this trainee; as if we don't have enough to do! But Jack merely smiled and asked, 'Penny, do you dive?'

'No,' replied Penny. 'I don't really like water sports.'

'What about sailing, do you sail or do you go cruising?' Jack asked.

'No, as I said, I don't really like water sports,' she repeated.

'So why join the Marine Investigation Unit?' asked Jack. 'I would have thought that you would be spending a lot of your time either on or under water in that Unit.'

'It's just a six week attachment,' explained Penny. 'The idea is that we move through the various units learning how they work. It's supposed to inform the other training and provide an overview,' she added.

Jack could now understand the comments from Charles. HM Border Force Officer P. Pendleton-Price would be just an observer. Sandro sensed the awkwardness between Jack and Penny and immediately changed the subject. He summarized the itinerary and outlined what they were planning to do. He went on. 'Did they tell you that the Pilipino Engineer from the *Lee Kwan Fong* took note of the GPS position just before the ship went down? He picked up the ship's log, scribbled in the date, time and coordinates, and stuffed it into his bag just minutes before she sank. It could have taken us weeks or even months to find the ship without the coordinates. We should be able to find it in hours,' he confided. 'If all goes well we should be able to wrap up the entire job in a week or so. Hey, if you want to learn to dive I can teach you,' he added with that winning smile.

Stilted conversation continued for the next half hour or so. It alternated between the transport arrangements to Lammu, the diving regime whilst on the boat and an outline of the inspection they would be making. It was a relief when the flight was called and Jack could escape to his own little cubicle on the plane.

Jack had to admit that the business class seat, or rather bed, was more comfortable than many ship bunks he had slept in. However, after the long flight, hanging around in Nairobi and then the ongoing flight to Malindi he was weary. The decision to have an overnight stay in Malindi before driving up to Lammu had been a smart one. He really didn't want to drive along unknown African roads, at night, when he was tired.

A representative from *Deep Sea Safari* was waiting for them in the arrivals hall with a big white plastic sheet and the

71

name *Marine Salvage & Investigation Company* written on it. He had a couple of luggage trolleys and porters who helped them load the diving crates, and all the other luggage into the open back of the Toyota pickup and tie it down, although it was only a short drive. The representative gave them a five minute animated explanation of the controls of the pickup as he negotiated the busy traffic; it was obviously something he had done many times before. He drove onto the hotel forecourt and then down a slip road towards the basement. There was a security guard, complete with rifle, next to a linked metal screen. A quick word and someone inside the basement garage hit the switch and the gate started to rise. The pickup drove through with the driver waving to the guard. He parked, nose in, into a space close to the elevator.

'I'll get a luggage trolley, but we may need three,' he said as he hopped out of the cab and to a hidden storage space next to the elevator. Kev and the driver started untying the diving crates whilst Jack and Sandro lifted them on the trolleys.

'Don't leave stuff in the back of the pickup,' advised the driver. 'Even in a place like this. If you leave it the rascals will steal it. If you leave the pickup on the street overnight they will have the wheels, battery and anything else they can steal in an hour. You will be safer in the bush, away from the city, but just be careful,' he added.

It was just an overnight transit stop but next morning Penny was transformed. She had changed out of the severe blue suit and was now in sandy brown trousers that stopped below the knee and suede boots, pale green shirt and a dark green neckerchief. She looked like she was going on safari.

Chapter 9

Rendezvous with the MV *Karwe*

It was already dawn when they assembled in the foyer and started to transfer all the kit to the pickup in the basement below. Kev said he would drive, Jack would navigate and Sandro and Penny could either sightsee or sleep until it was their turn to drive. Penny fell asleep within minutes which was much to Sandro's disappointment.

The Toyota was big, fairly new and surprisingly comfortable. The city certainly had that feel of a holiday, seaside resort with high rise, colourful signs and street vendors setting up their stalls. Soon the offices and shops, tarmac and concrete curbs gave way to smaller offices, to fewer shops and houses and to shacks and farmland. The colours changed as well. The raw, grey cement block barricades changed to terracotta mud block walls. The soiled, gaudy patchwork of building facades changed to a warm spectrum of colours from the palest yellow to brick red and through a hundred shades of brown. They sped by in air conditioned comfort, along the coast road, heading due north. The tarmac gave way to gravel but the Toyota simply glided over the bumps.

'It's all about finding the optimum speed,' explained Kev. 'Too slow and we'll be shaken to bits, too fast and we're out of control. Just right and we glide over the corrugations.'

It was about two hundred and twenty-five kilometres from Malindi to Lammu and it took over four hours. It was noticeable that the traffic eased quickly as they left Malindi. The further they got from the city the less the traffic. Conversation had been easy for the first hour as everyone introduced themselves, spoke of similar dive trips, about remote places they had worked or visited and about the forthcoming survey of the wreck. They tried to include Penny in the conversation but it soon became clear that skiing trips to the French Alps and cycling holidays in Sicily were about as far as Penny had ventured. Her working life could be counted in weeks rather than years. The conversation slowly dried up.

They changed drivers after two hours when they spotted a fuel station, complete with store, next to the road. They filled the pickup with diesel and themselves with Coke and Fanta.

Sandro was driving as they approached Lammu. The *Deep Sea Safari* representative had given them a map and directions on how to find the *Wise Buy* Supermarket, and the name of the manager. He would loan them polystyrene boxes into which they could pack frozen food for transfer to the boat. They were used to equipping sailing and diving trips. It was simply a case of looking for the landmark, the fuel station on the main road through town; opposite was the supermarket.

It took longer than expected to tick off all the items on the shopping list. To stack all the dry goods into plastic tubs and the perishables into polystyrene crates. Kev had done this dozens of times and knew what to buy and how much. He explained to Penny that he didn't want to use cardboard boxes and risk carrying cockroaches, and their eggs, onto the boat. He'd found to his cost that the little blighters burrow into every crevice. As the crates and tubs were ferried out to the pickup Jack and Sandro restacked them in the back. It was getting very full but they would only have to drive a short distance. It was also starting to get hot as they moved the boxes around in the full heat of the sun.

Without the sketch map they had been given it is likely they would have missed the unmarked turn from the main gravel road and onto the dirt track down to the fishing port. They had plenty of fuel, plenty of time and the Toyota could simply smash straight through the bush if they had to, but they crawled down the track. They passed the occasional house and decaying fishing boat and guessed they were on the right road. More houses and more vegetable gardens emerged as they caught a glimpse of the sea through the trees. There were chickens scratching around but no small children playing around the houses. There were rows of young plants but no one weeding them. It didn't look affluent, more like subsistence farming supporting the fishing or vice versa. A few more grass houses, and then suddenly they were in an open area perhaps fifty metres by thirty metres. Along two sides of the square were larger buildings made of mud brick or cement block. There was a store and perhaps a bar. Opposite, under some trees, it looked like a small market area, but no people. Off to the right they could see the sea and what looked like a pier; they drove slowly towards it. Suddenly they could see the MV *Karwe*. It looked completely out of place, but a welcome sight. In the strong sunshine the boat was a blaze of white. It looked big and chunky. A blue awning was spread across a frame on the top deck, next to

75

the for'ard wheelhouse. A yellow zodiac was suspended in a rear hoist and a row of port holes peered across at them. Sandro drove towards the boat but stopped short. The pier was made up of rows of crudely cast concrete beams, and they didn't look too safe. The beams were not level, some had lips several centimetres high and there were gaps wide enough for a foot or leg to slide between them. It all looked a bit precarious. The MV *Karwe* was moored against this pier.

Two men suddenly appeared on the upper deck, first waving, then disappearing, and then re-appearing as they hopped over the side and jogged towards them. Jack and the others started to get out of the pickup and stretch as the two men arrived. Big smiles and long handshakes all around. Both men were dressed in light blue polo shirts with an embroided logo of a leaping manta ray and the name of the boat, MV *Karwe*, in dark blue. It was the same shirt the representative in Malindi had worn. Mohammed was short and stocky with the odd grey strand twisting its way through his close cut hair. He announced that he was the captain, navigator and engineer and that he had sailed these waters for twenty years. However, the thing that Jack noticed was that his nose seemed so flat it was just a small bulge between his eyes and wide mouth. Kirru had to be at least a foot taller and several shades darker. His head was like a smooth black ball and it seemed so black that his skin had a blue tinge. Kirru was a Somalian not a Kenyan. He was the Dive Master, cook and "all things Mohammed not do". From Mohammed's reaction it was clear that the two men got along well.

Sandro carefully manoeuvred the pickup close to the rear of the boat. They started untying the ropes and manhandling the food on board. Mohammed simply stacked the plastic tubs on the dive deck whilst Kirru carried the polystyrene crates through to the galley and began unloading them into the freezers; there was plenty of space. Everyone was busy helping to manhandle the large aluminium diving crates from the pickup and onto the dock, that they hadn't noticed the four approaching men until they were close to them. The quiet was suddenly shattered by gun fire; so close that Jack crouched and put his hands over his ears. Before Jack could even straighten he received a sickening blow to his back, near his shoulder. He had tried to brace himself as he fell but was stunned and landed heavily face down, cracking his forehead against the hot concrete. As he rolled onto his side Kev fell almost on top of him. He had been hit by the stock of whatever gun one of the men was carrying. A bruise was starting to form on his cheek. In the confusion he heard a woman scream, it was Penny. One of the men had grabbed her shoulder and was wrestling her to the ground. Jack couldn't see Sandro. There was another burst of extended gunfire and then shouts. Jack didn't know what was happening but knew it wasn't good.

As Jack lay on the ground he looked around him and saw three men, all armed. They weren't military. The odd collection of clothes told him that much. Jack started to rise making sure he had his arms stretched out above his head in the universal surrender mode. As he turned, looking for Sandro, he could see that despite a bloody nose, he was all right and helping Penny to her feet. The sleeve of her crisp pale green shirt had been ripped at the seam and red welds drew vivid lines on her pale skin. The gangsters shouted and pointed until they had the four of them backed up against the tailgate of the pickup. A fourth gunman was shouting at Kirru. From the arm waving Jack guessed he was telling him to leave the boat and join them on the jetty.

Despite the blow to the side of his face Kev was saying he was OK; Sandro had his arm around Penny who looked bemused. It was then that Jack realised that Mohammed and Kirru were arguing with the armed men. Not just arguing, but screaming at them and waving their arms. Jack wasn't sure why Mohammed, and then Kirru, started moving slowly towards one of the gunmen; Jack was frozen to the spot. Almost in slow motion, and without looking directly at them, the gunman swung his rifle round, one handed, and fired a long volley at Mohammed and Kirru, spraying them with bullets.

Jack had never seen anyone shot and it wasn't like the movies. In real life each bullet that struck caused devastating injuries and tossed the two men around like broken puppets, as though being hit by a massive invisible force. The first impression was that Mohammed and Kirru had been offering the gunman a drink because it looked like fluid was being thrown into the air. As soon as the impression was formed it was dismissed; it wasn't water but blood. In the deafening silence that followed the smell of the gun smoke, and something else, drifted over them. Jack felt his stomach clench and burning vomit rise to his throat. He was about to be sick but forced himself to stop and force the rising mass downwards. It left an acidic, sour taste in his mouth. Penny was less fortunate; the vomit exploded from her mouth before she could stop herself. The gunman laughed and propped the rifle butt onto his hip like some movie star.

Jack, Sandro, Kev and Penny allowed themselves to be pushed into the back of the pickup and to be wedged with their backs against the cab. Jack could feel the hot metal of the pickup on his backside and back but gave no thought to it. Two of the gunmen climbed into the back and sat on the raised tailgate, their rifles pointing directly at them.

It was then that Jack noticed movement on the dockside next to the aluminium crates. It was Mohammed. He was trying to stand, his arm pushing himself up from one of the aluminium crates. One of the gunmen who was sitting on the tailgate had spotted Jack's glance, turned his head, and shouted something. There was another long volley of fire. The bullets kicked up chunks of concrete and dust. They thumped into the crate over which Mohammed crouched punching neat holes in the middle of a smooth dent. They also thumped into Mohammed and knocked him backwards. He wouldn't be getting up again.

Two gunmen on the dock strolled towards the murdered men and started to roll the body of Kirru towards the edge of the jetty with the soles of their boots. There was a dark smear left behind. It may have been the light but the smear seemed to change colour, and darken, as the body was rolled. Jack heard the dull splash as Kirru dropped into the water. Moments later Mohammed followed him. Jack couldn't believe what was happening. The two gunmen must have climbed into the cab because suddenly the pickup burst into life and they were bouncing back across the open ground and towards the main gravel road. Jack had no idea how long they were driving, not long, but they slowed and turned down a similar but somewhat wider dirt road. This time there

79

were women in the vegetable gardens, children playing and men mending nets but no one paid them any attention.

They arrived at another jetty, bigger and busier, but no one gave them a second glance. The pickup came to a halt towards the end of the jetty next to an old barge with a diesel powered crane. No words were spoken but from the waving and pointing they got the message. They were to get off the pickup and onto the barge. The gunman who had murdered Mohammed and Kirru motioned them to sit on the deck, side by side. Jack had noticed the sheen of diesel oil smearing the deck, and the fetid smell of sewage, but simply sat in the grime and filth. He almost laughed when he realised that Penny's smart light brown trousers would soon have a black bottom. He didn't laugh but bowed his head into his hands, took a deep breath, and wondered what would happen next.

Jack had lost all sense of time but the sun was still roasting and high in the sky. He heard a movement on the dockside, some activity. One of the gunmen, who had been sat in the shade of the pickup, suddenly tensed. A scowl formed on his face as he grabbed his weapon and assumed the "at ready position".

Jack turned his head to see who was coming but the light was so bright he had to squint. He could see several men getting out of some form of pickup and starting to unload cases. He then realised they were offloading large custom made aluminium cases; their diving gear! Once stacked by the pickup they walked purposefully towards the barge. What caught his attention, besides their diving gear, was an enormous African in the middle of the group. He was head and shoulders taller than the others and dressed as a soldier. Jack's first reaction was that the nightmare was about to end, that a local army officer had heard of their plight and was coming to sort it out. The flutter of relief was only momentary as he realised the clothes were an odd combination and of no army that anyone would recognise. Furthermore, his four companions were certainly not military but rather scruffy individuals in T-shirts and baggy trousers. The thing they had in common was that they were well armed.

He nudged Sandro and nodded towards the group. Sandro said nothing but it was clear he was suddenly wide awake. Penny remained comatose but stirred by the sudden noise on the dockside and activity onboard. Kev appeared to be still dozing.

With a great effort, and swaying unsteadily after sitting so long, Jack slowly got to his feet and turned towards the group of approaching men. The huge guy in the middle continued walking and in a fluid, nimble move simply hopped over the side, landed smoothly on his toes, and greeted Jack with a big, but less than convincing smile.

'This is your equipment,' said the big man. His voice was deep and gravel-like. It reminded Jack of an old TV interview he had seen with the Afro-American singer Paul Robson. He had that same deep, rich and resonating voice. However, the image was immediately shattered when the guy towered over him and said, 'I have job for you. You dive and get my container from the ship the idiots sunk. You will do it today or I will be very angry.' It wasn't just what he said but the menace he conveyed through his presence.

Jack should have been cowed and ready to agree to anything but he suddenly felt angry and belligerent. The mixture of eagerness and anticipation he had felt at the start of *Marine Salvage & Inspection Company's* first wreck inspection, coupled with the horrors he had witnessed a few hours ago boiled over. He looked straight at the big man and said. 'My buddy and I will be glad to try and retrieve a container for you, but not today.'

The reaction of the big African was immediate and swift. He flicked his right arm and with a snap of the wrist, slapped Jack across the face with a force that knocked him sprawling across the narrow deck. The sound brought everyone wide awake and alarmed.

'You dare to say no to me! Do you know who I am? I'm SAM,' he shouted, with spittle bursting from his lips as he stood over Jack with both his fists bunched.

The slap, on top of slight concussion, dehydration and a touch of heat stroke knocked the stuffing out of Jack. Bemused he lay on the filthy deck and tried to concentrate. Who was this brute?

As Jack took deep breaths, and tried to recover, he formed an image of the man standing in front of him.

Section 2

Soloman Abraham Mbano (SAM)

Chapter 10

Growing up quickly

Jack had to admit that SAM was an impressive sight.
However, there was no way he could have known the
background of the man who stooped over him.

SAM may have lost that magnificent physique of his
twenties and thirties and may have gained fifteen kilos or
more around his belly, but he still radiated a presence. SAM
wasn't just big he was huge! Standing in his size fourteen
suede Caterpillar boots, of which he was very proud, he was
over six feet four inches tall. So tall that he often had to duck
when entering rooms and typically slid through doorways
sideways. It wasn't just his height. He had been well
proportioned, with his upper body heavily muscled. His early
years clearing fields of trees and scrub in Malawi, Central
Africa, to extend the family farm, had been good preparation.
Even as a teenager he had the stamina and strength of a
mature man. Today he stood in jungle camouflage trousers
with a long bone handled Bowie knife strapped to his right
thigh, plain green, military style jacket with black webbing belt
and Russian automatic in a stained canvas holster. When the
pronounced scar on his left cheek was added he looked like
a film poster for some "over the top" action movie.

SAM had been a big baby. There were no records of his
birth weight. In family tales he was told that had it not been

for the Dutch Catholic nun at the nearby Mothers of Mercy convent, who was also a skilled and experienced midwife, he and his mother would not have survived the birth. They both survived but Daisy, his mother, could never have more children and lavished all her attention on SAM. Daisy and Doli, her husband, wanted more for their son than toiling in the fields as they and their parents had done. They believed SAM was something special, a gift from God. Unlike other children in the village they didn't get him to collect the firewood, feed the chickens and pigs, and weed the rows of maize day after day. Instead he went to the Kadenza Primary School, part of the Mothers of Mercy Convent which was just a short walk each day – four miles there and four miles back, carrying his little rucksack. That is after he had carried five gallons of water from the village pump in a World War II jerry can and made the same trip after he returned from school. At weekends and in school holidays he helped his father clear the scrub and trees around the farm to extend it. It was back breaking work but SAM loved it. He loved wielding the axe, chopping up trees and carrying them home at the end of the day. He even enjoyed digging out the tree stumps. He thrived on it.

SAM was in awe of the nuns at the convent school, in their white flowing habits, riding around on Honda motorcycles with their white headscarves billowing in the breeze. He was also in awe of the strict regime they imposed, and he thrived. SAM wasn't a brilliant student but he was smart and he tried. Since he was bigger than all similar aged boys, and many older, he was never bullied. He was popular and was always invited to take part and gradually emerged as a leader with his views sought by

85

many of the other boys and girls. This continued when he moved up to the Kadenza Secondary School where he was taller than the headmaster. Occasionally, when SAM looked back, these were idyllic days. However, this was before the Front for the Liberation of Mozambique (FRELIMO) freedom fighters began their war against Portuguese rule in Mozambique in the early 1970s. Before they started laying landmines in the road to Salisbury in Rhodesia and the ports of Beira and Lorenzo Marques. It was before men slipped across the invisible border between Malawi and Mozambique to take whatever they wanted with guns and pangas.

In the space of a few hours one dark November night in 1975 SAM's life was transformed. It may have been a group of renegade freedom fighters from FRELIMO, from the Mozambique Resistance Movement (RENAMO) or just an armed gang who arrived in an old Land Cruiser and two military looking covered lorries; the result was the same. The village was ransacked and anything of value was stolen. Anyone who stood in their way was shot or just clubbed to the ground. Daisy and Doli were shot dead as they tried to stop the gang carrying off the sacks of maize from the grain store. The maize that they had planned to sell in the market so that the family could survive another year. Other parents were shot as young girls were tied up and flung into the back of the lorry for later enjoyment. At their leisure they hog-tied the pigs and threw them all into the back of a lorry. It was the same across the whole village. Anything of value was whisked away, what was left was burnt, even his school books.

With no family and no home SAM was stunned as were the other survivors. It was only a day later, when he had no more tears left, that he believed he had only one option. He would work in the gold mines in South Africa. He knew there was a recruitment centre in Zomba and that the Wenela planes flew regularly from Chileka airport in the south of Malawi to Johannesburg to feed the need for young strong men to work in the mines. He had heard stories of men coming back after three years who were rich and who bought farms and wives.

The day after burying his mother and father, and as the sun rose, he started walking towards the Zomba road with all the food he could salvage in his rucksack and the few Kwachas that his mother always hid under the mud stove in the centre of their hut. He sat most of the afternoon by the roadside until the cream coloured bus, with luggage loaded on the roof, took him the rest of the way.

SAM had been to Zomba before and found the Wenela Recruitment office easily. Officially it was the Witwatersrand Native Labour Association but known generally as Wenela. It was just off the main tarmac street through the town and near the Sports Club where the white men played rugby most Saturdays with women in long dresses watching. What he wasn't expecting was the queue. He stood for hours in the queue as it crawled forwards. Overhearing the men alongside him he quickly discovered that he would have to lie about his age since he had to be at least twenty years old. SAM towered above all the other men so it was going to be an easy lie to tell. He also discovered that the *Bas Man* wanted men who had worked in the mines before since many couldn't cope with the sheer physical effort needed nor work in confined airless spaces in near darkness.

87

SAM could hardly remember what happened when he arrived in front of the *Bas Man* and white coated doctor, it all happened so quickly. He was young, fitter and stronger than most of the men in the line but the doctor told him he was underweight. He had no diseases, had all his own brilliant white, even teeth and was happy to sign on for the standard six month period. He could even write his address and sign his own name. That he didn't have identification documents was not a problem since few of the other men had them.

From the recruitment office he joined the others in an old bus that had "WENELA" painted in large red capital letters on the side and was ferried to Blantyre for a short stay in the barracks. SAM spent three days there. Most of the time was spent learning Fanagolo the *lingua franca* in the mines. SAM already spoke English and Portuguese as well as Chewa his native Malawian language and Fanagolo seemed easy. For a few days it was like being back at school. He was also introduced to the rudiments of mining and the regimes he would have to follow before flying down to Johannesburg. He liked the barracks and the lessons but remembered the flight as a nightmare. There were about sixty men crammed into a DC4 airplane that bucked and shook all the way to Johannesburg. Soon after take off grown men were being sick everywhere, moaning and pissing themselves. Within a short time the stench was overpowering; once one started vomiting others followed, including SAM. It wasn't a good introduction to working at the Transwerk Mine on the outskirts of the city. He was so pleased to get off the plane and like the others wash the vomit from his mouth and clothes. After that he simply followed the men in front and did just what they did. Eventually he collected work clothes, ate in the canteen, washed in the ablution block and ended up at the bunk to which he had been allocated in one of the dormitories. His first day was more queues, more questions and because he was young and strong, and had no mining experience, was attached to one of the Clean-Up Gangs.

After the rock had been blasted from the head of the shaft, mechanical shovels moved in to transfer the ore bearing rock to huge metal skips on rubber wheels. They could pick up most of the ore but it was left to the Clean-Up Gang to move in with crowbars and picks, sledge hammers and shovels. They pried loose the rocks that hadn't fallen, smashed the ones they couldn't lift and generally cleared the rubble. Other teams would take over to extend the air hoses, the electricity cables and shore-up the roof and walls.

On his first morning SAM attacked the rock face like the bush around his former home. He dodged the rocks that he levered from the roof; rocks that would have crushed his feet had they hit them. He lifted rocks and threw them into the skip that other men spent half an hour beating with sledge hammers. He worked stripped to the waist. He peeled off the top of his boiler suit and tied the arms around his waist. He was covered in dust and sweat but with a big smile and flashing white teeth, a tin helmet perched on the top of his head.

It was at his first lunch break that a worker from the same dormitory sat beside him and told him to slow down. 'Man, you are working too hard. You never keep up that pace for six months, you hurt yourself, and you make us look bad!' whispered his team mate.

SAM did what he was told and the team thanked him for it. He still did the work of three men but it wasn't at the same

89

frantic pace. Indeed, they all realised that SAM was an asset to the Gang. They always cleared the blast space, never delayed the next team and had an easier job because of SAM. In a place like the Transwerk Mine it was in their interest to keep him safe. They had all guessed that SAM was just a big boy, pleasant but naïve. They steered him away from the whorehouses and shebangs – the drinking dens that surrounded the mine. They steered him away from the gamblers and the dagga; they kept him safe, they kept themselves safe.

After three months of physical toil, an endless supply of food and ten hours sleep per night SAM had been transformed. He had put on weight, not fat but solid muscle, but was bored. He enjoyed the weekly film shows and at first the nightly TV programmes. SAM wasn't a big reader and whilst he had enjoyed listening to the stories of the other men in the dormitory after a while they were the same stories. He had taken a trip with the Clean-Up Gang into a township on one of his first days off but didn't enjoy it. Too crowded, too noisy and too expensive!

It was more by accident than design when one evening he stumbled into the Mine Gym. He wasn't intending to go, he was just curious and bored. Inside it was just another dull dormitory but without the bunk beds. There was a boxing ring on a raised plinth, a line of leather punch bags hanging from the ceiling, wall bars, soft mats scattered around, strange looking equipment and near the door sets of weights. He had seen weightlifters on the TV and so recognized the array of dumbbells and bars with disc shaped weights at each end. There were about twenty men in the gym. A few seemed to be just standing around talking, some were doing exercises on mats and others thumping punch bags. There were two men boxing in the ring with guys hanging on the ropes shouting. Near him there was a muscular man crouching. He had one hand on his knee and a short dumbbell in the other as he bent his arm backwards and forwards. SAM could see the bulging biceps and sweat shining under the lights.

More in curiosity than anything else SAM moved over to the bar and weights, bent down, picked it up and pushed it over his head like he had seen on the TV. He had just lifted two hundred pounds! 'Vut the fuck are you doing?' shouted the Afrikaner, in a strong accent, who was wearing a dark blue tracksuit; a man that he hadn't seen.

SAM froze with the bar above his head.

'Put the fucking thing down and come here,' the man demanded.

SAM replaced the weight and walked to the man who had shouted at him. He looked down with a neutral expression. It was the expression he had perfected when the *Bas Man* was passing by or giving orders, 'Och Man, if you are going to lift weights you need to keep your back straight and use your legs to lift and spring the bar up. I'm surprised you didn't hurt yourself, and in my fucking gym!'

SAM said he was sorry and continued to look down. It was then that Jannie van Scullkvek, who ran the gym, noticed the boots, 'Shit, man, and don't come in here in those bloody boots, you're going to rip up the fucking mats. Get yourself some trainers,' he shouted.

Jannie turned away and walked towards a tall plastic bin set against the wall. He up-ended it and out poured a drab collection of worn sports kit. He reached down and pulled out a pair of dark green rugby shorts with a gold stripe down the sides that was on the top of the pile. SAM was still stood motionless behind the bar. Jannie walked towards SAM and threw the shorts towards him. 'Here, I reckon these will fit you. They are too big for anybody else who has been through here in the last couple of years. You can change through there (pointing to the back of the hall). Oh yis, and leave those bloody boots with your gear, you can work out in bare feet,' said Jannie.

SAM emerged from the changing rooms and walked back towards Jannie. Jannie couldn't believe his eyes. Bare chested, bare footed, towering over him and wearing Springbok style shorts with a sheen of sweat on his body SAM looked the epitome of an athlete.

'Do you realise how much weight you have just lifted?' asked Jannie.

'No, it didn't look that heavy,' said SAM.

'Shit, man, that bar has two hundred pounds on it. It's heavier than many professional lifters could manage, and you did it with fucking terrible technique! If you are interested in lifting weights I'll teach you,' offered Jannie.

Chapter 11

Survival skills

SAM returned to the gym every night. At first he practiced lifting light weights, and grooving the various techniques. He practiced the explosive snatch and spring into a crouch, the bounce as he sprung the weight from his chest into the air. Jannie also got him to exercise other muscles that would allow him to control the bar with his arms, shoulders and core body muscles. SAM practiced all of this during the day with the Clean-Up Gang. He also realised that he had been lucky so far. He had been carelessly lifting rocks that could have injured him permanently. After a while SAM realised that he was getting bored with lifting weights. He wanted to try something different and at the end of his last repetition with a pair of weights walked over to Jannie and asked if he could try boxing. Jannie smiled and agreed because boxing was his first love.

His first boxing session with Jannie was the most frustrating experience SAM could remember. With huge padded gloves, bulky head guard and uncomfortable leather protector covering his lower stomach and groin SAM felt awkward. Jannie was kitted up the same but looked completely comfortable. Jannie had explained that to score a point he had to hit his opponent with the knuckle part of the glove on the body (above the waist but not the back or kidneys) or on the head (but not behind the ears or back of the head). With his massive height and reach SAM should be able to do that easily and smiled, his perfect white teeth sparkling. What he didn't know was that Jannie had been a Physical Training Instructor for twenty-five years in the South African Army. Twenty years earlier Jannie had been middleweight champion of the Army!

'First to ten points wins,' announced Jannie as he bounced around the ring, ' . . . en put yer gum shield in,' he told SAM.

Try as he might SAM simply couldn't touch Jannie. He poked out his arm, sure that he would tap Jannie on the chin, but Jannie's head wasn't there! He tried again and got a face full of glove. It wasn't hard but enough to jolt SAM's head back. He swung a huge right arm that sailed over Jannie's head, only to be tapped in the middle of the chest by Jannie. It was a two minute one sided contest. SAM was pouring in sweat at the end of it, Jannie wasn't even breathing hard.

'Ock, man, you were shit,' laughed Jannie. 'It's all about technique, just like lifting,' said Jannie as they climbed between the ropes and out of the ring. 'You've got to be on your toes, balanced, ready to move forward or back, to one side or the other. You were flat footed, that's why I caught you. You've got to watch your opponent and keep your head moving. If you stop moving you're going to get hit,' explained Jannie.

SAM didn't get back into the ring for another three weeks. Jannie had him twirling the leather skipping rope and moving around the floor whilst he did so. At first it was laughable. SAM had seen young girls skipping in the village but had never done it himself; he thought it was a girl's game.

However, if anything it was more frustrating than the sparring and just as tiring. However, with perseverance he mastered the skipping rope, and the speed ball and found himself on his toes dancing around the ring rather than shuffling around flat footed. After a month or so the two minute sparring sessions with Jannie were getting closer. SAM soon realised what an advantage his height and reach gave him. He could simply fend off Jannie and keep him at a distance. However, he couldn't land many, if any, blows. It was then that Jannie gave him an insight into strategy.

'Ock, man, you are doing well. You are getting sharper all the time and moving well, but you are always going for my fucking head! What's wrong with the body? A tell yer man, kill the body and the head will fall. The body is big and doesn't move much. You may not hit him where you plan, but where you hit him will hurt. The head is much harder to hit and moves much more. Keep missing the head and you tire yourself out. Work on the body at first, slow the guy down. When his head goes down knock the fucking thing off,' Jannie explained with a big smile.

The weeks passed and SAM became more confident moving around the ring, jabbing at the body and slipping punches. He was sparring with smaller but quicker men and quickening his reactions all the time. SAM was enjoying it. One unremarkable night, within weeks of the end of his six month contract at the mine, SAM had showered, changed and was off back to the dormitory when Jannie caught him at the door. Jannie explained that there was an amateur boxing match coming up in Pretoria in a couple of months and the mine always entered a couple of boxers; did SAM want to enter? SAM was confused. He told Jannie that he had never

95

thought about an actual fight and his contract finished in a couple of weeks, so he couldn't box. With a grin Jannie explained that he had checked with the shift manager, a boxing fan, who was happy to extend his contract for another six months and happy for him to represent the mine at the forthcoming tournament. SAM was happy with the six month extension and agreed for Jannie to enter his name. The next six weeks were a mixture of training and sparring, moving smoothly around the ring, firm but not hard punches to the body, ignoring the head.

The fight was on a Saturday night and Jannie drove SAM and two of the other boxers the hundred or so kilometres to the Sports Hall in Pretoria. Only one of the two other boxers had a bout, the one who didn't would act as another second in the corner of the ring.

It was shortly after arrival, and when he was in the changing room, that Jannie came in. He looked flustered. 'Ock, sorry, man, change of plan,' blurted out Jannie. 'The man you were going to fight has just pulled out. They want to replace him with Amos Simbaye. He's a black South African and a heavyweight just like you. I've asked around and my friends confirm what I had picked up. They tell me he's a dirty fighter. He's also had twenty-six bouts, won twenty-two, lost three and drawn one. You're not ready for him SAM, he can hurt you. I'm going to call it off,' Jannie announced.

SAM sat on the bench against the wall, a set expression on his face, staring into space. 'I want to fight him, tell me what I have to do,' said SAM.

Jannie's shoulders slumped as he breathed out. 'Look, man, this was supposed to be a gentle introduction between two novice fighters, just to get the feel of a real fight. This guy is bad news, that's why he's trying to pick up fights whenever he can,' explained Jannie.

'But you thought I was ready. I want to fight tonight,' pleaded SAM.

'You were ready for another novice fighter, but not this guy,' explained Jannie.

'I want to fight him, Jannie, tell me what I have to do,' repeated SAM.

Jannie breathed out heavily in a resigned gesture. 'OK, man, this is what you do, are you listening?'

Chapter 12

A brutal lesson

SAM remembered waiting a long time in the dressing room as the bouts were fought. As the only heavyweight on the bill SAM was going to be the last bout. When he finally entered the ring SAM was surprised at the number of people in the audience. Somehow he had never thought there would be so many even though he had heard the cheering earlier. Jannie told him there were even men from the mine in the audience who had rented a van to bring supporters. SAM beamed with pride.

As SAM sat on his stool, before the opening bell, Jannie kneeled in front of him, holding SAM's head in his hands. 'Listen, man, do just what we have practiced. Stay on your toes, move around, don't stand still. First round go for the body, slow him down. Don't start mixing it with him, I've heard that's what he likes, keep him at range, use your reach, do what we have been practicing,' urged Jannie.

The first round felt strange. The big black South African, Amos Simbaye, simply marched forwards and started to swing punches whenever he thought he was in range of taking SAM's head off. SAM simply moved his head out of the way, dancing one way, then the other before jolting the guy with solid straight lefts to the chest. Towards the end of the round SAM could see the frustration in his opponent's eyes mounting as he swarmed towards him and trapped him in a bear hug before throwing him onto the ropes and catching him with a glancing blow to the shoulder. Feeling elated, but covered in sweat and breathing hard, Sam returned to his stool.

'Man, that was fantastic. He never laid a glove on you. It was at least a six points to none round. But SAM, listen to me, man. This guy is dangerous, he is still strong and he's mad. Do just what you have been doing. Keep away from him, let him swing and miss and poke out that left, let him tire himself out,' said Jannie.

Round two was a carbon copy of Round one. The more Simbaye marched forwards the more he was caught with straight lefts to the body. Twice he managed to dive forward and catch SAM in a clinch, trying to rub his head into SAM's face. It was only by leaning backwards that he avoided being butted and before the referee stepped in and called them to break. SAM ended the round on his toes, jolting his opponent with solid straight lefts to the body whenever he came close.

'Great, man, tremendous,' shouted Jannie over the screams in the crowd. 'He's tiring, you've slowed him down but he's getting more dangerous. If he catches you with that head butt he can split your eyebrow and it will all be over. You are miles ahead of him. Just one more round, do the same,' urged Jannie.

Something had changed at the start of the last round. Simbaye was no longer marching forwards. He appeared to be gasping for air and just standing still, bobbing and weaving but making no attempt to fight. SAM didn't know what to do. He danced around, prodded out the left hand but with no real force behind it. There was no response from

Simbaye, he continued to gasp and to weave. SAM made another tentative straight left, made contact with nothing coming back. He tried another, and then another when suddenly Simbeya sprang into life. From a crouching position he flung a vicious over arm right at SAM's head, springing off his feet as he launched himself forward and upwards. SAM was caught off guard and tried to twist his head away, but not in time. The glove brushed SAM's face but was followed immediately by a violent elbow crashing into his face and breaking his cheek bone. SAM reeled backwards, his vision blurred by the tears in his eyes. His face was numb and he touched his glove to his cheek; it was smeared in blood. He sensed Simbeya marching towards him swinging punches left and right. He backed away flat footed trying to protect his head with his gloves. Simbeya was battering him with vicious lefts and rights. Some of the punches missed the target, hitting SAM on the arms and gloves, but lots hit. SAM grunted in pain. In desperation SAM lunged forwards and grabbed Simbaye in a bear hug, just trying to hang on and let his head clear. His saw blood dripping from his face onto the shoulder of Simbeya.

Then, suddenly, Simbeya was talking to him! 'How'd you like that, boy?' snarled Simbeya. 'You fell for it eh. I bet that elbow has broken your fucking jaw, years of practice eh,' laughed Simbeya as he struggled to release himself from the clinch.

SAM suddenly realised he had been fooled and that Simbeya had hit him with an elbow deliberately. He was angry. His head had cleared and he jumped backwards out of the clinch. He stood flat footed, square on to his opponent, both hands raised and a scowl on his face. It was then, as he looked into the face of Amos Simbeya, that he saw he was smiling, this is what he wanted. 'Come on, boy,' invited Simbeya and SAM was just about to stride forwards when he remembered Jannie's advice.

'Never get mad in the ring, get even. An angry fighter is a bad fighter, use your head.'

Instead of marching forwards SAM sprang backwards and went up onto his toes just as a haymaker right whistled past his nose. The crisis was over, SAM was moving just as smoothly as before, dancing first one way and then the other. But Simbeya wasn't finished, he came swarming in, gloves flying and screaming through his gum shield.

SAM had not thrown a single right hand in the whole contest, it had been straight left after straight left all night. He suddenly realised Simbeya wouldn't expect a right hand punch. SAM jinked to his left and shaped to send out yet another straight left. Simbeya was expecting it. He started to anticipate the punch and was moving his left hand across his body to swat away that irritating punch that he knew was coming. He was going to finish it with a massive right hand. But the straight left never came. SAM began to swivel his hips to the left, his right shoulder followed and with increasing speed his right fist flashed across the narrowing space and exploded against the side of the head of Amos Simbeya. Simbeya was unconscious before he hit the canvas and skidded across the ring, ending almost below the bottom rope. The referee didn't even start the count but rushed to the boxer, turning him on his side, and pulling out the gum shield. At the same time he was waving to the ring side doctor to come and help the helpless fighter. It was all over.

They told him afterwards that the hall erupted in cheers, but SAM couldn't remember any of it. He allowed Jannie to lead him back to the changing room he had left less than fifteen minutes ago and just sat there angry and bewildered. After some time, SAM couldn't say how long, a doctor appeared and examined his face.

'You've got a depressed fracture of the cheek bone. It will need to be reset tonight at the clinic in town, I'll arrange it,' announced the doctor dispassionately.

Later still Jannie returned to explain in a very matter of fact way that since SAM was representing the mine, the mine would pay for his treatment at the clinic. He couldn't go to the Whites Only hospital in town, but the clinic was good. Jannie also told him it was likely he would have to stay in the clinic for a couple of days but he would inform his shift manager at the mine. Jannie then smiled. 'A tell yer, man, you were fucking fantastic. All that training paid off, you had him pinned on that straight left for the first two rounds. But when he caught you with that elbow, gheeeeeeeeeeeeeeee, I thought you were going to lose it, and that right hook was a peach,' grinned Jannie.

SAM allowed himself to be ushered from one place to another over the next few days; he just went along with it. He woke up in a clinic bed on Sunday morning after the operation to fix his cheek. At first he didn't know where he was and felt confused, but the gauze and plaster over his face reminded him. He had never slept on a proper mattress with white sheets before, nor with a white pillow. He had never had people bringing him food and juice to drink and asking if he was OK. It was all very strange and it gave him time to think.

102

Chapter 13

A new SAM

SAM was discharged two days later; there were no complications, just a face swathed in bandages and tape. Jannie collected him from the hospital and drove him back to the mine. 'Great news, SAM. Your shift manager, van de Valke, was in the crowd on Saturday night and thought you did the mine proud. He asked me to tell you that you have the rest of today off but to report to the training office tomorrow at eight a.m. sharp.'

The next time Jannie met SAM it was clear that something was wrong. SAM had changed, he was sullen and cold, and that bright, chirpy demeanour had gone. He wasn't the happy, open young man that had stumbled into the gym months ago. He had seen it with other fighters who had got hurt, but didn't expect it with SAM but he let it go.

The shift manager had arranged "light" duties for SAM until his cheek bone healed. He had been sent to the training centre so that he could be taught how to drive the tractor or mule that pulled the metal skips along the shafts. He enjoyed it for a few weeks as he moved around the mine and met other workers, but he missed his friends in the Clean-Up Gang. The nurse in the first aid room at the mine changed the bandages every day and said it all looked good. There was some bruising and swelling but it was fine.

At the end of the month a check revealed that the cheek bone was healing and SAM asked if he could return to his gang. But the shift manager had other plans for SAM. He had enquired and learned what a good worker SAM was and the initiative and leadership qualities he had shown. He made SAM an offer. Would he like promotion to a gang supervisor and a pay rise? He would fill in for a worker in a gang who was sick, injured or whose time was up. He would also report on the work of those in the teams; those who weren't up to it would be transferred to other jobs.

SAM had no hesitation, it was what he wanted. He wanted what he had seen in the clinic. Polished leather shoes, clean shirts, eating food off white plates rather than the metal ones in the canteen. He wanted to live in his own home with his own friends; not the dust and grime of the mine and the stink of unwashed men around him. He accepted the offer and could go home a rich man.

It was now over a month since SAM had agreed to the boxing match in Pretoria. It was also the first week of his job as gang supervisor as he returned to the gym to be greeted by Jannie and the others he had come to know. The other boxers gathered round, slapping SAM on the back, congratulating him on his win and miming that right hook that had demolished Amos Simbeya.

'Ock, great to see you, man,' said Jannie.

It was then that he saw the scars on Sam's cheek; a pink stripe along the line of his cheek bone and a vivid crescent scar across the middle of his cheek. Whilst the surgeon may have done a good job on resetting the cheek bone the guy who stitched SAM up hadn't done the best of jobs. Slightly taken aback by the intimidating appearance that SAM now exuded, Jannie announced with a smile, 'I see you are ready to start training,' as he strode over to the group. 'What's it to be?'

SAM placed a huge arm over the shoulder of Jannie as he steered him away from the group. 'I don't want to box anymore,' announced SAM. 'I want you to teach me how to fight'.

'I don't know what you mean,' puzzled Jannie. 'That guy was just dirty. I don't want to teach you those tricks,' he said.

'No, no, not in the ring,' explained SAM. 'They've made me a gang supervisor and I can tell some of the men don't like it. I've already had some trouble and there will be more. These guys don't come at you with fists up, they come swinging a sledge hammer or come at you with a knife. I don't know what to do,' confided SAM.

Jannie paused, his face set, he looked down. He knew what happened in the dark tunnels in the mine when "accidents" happened. When, apparently, a loose rock just happened to fall at the wrong time to crush someone's skull. Was it a rock? When an arm or leg was broken. Did he trip? When scores were being "settled", "justice" delivered or when a message was "reinforced". As big and strong as SAM may be he couldn't watch his own back all the time and there would be no one to help him in those dark corners.

'Gee, man, in the army I used to teach unarmed combat, but that was a long time ago. I can teach you some of the techniques but I'm rusty. Let me make a few phone calls and see what I can do. Come back tomorrow,' promised Jannie.

Jannie was as good as his word. The next night an average looking, red faced, South African in crisp olive shorts and an olive T-shirt was waiting for him alongside Jannie.

105

'So, you want to learn about unarmed combat?' said the sharply spoken man with a strong Afrikaans accent. 'Have you got what it takes, 'cos it's not about strength but skill.'

'I want to learn, sir. I'll do what you tell me to, I'll try, sir,' said SAM.

'I'm not a fucking sir, call me Piet and grab this,' said Piet as he tossed a wooden stick shaped like a dagger towards SAM. 'Now, act like you are one of those black bastards in the mine coming to stick that knife into my gut. I'm going to teach you what to do.' With that Piet sprang to the side, on his toes, hands held high but relaxed. 'So come on and stick it into me,' shouted Piet.

'I don't want to hurt you,' said SAM.

'You stupid black bastard. You aren't going to hurt me. I'm going to hurt you!' he shouted back.

Stung by the comment SAM lunged forwards with the wooden knife, aiming for the middle of Piet's body. Next minute SAM was on the floor, face down, his arm was up his back, he had lost the knife and Piet had a knee in the small of his back.

'OK, get up, let's go through this again,' said Piet as he helped SAM from the floor.

For the next ninety minutes Piet explained and demonstrated the way he could use the momentum of his attacker against the attacker. It was skill and technique, not strength, that was important he stressed. He went through the movements in slow motion, with a knife attack from this side, from the front and from behind. SAM was impressed by the way Piet, with seemingly effortless ease, could deflect what SAM was trying to do, the way he used his own body weight and movement against him. SAM was totally committed.

Every night for the next six weeks SAM was slammed to the floor, had his arms twisted, folded and held against the joint. He was tripped and rolled, sent stumbling or held paralysed by a few fingers by a man thirty centimetres shorter and half his weight. But SAM learned. He was also putting these skills into practice in the mine. The day after he had recommended that a man on Green Shaft, Level five be replaced in one of the Clean-Up Gangs he was walking through that clean up area as the men worked. He wasn't sure how but he sensed it, something wasn't right. The big Ugandan to his left was holding the crowbar strangely and wasn't standing normally; something was wrong. One of the men with a shovel wasn't scooping up the loose rock and throwing it into the skip, he was stood looking. SAM continued walking through the rubble, not changing his stride, but watching the Ugandan in his peripheral vision. He was almost level with the man when the Ugandan struck with the crowbar; it whistled through the air promising to decapitate SAM.

In one fluid movement, that he had practiced with Piet and Jannie, SAM smoothly intercepted the bar with both hands but didn't try to stop it. Instead he twisted and with his hip simply rolled the Ugandan off his feet, as though the weight of the crowbar was pulling him. As the Ugandan began to fall Sam clubbed him at the back of the head with the crowbar; the man collapsed face down in the dust. It had taken less than a second and the whole team just stood in silence as SAM dropped the crowbar to the ground with a clatter and said, 'When he wakes up tell him to be careful not to trip over again. Next time he trips he could get really hurt.'

Over the next couple of weeks SAM realised that it was the crowbar rather than the shovel, pick or sledge hammer that was the weapon of choice. He also seemed to have developed a sixth–sense when something wasn't right; when someone was going to try and take him out. There were two more attempts to injure SAM before they gave up. Each time he anticipated the attack and left the man unconscious but with nothing broken. There was a general consensus amongst the Clean-Up Gangs that SAM could have killed the men who attacked him, but he didn't. He didn't report them to the *Bas Man* and did more than his share of the work when he was replacing someone in the gang. The men both feared and respected him.

After three months SAM was becoming a match for Piet, just through what he had been taught and practiced. In terms of skill and technique Piet was better, but what SAM lacked in these areas he made up for in sheer strength, aided by his amazing reach. It was impossible to get close to SAM without those huge hands grabbing you and doing what Piet had taught him. Piet was also intrigued by SAM. At first it was just a favour to Jannie. He would give the boy a few tips and leave it at that. But SAM's determination and progress made Piet want to see how far this boy could go; he was already one of the best recruits he had taught.

It was just another one of those cold, wet October days when SAM turned up at the gym. Piet announced that this would be the last week but with a different focus. For the rest of the week they would be practicing the stuff not taught in the manual.

Piet faced SAM across the mat, this time with a heavy chain in his hand, swinging it from side to side. As SAM steadied himself to respond to the swinging chain Piet suddenly threw a handful of sawdust into his face. He wasn't expecting it, his eyes clamped shut at the sharp pain. He instinctively brought his hands to his face . . . then felt a firm hand on his chest pushing him backwards, tripping over an outstretched leg, onto his back. Piet was standing over him saying 'Clunk, clunk, you're dead.' SAM was spitting saw dust out of his mouth, blinking his eyes and rubbing sawdust from his face. 'Sorry, man,' said Piet. 'I knew a man in Pietermaritzburg who carried dry sand in his left trouser pocket, just in case he needed it. These are some of the tricks you are going to meet and better you meet them here with me than in the mine.'

The rest of the week Piet showed him the tricks and ruses that street fighters use. The glance from the face to over the shoulder followed by a kick to the balls. The "I'm sorry, let's be friends handshake" that is followed by an elbow to the throat or head butt to the bridge of the nose. It was a world he knew existed in the mine but he had yet to experience. At the end of the week Piet and Jannie sat down with SAM next to the boxing ring. It was late and all the others had showered and gone back to the dormitories.

'Well, man, that's all I can teach you,' said Piet as he raised the bottle of water to his mouth and half of it gurgled down his throat. 'The rest is practice. But just a couple of last tips. When you are really up against it don't be polite. Don't wait for the other guy to hit you 'cos once you are on the floor you're dead meat. Get your man down as quickly as possible and make sure he doesn't get up. Oh yis, and try not to kill him hey,' as Piet smiled.

Jannie didn't smile. He had noticed the change in SAM since the boxing match. The smiling, friendly young man had gone. That had been replaced by something a lot harder, far less forgiving and ruthless. Jannie began to wonder if he and Piet had created a monster. Certainly, the gossip he had picked up told him that SAM was already taking the advice of Piet; he was getting his retaliation in first.

Chapter 14

A view of the future

SAM continued to visit the gym most nights, but not all of them. He still avoided the gambling dens and dagga but enjoyed the occasional beer and weekly trip to the whorehouse. His next six month contract began to follow a routine. He knew his way around the mine. He could spot the men who may cause him trouble. He also realised that the men around him, like lots of others, could spend all the money they had earned in a week in a few hours on whores, drink, gambling or dagga. When he left the mine he was going to be the man taking their money.

SAM finally said no to further extensions of his contract and in November 1978 completed three years at the Transwerk mine. With all the money he had saved, and a kitbag full of clothes, he set off for Beira; the major port in Mozambique and a city of more than one hundred and fifty thousand people. His journey by numerous buses was long and uneventful. His attempts to get work was depressing, especially as he had arrived in Beira in December, almost at the height of the rainy season. He had walked for hours around the docks, asked about work in bars and sawmills; there was nothing. Men in the dormitory had told him Beira was booming and there would be lots of jobs, but they were wrong. The start of the civil war between FRELIMO, which controlled the government, and the RENAMO rebels was bringing chaos to the country and to Beira. He could see the effects of hunger and disease on the streets. SAM had heard about famine but never seen it. It was when he walked into the famous Grande Hotel in Beira that he realised that coming to the city had been a mistake. There would be no work, the hotel was full of homeless people.

The rain dropped straight out of the sky and turned the red soil into a mudbath. His new Caterpillar boots, a present to himself, were covered in mud. The rain also ran down his thigh off another present, the long bone handled Bowie knife that was strapped to it. It was like the one he had seen in one of the cowboy films he had watched at the mine. To get out of the rain he ran into one of the bars just past the Grande Hotel. Wet and miserable he sat by himself, in a corner, sipping a lukewarm beer that cost twice as much as in Johannesburg. SAM was wondering what to do next, where to go.

He was thinking of going back to the mine when, initially unnoticed, three men walked up to the table and one of them kicked a table leg rocking his bottle of beer and nearly knocking it over.

'Hey, you, this is our table – *voertsek*,' shouted the man in the middle as he placed both hands on the table and thrust his face in front of SAM. It was the derogatory South African slang typically shouted at dogs.

All the pent up frustration, the anger at being misled, his prized muddy Caterpillar boots, exploded. No one saw SAM's right fist execute a perfect upper cut as it connected with the point of the man's chin. No one could see the jawbone dislocate and twin spears of bone being driven up into the man's brain. Few witnessed the straight left that smashed into the face of his companion, breaking his nose and knocking out three teeth. What onlookers did hear, however, was two men falling to the ground, one dead, one unconscious. In another bar, in another town, in another country SAM would have been in trouble, but not today in this bar, in Beira. It was just another brawl and it was all over, back to drinking.

SAM pushed back his chair, picked up his beer and took a long swig finishing the bottle. 'You can have your table, I'm going,' said SAM as he started to get up.

The third man was staring at his two friends, only one of whom was stirring, and then switched his attention to SAM. 'Do you want a job? We are now a man short,' he announced with a forced smile. 'I've got a pickup outside, give me a hand, we need to get these two cleaned up.'

The tone and expression told SAM that this man knew one of his companions was dead and was offering to get him out of the bar and away.

The man with the broken nose and bloody mouth was helped to his feet by his friend, still groggy after the punch. SAM grabbed one arm of the other man and slung him over his shoulder. 'Where to?' said SAM as he was led outside.

SAM had seen dead men in the mine. There was looseness about the way they laid and odd movement when they were carried or lifted that shouted it at you. SAM knew the man he had hit wouldn't be waking up. He also knew he had to get out of the bar and away from Beira as soon as possible. The pickup could get him away.

'I'm Souha,' offered the third stranger after they helped the injured man into the back of the pickup and draped the

113

corner of a tarpaulin around him. The second man was laid out and the rest of the tarpaulin thrown over him. 'We work for Jammal, he's a ... er ... businessman. He sent us to find someone to help us in the ... er ... business. I think you are what we need,' he said with a smile.

Souha didn't seem upset by the way SAM had beaten his two friends and made a snap decision not to bail out of the Mitsubishi pickup but to see if there was a job after all.

It was only a short drive along the docks, where he had walked through the rain. Souha drove down a side street and stopped next to a pair of peeling warehouse doors. They had been blue at one time but now there was more wood showing than paint. They were big enough to allow a truck to drive through. Souha knocked and after a short delay a small side door was opened. Between them they helped the man with the bloody face out of the Mitsubishi and manoeuvred him through the side gate; they left the other guy under the tarpaulin. They both knew he would be going somewhere else fairly soon.

There were two other Mitsubishi pickups inside, all with the tell tale signs of hard wear. Scraped body work, broken tailgates, rusting hinges and crude attempts to paint out previous signs on the doors. Was it a warehouse, was it a store, was it a barracks? It was difficult to say at a glance, but obviously lived in. SAM could smell the food and suddenly realised how hungry he was. As he glanced around he saw three men sat at a long table near a window; it looked like they were eating. There was a large cauldron on the table with steam rising, flat loaves of bread and bottles of beer. The men rose and turned towards SAM and Souha. The man in the middle looked like an Arab and was wearing a pale

114

brown jalaba and dirty white turban. His face was weathered and thin, the other two were mestiço; mixed race. What he did notice was that the two either side of the man in the middle looked well fed, they were wearing fancy boots, an odd collection of clothes and were both carrying knives in curved sheaths on their belts. One of the mixed race men was slightly built, had a striped shirt without a collar and a stained maroon waistcoat. He had a piece of black cloth over his hair, tied back to make him look like a pirate. SAM smiled. Not at meeting these three men but thinking about the nuns at the Mothers of Mercy Convent with their headscarves; he liked theirs better. The other was heavier, had an untidy beard and was wearing what looked like a football shirt tucked into heavy canvas trousers.

They left SAM standing on his own next to one of the Mitsubishi pickups whilst Souha spoke in whispers to the man in the jalaba. SAM assumed this was Jammal. The other two just stood and smiled at him, but without any warmth.

'So, you have killed one of my men, badly beaten another and want a job,' said Jammal in a sharp accented voice that SAM struggled to follow.

'They started it. I only hit each man once,' replied SAM.

Jammal smiled and looked at the pirate with the soiled waistcoat. He turned back to SAM and said, 'A little test my big friend. This is Ahmed,' pointing at the pirate in the soiled waistcoat. 'Take the knife away from Ahmed, without getting cut, and you have a job. But be careful, the knife is sharp!'

Chapter 15

Passing the test

Ahmed stepped forward and with a slow and deliberate action pulled the curved knife from its sheath; he smiled at SAM. It was then that SAM noticed his sharp stained teeth, like the rats in the tunnels of the Transwerk mine. His eyes were bloodshot but Ahmed didn't bother to look at the knife as he flicked it from one hand to the other, his smile increasing. Ahmed sank into a crouch as he advanced on SAM. Like a training session in the gym thought SAM as he backed away from the pickup into an open space. He was glad he had remembered to brush the mud from the soles of his boots; he didn't want to slip now. SAM also remembered the coaching Piet had given him that last week. He glanced nervously over his shoulder giving the impression he wanted to run. He wasn't nervous, he just wanted to check for rubbish on the floor. He wanted to note things to slip on, things to snag against.

'Nowhere to run, my big friend,' called Jammal from the side lines, the other men spread out around the sides of the space.

SAM continued to back away as Ahmed slashed the knife left handed through the air. The slash was not to cut SAM but merely to intimidate and back him against the wall. He prodded the knife towards SAM's face as SAM backed away, but towards the middle of the open space. Suddenly Ahmed sprang forward, the knife arrowing towards SAM's throat. But rather than jumping backwards SAM moved forwards and grabbed the left wrist of Ahmed pulling him off balance. As Ahmed stumbled forwards SAM cushioned his head in his huge right hand, flicked Ahmed's legs away with his own right boot and slammed him face down onto the grimy concrete floor. In an often practiced, fluid movement he dropped his knee and his whole weight into the middle of Ahmed's back and drove the air out of his lungs. SAM plucked the knife from Ahmed's still hand and stood up. Ahmed lay stunned on the floor gasping for breath. SAM reached down, grabbed him by the scruff of the neck, and hoisted him to his feet. Half lifting, half pushing, he guided Ahmed to the bench next to the table, sat him down and propped him against the table edge. As Ahmed swayed and brought his hands to his face SAM picked up a bottle of beer. Holding it by the neck he levered off the cap with the back of the knife, flicking it onto the floor. He picked up a second and did the same, setting it down next to Ahmed. SAM then dropped the knife, point down, and stuck it into the table top.

'I think this is yours, my friend. Have a beer, you'll feel better,' said SAM.

But the tone didn't sound friendly and gave no impression that he was even bothered if Ahmed felt better or not. SAM stood waiting for a reaction or another attack. He turned to Jammal and the others who stood with mouths open. Ahmed had never been beaten in a knife fight; he was the best they knew, until now.

'Do I get the job?' SAM asked.

Beyond the table and benches, at the back of the warehouse, were two separate doorways. One led to a series of rooms where Jammal and his two wives lived, the other to a well lit bunkhouse with two, two-tier metal bunks against one wall. Two other long, low cots, that looked like military wood and canvas collapsible bunks, were lined up against the other wall. Two large windows allowed sunlight to stream into the room. Next to the bunks were a motley collection of small cupboards, most of which had the doors missing. Another large table and benches filled the middle of the room; it was like a small barracks.

'You can have that one over there,' said Souha pointing to one of the low cots on the far wall. 'The man you killed had it,' he said.

It was no secret what "business" Jammal was running. He supplied illegal alcohol to the drinking dens around Beira as well as running a number of brothels attached to them. He also bought almost anything stolen from the docks and resold it either in the city or in Rhodesia or South Africa. SAM was to be the muscle if problems arose as well as doing the fetching and carrying.

The first few weeks followed a similar pattern. SAM would stack maize baskets and blanket rolls into the back of one of the old Mitsubishi pickups and cover it with the patched tarpaulin; it kept out most of the rain. He would then be driven with Jammal out into the bush to isolated villages. It varied, but it was typically a round trip of three to four days depending on the weather. Two of the others in the group had similar routes. Once in the village they would meet with the suppliers of Kachasu, the illegal alcohol brewed and then distilled from maize, finger millet or bananas. SAM had seen neighbours, back in the village in Malawi, brewing beer for festivals and distilling it to boost the alcohol content. Drink too much, especially on an empty stomach, and it can kill you, but the men and the women loved it. He remembered his neighbour showing him and the other boys how strong it was by pouring a drop of Kachasu onto a tin plate and touching it with a match. A blue flame licked around the plate until it had all gone.

They would drive into the village. SAM and the driver would shelter under a tree or just sit in the shade of the Mitsubishi whilst Jammal haggled with the women over the price for the liquor; it could take hours. It took time because the Kachasu was in dozens of bottles of different shapes and sizes, from beer bottles to wine bottles, jam jars to gallon sized plastic tubs. Each different sized bottle was haggled over. They would then stack the bottles in the maize baskets, wedge them with grass, and drive to the next village. SAM soon discovered that loose plugs and poorly packed bottles had Kachasu running off the bed of the pickup as they bounced along the muddy dirt roads.

Back in Beira they would drive round their network of shebangs to sell it, and go through the haggling all over again. The rains had turned the country roads into red quagmires and after two exhausting wet trips Jammal decided he preferred the warmth and comfort of his bed and that from now on SAM could make the weekly collection of Kachasu. He gave him instructions on the price he should pay, gave him a thick wodge of escudos, and told him how much he expected SAM to bring back. He also warned, 'If you are short I'll take it out of your wages,' with a challenging tone.

Two days later SAM drove off on his route with eighty cases of empty beer bottles strapped into the back of the Mitsubishi, together with six live chickens and sacks of cassava, sweet potato and chickpeas. He had also acquired one thousand crown corks, stolen by one of the employees of the Castle Brewery in exchange for one bottle filled with Kachasu.

At the first village on the route the absence of Jammal and threatening presence of SAM was soon dispelled. SAM presented his supplier, Effi Ngulube, a toothless middle aged uneducated mother of five, with a live chicken and enough cassava, sweet potato and chickpeas to feed the whole family that afternoon as well as SAM and the driver. However, her surprise turned into delight when SAM stacked five crates of empty beer bottles next to her hut. Collecting empty bottles was her biggest problem.

She shrieked in amazement when SAM filled one of the bottles with water, put a crown cork over the top and with a piece of metal tube and piece of wood crimped the crown cork in place before twisting the tube free for the next bottle. SAM showed her that the water couldn't get out. He then caught the edge of the bottle top on the edge of the crate and with a practice punch with the heel of his hand, knocked off the bottle top and poured the water out. He then gave Effi the bottle, a new crown cork, metal tube and lump of wood and told her to practice. Effi again laughed out loud as she tried to coordinate the holding with the hitting. With one of her children holding the bottle, and half a dozen attempts later Effi had mastered it.

Having created such a good atmosphere it didn't surprise SAM that he and Effi soon agreed the price for each full

120

bottle of Kachasu and that if she and her friends could make more, of the same quality, he would buy it at the same price. It was some time later that Effi realised that she had agreed to sell her Kachasu for less than before, but she knew of other villages that could supply her. She could probably make even more money and it would be easier.

SAM repeated the same process along his route and each week brought a chicken or salted fish as a present each time. Instead of being a frustrating and tiresome business his weekly rounds became a pleasure and the network increased. It was very different from "persuading" reluctant bar owners to pay cash for the kachasu or dissuade the competition. Within months SAM was bringing in more kachasu than ever, at lower cost and with no breakages. Jammal was not pleased as he saw his authority being eroded, despite making more money.

At the end of the rains Jammal decided he would resume the kachasu collection; SAM could accompany Ahmed and collect the takings from the three brothels he owned. They could also track down and break the fingers of those men who had slapped any of the girls around; damaged girls were bad for business. They could also warn off any freelance girls who would hang around the shebangs.

Chapter 16

Facts of life – and death

SAM's job was to move between the various shebangs and brothels that Jammal owned. Just maintaining a presence in the wild town reassured many of the customers. Occasionally there would be a drunk to throw out or a fight to stop; it was a case of being vigilant. Over the months he formed a pretty good idea of how much kachasu was being sold and how many men were climbing the stairs to visit the girls. He knew the price of both. He was also aware of the worsening situation in Beira; it was getting more lawless and chaotic with armed confrontations between the FRELIMO based government and the RENAMO rebels. This was mainly in the countryside as each group vied for support, but it was spreading to the towns. He had already been stopped by a RENAMO roadblock and only got through when he presented each soldier with a bottle of kachasu. It was around this time he had noticed a police officer in one of the shebangs and seen money change hands. He reckoned it was just a matter of time before the police or the paramilitary took an interest in the kachasu sales and wanted part of the profit from the brothels.

Before he joined Ahmed to collect the takings from the brothels he had mentioned the policeman and what looked like a pay-off to Jammal, who had dismissed it.

'I have it all under control. You just do what I tell you. I'm running this business,' he smirked.

SAM was pretty sure he didn't have it "under control" and it was just a matter of time before they attracted attention.

An incident with Ahmed, collecting money from the brothels, was the spark that soon created the explosion. They had driven to the first brothel to meet with Estella who ran the place, kept the girls in order, looked after them and collected the money. SAM had seen Estella many times before and didn't like her. She was a shrew of a woman: tall and skinny with a shrill voice. She always appeared to be complaining about somebody or something. Wanting others to sort out what she should be sorting out. SAM was aware she had favourites and treated other girls like slaves. SAM had asked Ahmed how much money he usually collected each day and was surprised. In the evenings, as he sat in the entrance hall, he had seen the steady flow of clients. Busy at the weekends but steady during the week. He had a pretty good idea what money was being earned.

They ducked into the shebang and walked past the bar and through a curtained door that led into a large open room. A wide staircase led from the room and then turned upwards to the rooms upstairs. It had once been a very smart room. But the large single chandelier was covered in dust and at night nearly half the light bulbs were either missing or not working. The velvet curtains had been bleached by the sun and hung in irregular loops from wooden poles. The windows were dull and covered in hard baked dust. The two and three-seater leather button backed chairs had once been grand but had suffered hard wear and neglect. Parts of the backs, arms and seats were shiny with regular use but

123

otherwise drab and scuffed. The large Indian rug on the floor, once bright, had seen better days; it looked as if it hadn't been brushed for weeks. The brightest sight in the room were the eight girls. They were young, attractive but subdued, talking in earnest whispers rather than girlish ways.

Estella was expecting them. She greeted Ahmed with a big false smile and peck to the cheek but her smile disappeared as she turned and almost scowled at SAM. Estella had a roll of escudo notes in her hand and held it out to Ahmed saying, 'Slow time last night.'

Before Ahmed could reach out to collect the money there was a blur of movement as SAM's hand chopped down on the outreached arm. The two bones in the arm snapped like dry twigs as Estella cried out in both surprise and pain. She stood holding her elbow as the forearm dangled at a grotesque angle.

'The money is short and this place is a shithole,' announced SAM. He grabbed Estella by the throat and pulled her towards his face, stooping to meet her face to face. In a low threatening tone SAM was almost spitting into her face, saying, 'I've been counting your customers and I know how much money should be in that roll. I'm going to come back at midday to collect the rest. Don't disappoint me otherwise I will break your other arm,' and he pushed her away.

SAM turned and shouted for Ndele, the black South African who did all the cooking and cleaning in the place. He shouted again as Ndele shuffled into the room, his eyes drawn to Estelle who was stood to one side sobbing and being comforted by two of the girls. SAM took one pace towards him and grabbed him by the collar. 'This place is a shithole. You're going to do what you are paid for and clean it

124

up. Are you listening to me?' glared SAM. 'Before it gets dark you are going to wash down these walls and clean that light. You are going to wash these chairs, the floor and the rug. Are you listening to me?' snarled SAM as he shook Ndele by the scruff of the neck, with Ndele trying to nod. 'And I'm coming back for something to eat with the girls but not that shit you serve up. I want piri piri chicken and sweet potato, bananas and sugar cane. These girls are valuable, more valuable than you, and I want them well fed and happy. And if I don't like it I will cook your hands and make you eat them. Do you understand?' glared SAM as Ndele shivered with fright. 'What time do you eat?' he asked the girls as he picked up the roll of money, handed it to Ahmed and walked out into the sunshine.

Outside Ahmed couldn't contain himself. Jammal will go mad, what have you done?' asked Ahmed.

'Estelle has been cheating us for months if not years,' said SAM, 'and Jammal didn't even know.'

SAM and Ahmed went, in turn, to the other two brothels and SAM repeated his performance. At the second brothel he grabbed the hand of the madam as she offered the money to Ahmed and crushed it in his own until he could hear bones break. The cleaner / cook was slapped to the ground with one blow when he started to argue with SAM. He didn't argue any more as he felt loose teeth with his tongue. The third madam had her shoulder dislocated as SAM made his demands clear. The cleaner / cook backed away promising the floor would be so clean that he would eat off it himself. SAM told him that if it wasn't clean he would eat off it – without his teeth!

SAM and Ahmed returned to the first brothel in the late afternoon as promised, just as the early supper was about to be served. The transformation was astounding. The chandelier twinkled as sun blasted through sparkling windows. The walls and floor showed smears where the water had dried but the result was still noticeable. The place smelled clean and fresh. Even the carpet looked brighter from its washing, even though it wasn't fully dry. But it was the smell of the piri piri chicken that both Ahmed and SAM immediately noticed as saliva started to flow.

SAM had expected the girls to be subdued, like they were when he arrived that morning, but they were not. He was suddenly taken back to Kadenza Secondary School and the sound of girls chattering excitedly with occasional giggles as he and Ahmed joined them in a back room to eat. The piri piri chicken looked and smelled delicious and he called Ndele in to tell him so. Ndele smiled like a little boy at the praise. As they were eating Estelle walked into the room on unsteady legs. Her face was pale and strained, a patterned scarf acted as a sling. She had been into the market and the traditional medicine man or curandeiro had set the two bones and given her *muti* to dull the pain.

'Where's the rest of the money?' demanded SAM without even looking at her.

Estella crept forwards and dropped a cloth bag on the table, across from SAM. 'I only took it for my children,' pleaded Estelle as she backed away. 'That is all I took,' she said.

'I'll be checking and if I find you have cheated us I will break your other arm,' threatened SAM.

Estelle turned away and left the room.

There was a moment of quiet before everyone resumed eating. Within minutes the girls were telling SAM and Ahmed that they knew Estelle was stealing the money, but they were too afraid to tell anyone. Before the end of the meal they were telling him that the beds were old and broken, the sheets were thin and ripped … they wanted mosquito nets … and proper soap … SAM escaped as soon as he could but with a big smile on his face. The girls were happy and more money would come in.

The one person who wasn't happy was Jammal. The news of the broken arm, crushed hand and threats had reached him. SAM and Ahmed had driven back to the warehouse and walked in as Jammal and the others were stood around the table with a large map of the city spread out on it. Ahmed approached Jammal with the cloth bag and rolls of notes from the takings of the brothels.

'They have been stealing our money,' blurted Ahmed. 'SAM got it back, there are thousands of escudos here,' he said as he placed the money on the table in front of Jammal.

'Did you have to break arms and crush hands to get the money,' said Jammal in a dismissive tone. I've now got to find replacements.'

SAM shrugged off the criticism; everyone in the room knew that they would have done the same, if they could. He walked to the side of Jammal as he returned to the map and his plan to attack a rival kachasu business. The plan was to steal their supply and put them out of business, permanently. It was a crude plan and after a few minutes listening SAM said so.

It was as though Jammal had been stung. He turned and with the back of his right hand clipped SAM across the face

127

saying, 'When I …' The words froze on his lips as SAM reacted to the insult. SAM's body turned, his shoulder and arm followed as the long Bowie knife snaked out of the leather sheath and plunged into Jammal's chest. The blow sounded like an axe on a tree; solid and dull. Jammal was driven upright, his head snapping forwards and an explosion of breath burst from his open mouth. Jammal was pinned like an insect. The knife was buried up to the brass hilt, the tip of the blade creating a small tent-like fold in the back of his jallaba. SAM held him upright with one arm and then flung him towards the wall, pulling out the knife at the same time. It emerged with a strange sucking sound. Jammal fell to the ground; he looked like a pile of dirty clothes. There was no other sound in the room. SAM reversed his grip on the knife and drove it into the table top. Blood from the blade ran down and formed a small pool around the tip.

Chapter 17

The criminal empire starts

'This is what I suggest,' said SAM.

SAM suggested a "carrot and stick" plan similar to the ones he used in the mine and in the brothels that morning. He knew that Jammal had "acquired" a fairly new Toyota Land Cruiser from his contacts at the docks; one that was being exported by a Portuguese settler who was deserting the country. It would simply fail to be loaded onto the freighter and never found again. Jammal had planned to sell it in Rhodesia. SAM suggested abducting and killing the main man, but at the same time making a present of the Land Cruiser and crates of empty beer bottles to the others and inviting them to work for him. Of course any who said no would join their former boss at the bottom of the bay. They would soon start to control all the Kachasu in Beira as well as the price; it was good business.

'Think about it,' asked SAM as he turned to Ahmed.

Like everyone else he knew Jammal kept a bronze key round his neck. It was on a thin strip of leather and opened the floor safe cemented into the warehouse floor. Like the others he guessed what was in it.

'Give me a hand with him,' said SAM to Ahmed. 'We'll lay him out in the back of the Mitsubishi. His wives can decide what they want to do with him.'

Jammal wasn't heavy and his shirt was open at the neck as SAM tried to find the key. As the Bowie knife had plunged into Jammal's chest it had cut the thin leather cord that held the key, before it tore through his heart and out of his back. Jammal had died almost instantaneously. There was little blood from a heart that had stopped so suddenly. SAM quickly found the key and he and Ahmed walked to the back of the warehouse where the safe had been sunk into the floor. It looked like an old battered metal plate. It had once been painted green but now there was more rust and metal showing than paint. An oval plate had once been riveted to the middle of the safe but had been chiselled off years ago. There was a brass oval latch covering the keyhole. The bronze double edged key slid into the safe and turned smoothly. Ahmed grabbed the recessed handle and pulled the door open. Inside was a dull metal box that Ahmed pulled out with the thin brass handle that was attached. As it came out SAM turned to the others who had gathered.

'Let's see what the old bastard had in there,' said SAM as Ahmed carried it across to the table.

Over the next half hour Ahmed and the others counted out over US$44,000 and hundreds of thousands of escudos; they were set out in piles on the table.

'Ahmed, divide the dollars into equal shares for all of us with a share each to Jammal's wives. The escudos we will leave in the safe to run the business. Anyone not happy with this?' challenged SAM.

There was no dissention.

Throughout the civil war in Mozambique the business prospered. By the early 1990s SAM had a monopoly of the kachasu trade and whorehouses in and around Beira. He had expanded and taken over the bars and was running dagga into Zimbabwe and South Africa as well as to the north into Malawi and Tanzania. He had discovered that looting the docks could bring trouble; it was bad business and he avoided it. He had systematically eliminated the opposition and found it easier to bribe government officials rather than kill them. But in the mid 1990s Mozambique was changing. As the civil war ended and as reconstruction money poured into the country the police and army were being reformed, trained and equipped. With outside advisers they began to wrestle control from the gangs and warlords and were closing down the illegal bars and whorehouses. Beira was becoming respectable and shipments of dagga and kachasu were being intercepted and profits reduced. SAM and his business was being squeezed. It was confirmed in a meeting with one of the senior police officers he had been cultivating, and then bribing, for years. It had been easy. Feed a young and ambitious officer with information about murders, robberies and kidnaps, and occasionally the activities of his competitors, and see his career blossom. Supplement this with occasional cash gifts and free "entertainment" in one of the best brothels in Beira and you had an ally. It was to their mutual advantage to cooperate. The Police Commander had whispered to SAM that a paramilitary unit was being formed and would be funded and trained by special Portuguese forces. The plan was that they would then target and dismantle the criminal groups. Any resistance would be met by overwhelming force; they were to be eliminated. SAM and his group were on that list and there was no way the Police Commander could get him off it.

SAM hadn't anticipated this development. He thought the police and army would gradually get stronger and that in a few years he could even become legitimate. The demand for dagga was increasing all the time and could fund his move into a respectable business. He could turn the shebangs into official bars and whorehouses into hotels. However, the Police Commander had made it perfectly clear that the only way anyone was going to get off the list was when they were dead or out of the country. He told SAM that the Minister of Justice had announced, in a meeting two days ago, that he wanted all the gangs wiped out, and that is what the paramilitary unit would do.

In the days after the meeting with the Police Commander SAM was in a dark mood; even Ahmed learned to keep away from him. SAM considered his options and soon realised that he wouldn't be able to bribe the Minister of Justice or other officials to get his name off the list. Equally he wouldn't be able to fight a well armed paramilitary unit, especially if backed by Portuguese Special Forces. However, he did have plenty of money, he had established networks for the dagga trade into neighbouring countries, girls into the whorehouses and kachasu into the shebangs. All of these were running smoothly and he had men who could run these for him. He began to plan his departure from Beira. Years ago he had bribed officials to get official South African and Malawian passports; he had travel documents for Mozambique. He had also systematically converted all his cash into US dollars. Some of this was stacked in the floor safe and knew he could either sell his bars and whorehouses quickly or leave a small team behind to manage them. However, he needed transport to leave Beira and a plausible disguise when crossing borders. It was then that he recalled the TV programme at the mine about gangs of men in Brazil who were employed to fell whole sections of forest ready to be transported to sawmills. He and his key men could dress themselves as woodsmen, stack saws and axes in pickups, and simply drive out of the country.

Although SAM had resisted looting the docks he knew what was possible. Within days his contacts had discovered that a consignment of new, pristine white UN Land Cruisers was on route to the docks. The four wheel drives would equip the various UN teams with the transport they needed to access the interior of the country. In the bustle of unloading and moving consignments it was easy to have three of these vehicles "disappear" within hours of unloading only to reappear days later.

SAM eventually found what he was looking for; a dilapidated garage and paint shop on the outskirts of the city. It was partially hidden behind a row of mango trees and a couple of village stores. It was one that he had never used before. The discarded metal skeletons of old saloons, pickups, vans and truck beds littered the approach. A space between the debris led to a large wide gate, made from rusting corrugated iron sheets; the entrance was marked by an old Renault saloon, without doors, seats or wheels balanced on bald tyres. It was clear that anything of use had been stripped away years ago.

Late afternoon, two weeks after he had heard about the paramilitary plan, SAM banged his fist on the corrugated iron sheets, calling out for anyone inside. After a few minutes a tired looking, skinny Indian man, emerged followed by his equally skinny teenage son. It was clear that Pratek Patel had been sleeping and from his stale breath SAM could guess what he had been drinking to make him sleep.

'I've got a job for you if you're interested,' said SAM.

'What sort of job?' asked Pratek.

'It's a spray job and the fitting of roof racks, and rear fuel racks,' explained SAM. 'I've got three new Land Cruisers, white, that I want resprayed light brown. I want everything that is currently white to be brown, inside and out. I also want you to paint on my company name, phone and fax numbers on the doors. When you've done that I want full roof racks on each of the Land Cruisers and racks for four, five gallon jerry cans on the back.'

Pratek smiled and exposed a jumble of stained teeth, two broken, and said, 'You say these are brand new Land Cruisers … white. Do they have any logos that need to be removed?'

New white Land Cruisers only meant one thing in Beira – United Nations vehicles. Pratek had immediately guessed that these would be stolen and he was being asked to mask their identity. It also sounded as though they were being prepared for some long distance driving.

'I could respray them for you and make up the racks. But how quickly do you want the work done?' asked Pratek.

SAM explained that he could deliver the Land Cruisers in a few days and would like the work done as quickly as possible. SAM had a pretty good idea of what the going price of a respray would be and was prepared to double it for a quick job. Pratek turned and beckoned SAM into the compound, walking slowly towards a far workbench with greasy tools scattered everywhere.

Beyond the gates was an open area of hard packed earth. Here the innards of the dead vehicles lay scattered around. There were engine blocks some with pistons still in place, gear boxes and rear axles that would never turn again. Oil had seeped away from the discarded metal and left behind dark smudges which were now partly covered in red dust. Pratek Patel and his son lived alone in a single storey mud brick building that linked to other more flimsy constructions. These were enough to shade them from the sun and shield them from dust when spraying.

'I can prepare and respray them in three days,' announced Praket. 'It will cost you US$3,000; half now and the rest on collection.'

This was much more than the going rate but SAM didn't react. He simply smiled and reached into one of the thigh pockets in his jungle fatigues, pulling out the money and handing it to Praket. What Praket didn't know was that SAM had different amounts of cash in different pockets. It was just a case of remembering how much was in each. What he also didn't know was that SAM had no intention of paying for the resprays.

'I will deliver the cars next Wednesday night, before midnight – be here. I will collect the cars on the following Sunday evening. Do not disappoint me,' said SAM.

With that SAM scanned the compound and called out to unseen men waiting outside the gates. 'Oh yes, two of my men will be staying with you from now until I collect the cars. They are interested in how cars are sprayed and want to learn from you,' he said in an unconvincing tone.

It was clear to Praket that this intimidating man was going to ensure that all their attention would be on respraying the three Land Cruisers and not doing anything else.

The next few days were not particularly busy and so the time dragged. SAM had already coordinated the collection and delivery of the Land Cruisers to Praket's workshop. He had almost completed the cash sale of his shebangs and brothels to a "businessman" in Lorenzo Marques. It was just a matter of deciding how the money would be handed over and how many of the men and women who worked for him would remain, and how many would join him outside Mozambique. SAM finally selected his best twelve men; men who would join him on the journey out of the country. They were currently buying axes and chainsaws, ropes and sledge hammers, hard hats and work clothes, harnesses and gloves, stores and fuel for the journey. He was anxious because of the delay in obtaining passports and travel documents for all the men who were to leave Mozambique. Obtaining forged documents to enter Tanzania under the guise of a forestry team was taking longer than expected. He was also anxious because his friendly police commander had told him that the Portuguese forces were due to arrive at any time.

SAM was not a superstitious man but felt his ancestors were smiling on him; everything was going as planned. He had heard that the Land Cruisers would be offloaded on Wednesday, sometime in the afternoon. He had arranged that these would disappear from the docks and reappear in a warehouse close by that night. His negotiations with the "businessman" from Lorenzo Marques were complete and he had a new strong box, the size of a small suitcase, that contained all his dollars. SAM was a wealthy man; he just had to stay alive for the next few days. All was in place.

SAM savoured the last few hours in Beira. He didn't normally use the brothels he owned but after his favourite meal of piri piri chicken and sweet potatoes, and a couple of bottles of beer, he drove round with Ahmed and two of his enforcers to the brothel where he had broken Estella's arm. The girls were always pleased to see him and tonight two of his favourites would make it a night to remember whilst Ahmed guarded the door and his men covered the bar.

SAM was relaxed as well before midnight he and his men drove out to the workshop to collect the three Land Cruisers. The area was in darkness but there was a light in the workshop compound. SAM revved the engine once and switched off, pausing before he climbed out of the pickup and slammed the door. A village dog moved silently in the darkness and hundreds of cicadas created a wave of noise. SAM glanced towards the gates but didn't even have to bang on them as his men started to open them; the last man in closed the gates behind them.

Pratek and his son were waiting in the middle of the compound, two of SAM's men behind them. To one side were the three Land Cruisers, lined up side by side; they looked huge. SAM walked forward and offered his hand to Pratek, smiling.

'It looks like you've done a good job,' said SAM as his eyes scanned the new sand coloured paintwork and dark green painted racks. He smiled again as he saw *Kadenza Forestry Company* and a string of telephone and fax numbers painted in dark green on the side. He noticed that Pratek had also fitted mechanical winches on the front of each vehicle. The four wheel drives looked impressive and sturdy, as though they could simply drive through the forest and over anything.

Pratek was smiling broadly as he showed SAM around the vehicles, pointing out how he had masked the pristine white paint with light brown, how he had fitted the storage and fuel racks and how it was impossible to see, even at close inspection, that the Land Cruiser had originally been white.

'This is my best work,' Pratek beamed as he wrapped an arm around his son.

SAM smiled and pulled US$1,500 from his jungle fatigues. Just as Pratek was about to take the money from SAM's hand the two men behind sprang onto the backs of Pratek and his son. They wrapped their legs around their waists and pinned their arms to their body. They simply collapsed under the weight and fell to the ground. But before they hit the ground SAM's two other men jumped forward and clamped a hand around the mouth and nose of Pratek and his son. Pratek was no match for the two big men. With his mouth covered and nose pinched his eyes bulged as he fought for breath that would never be drawn into his lungs. There was barely any movement from his son as he too was quickly suffocated. It was all over in minutes as SAM watched.

It didn't take very long to find the hiding place for Pratek's money; stashed in a money box in a cupboard. The US$1,500 and a wodge of escudos were there. It was not very much. They took the US dollars and left the escudos so that it looked like an accident not a theft. It didn't take long to strip them both, drop their clothes on the floor and lay them in their beds. A paraffin lamp, smashed between the beds was enough to get the fire going. With cans of fuel, paraffin, oil and grease everywhere it would only take minutes for the fire to take hold within the compound.

SAM, his men, and the three Land Cruisers drifted out of the compound and into the night. They weren't around the next day or the days after. They didn't see the blacked, twisted shell of the workshop with anything that could burn merely ash. It seemed that the corrugated iron sheets had protected the neighbours and created a chimney for the flames. It was surprising how well the car parts and mud building had burnt and how little was left. By dawn SAM, his three Land Cruisers and men were waiting for the pontoon to take them across the Zambezi River, north of Matondo, and on to Quelimane. The next two days they drove steadily north, along gravel roads, towards Tanzania and the coastal border crossing at Mwambo. Apart from occasional stares the trip was uneventful. The border guards paid little attention to the mini convoy, the papers were given only a cursory glance; probably encouraged by the distribution of bottles of kachasu.

Chapter 18

New town – new opportunities

SAM had decided to make their base in a large warehouse by the docks in Dar es Salaam. It took a large part of the cash he had accumulated but reckoned it was a good investment. Dar es Salaam was the major port in Tanzania with plenty of men wanting to buy the things he could provide. Their previous network had stretched to Dar es Salaam but they did limited business. However, SAM and his team knew precisely how to develop it, how to remove the competition, bribe officials and create a thriving business.

Nearly twenty years after escaping Beira SAM was in control and one of the most powerful men in the city but not the most prominent. The seedy drinking dens had been replaced with bars that offered anything a customer wanted, at a price. The whorehouses had been replaced by hotels but with few people ever staying for breakfast. This was the visual part of SAM's world. What wasn't so obvious was the dagga that had been replaced by tablets and syringes and his role as middle man for anything that could be stolen and resold. This ranged from UN famine relief supplies to cars, young girls to young boys. The liquor, sex and drugs provided the basis for his growing empire; the arms and munitions was a profitable addition.

In the proceeding years there had been no shortage of buyers for weapons of all shapes and sizes. There were ethnic groups in Rwanda and the Congo, separatist groups in Eritria and Sudan as well as would be Warlords and Gangsters. Weight for weight explosives, guns and ammunition provided a great return. Furthermore, SAM had the network to provide almost whatever the customer wanted. However, SAM had a guiding principle when it came to arms and munitions. He dealt in what could be carried by men. So heavy machine guns and mortars, land mines and assault rifles, side arms and grenades were his specialty. Tanks and armoured cars were out of his league. It was thus with little surprise, when, through a screen of contacts, he was approached with a request for a meeting with a businessman. The meeting was set for a private room in the Mount Kilimanjaro Hotel in Dar es Salaam. The contrast between the two men was startling. SAM had lost much of his athletic build but was still a massive man that radiated a presence. When in the city he discarded the military fatigues, tunic and weapons, in favour of the old style safari suit and suede desert boots; it drew less attention. He could now afford for others to do "the wet work". He had grown tired of actually wielding the panga or cutting a throat; it was a messy business. Across the table was a slim, effeminate looking young man representing an unknown client. Clean shaven with a calm, olive face as smooth as a young woman. Long thin fingers, that seemed to be paler than his face, and which appeared to be constantly writhing as he held a glass of water. He seemed out of place. His pure white shirt, colourful tie and dark suit jarred with the surroundings. He would have seemed more at home in a bank. However, his voice was

141

strong and confident as he outlined the request for shoulder launched anti aircraft missiles. His client was prepared to pay between US$100,000 to US$150,000 each, depending upon which generation of missile were provided.

SAM filled one of the large easy chairs that were positioned around a low table in the middle of the room.

'How many do you want? When do you want them, and where are they to be delivered?' asked SAM, as though he was talking about sacks of maize.

Without looking at SAM directly the young man paused and then, speaking softly, said, 'My client will purchase as many as you can supply,' in a tone that was almost dismissive. 'There is no minimum number but tens rather than hundreds of missiles would be preferred. They are also to be delivered here in Dar es Salaam at a time and place you can fix.'

The young man took a sip from the glass of water, his fingers almost caressing the glass before he placed it on the table by his side. He brushed back his black hair away from his face and gave his head a slight shake. SAM thought it the gesture of a woman not a man.

'However, the order is valid for only six months. If you cannot deliver the items in this time then the order is cancelled.'

The young man then slid his hand into his jacket pocket and pulled out a slim, dull red wine coloured mobile phone, placing it on the table next to the glass of water, and went on. 'When you have acquired the items please phone the only number stored in this phone; any time night or day. When you speak merely give a number and a date – say nothing else. Do you understand? Just give the number of the items you have and a date for collection, that is all. The person on the phone will repeat the number and the date. You will confirm, switch off the phone, and then destroy it.'

The young man paused, almost for effect, and went on. 'I will return to this hotel one day before the items are due to arrive in the city; I will be your guest.'

The young man turned his head towards SAM and asked, 'Is that clear?' Suddenly the young effeminate man had changed. He revealed what he was - hard and cold beneath a soft and smooth exterior. SAM simply nodded and confirmed all was clear.

'When you have the items at a secure location my client, through one of his representatives, will check them to confirm that they are operational. For current generation weapons, those held by the major powers, we will pay US$150,000 for each operational missile. For any previous generation weapon, that is operational, we will pay US$100,000 each. You may have this money in any currency. We can make payment here or in any country in the world; it will be your choice. When you have confirmed that the money has been transferred I will check out of the hotel. If the transaction works out well there will be other requests in the future. If you deviate from this agreement my client will regard this as a hostile act and respond accordingly.'

With this the young man smiled. He had changed again. The hard cold expression had become almost sensual.

'I will phone the number as soon as I have the weapons and when I have arranged delivery,' replied SAM. With this SAM levered himself out of the chair. He picked up the mobile phone and, without a handshake or any recognition, turned and walked from the room. His two men followed.

143

Chapter 19

Just a delivery job

What the strange young man didn't know, and couldn't know, was that SAM already had twenty missiles stored in a secure place; in his date farm in Western Libya. He only needed to make a few arrangements; it was a delivery job.

Wherever there was conflict SAM had a team on the edge of it. This was either acquiring arms and munitions or delivering them, at a price. When the revolt started in Benghazi in early 2011 he thought the General would crush it within hours. But General Gaddafi didn't and the unrest spread. Over the next few months the contacts SAM had informed him of soldiers deserting their posts and joining the rebels. Even the heavy weaponry of the army wasn't quelling the rag tag groups. One month later SAM had one of his teams driving a convoy of four non-descript, canvas covered trucks north from Niger to his farm, east of Gadamis. It was to be their base as they decided who would be buyers and who would be sellers.

SAM had learned a lesson from his days in Beira. He always had an escape route; a place to go to and regroup. He had decided that if Idi Amin could find sanctuary in Libya so could he, but as an anonymous farmer not former dictator. He had carefully marshalled his funds and bought an old but functioning date farm and part of an ancient wadi some six hundred and fifty kilometres to the south of Tripoli and due east of Gadamis. He was an absent owner but had his own men supervising the workers. It was a low key, benevolent regime that attracted no attention and made little profit. SAM had discovered that Gadamis was famed as an ancient underground town and the generations of owners of the date farm had excavated a warren of rooms, beneath the main house, to store the dates in a cool, dry temperature. It was ideal for weapons of all kinds. His men ensured no one got close to the house or those particular stores.

SAM had picked the farm because it was isolated and yet close to the Tunisian border. It was also within a few days drive of several ports - it didn't hurt to have multiple exit routes. He also picked it because his contacts had repeatedly told him of the opportunity to bribe Libyan military officers and the chance to acquire modern weapons for cash; weapons that had officially been written off as damaged or destroyed.

SAM had learned of the military store at Mizdah, about two hundred kilometres miles due south of Tripoli. He wasn't sure what the base contained but it was small stuff; it wasn't tanks and heavy equipment. It was probably a mixture of food, clothing and arms; a mixture was typical. Even before SAM's team trundled off the main gravel road and onto the dirt track that led towards the wadi, there was expectation in the air. After the success of the freedom fighters in Benghazi whole regions came out in support of the revolution. In a band that spread steadily south and west from Benghazi, town after town confronted the military.

SAM's team soon made contact with the rebel groups forming to the south of Tripoli. The offer to transport a group of them to Mizdah, to link up with other groups, and help in persuading the soldiers to defect or storming the supply base if they didn't, was too good an offer to refuse. It took only two days to negotiate the sandy track east of Gadamis to Mizdah and even less to locate the local rebel group. The Al Sawadi Group in Mizdah knew the commander of the base. They knew the indignity he felt by being relegated to an outpost and the delights he enjoyed even in a small town like Mizdah. It wasn't too difficult to interrupt his nightly pleasure and make him an offer he couldn't refuse. SAM's main man outlined the plan. Tomorrow evening the base would receive an urgent phone call from Army Headquarters in Tripoli. In reality one of the local rebels, a telecommunication engineer, would intercept the phone line and simulate the call. The commander would be ordered to form heavy machine gun teams from the soldiers at the base and dispatch them immediately in trucks to Tripoli for deployment. It would be stressed that the three-man teams should be equipped with four cases of ammunition, sufficient for the first phase of the deployment. He would also be told to leave the base lights on to suggest everything was normal but to leave only three men guarding the gate. They would be reinforced in hours - reinforcements were already on the way. All the commander had to do was to confirm the order by phoning Army Headquarters and then respond to it. As he left the depot with his driver, he should make a detour via his "friend's" house. He would receive US$250,000, in cash, in a military bag. They would never meet again.

Colonel Mohammad Bin Garhi, the base commander, was a realist. He knew the regime was finished. Any government that uses tanks and planes to fight fellow

146

countrymen was doomed. He had been following the rise in rebel activity and was thinking about ways to extricate himself from this predicament when the offer was made. He accepted and knew precisely which direction he would be heading tomorrow night.

The rebels made the call late afternoon and Colonel Mohammad Bin Garhi went through the process of confirming the order by phoning Army Headquarters directly. Only he knew that he was not talking to the Army in Tripoli. Within hours all the men had been mobilized, equipped, allocated transport and the convoy directed to Tripoli. As a twist Colonel Garhi told his drivers not to break radio silence until they reached Tripoli in case rebel groups intercepted the messages and tried to ambush them. He was pleased with what was happening and was smiling broadly as he started to slip the bulky medical bag off his shoulder. As he gripped it in both hands SAM's main man moved behind him and slipped a wire noose around his throat and strangled him. The colonel's driver followed moments later. The colonel's car, returning to the base so quickly, didn't alarm the three guards who were lounging at the gate. They didn't seem alarmed when two men, in Libyan Army uniform, got out and called them over. The only alarm they showed was when automatic pistols emerged in the hands of the visitors and gunshots turned everything into darkness for them.

SAM's team, in their four trucks and armed with crowbars, headed straight to the storage buildings, forced open the doors and backed in; the rebels in four cars and an old van followed. For SAM's team it was business. The stores were full of new wooden packing cases with Chinese characters printed all over them; they had no idea what they

147

contained. They had to lever open the cases, assessing what was inside, before deciding what to load. Within the first half hour they had located the assault rifles and side arms, the mortars and landmines, the grenades and explosives, the heavy machine guns, tripods and ammunition. Previous experience told them to take a limited amount of ammunition. Their buyers thought about guns first and ammunition second. Ammunition was also heavy and yet fairly easy to obtain elsewhere. Working in four teams of two they dragged and lifted, stacked and secured until they were all dripping in sweat. They could relax later.

For the members of the rebel group that accompanied them it was like entering Aladdin's Cave. There was so much available, so much to grab, so much laughing, back slapping and posturing. However, there was only so much they could fit into the boots of the cars and the van! Quite quickly they realised their mistake and instead of loading crates simply broke them open and threw the rifles and guns, mortars and rockets into the cars. It was only when the suspension of an ageing Ford pickup groaned that they realised they would have to be selective in what they stole.

SAM's team knew the clock was ticking. It was just over three hours driving time from Mizdah to Tripoli. It would be three hours before the alarm would sound and probably minutes before fighter planes would be overhead blasting anything that resembled a truck travelling at night. In less than ninety minutes the four trucks were almost full. But towards the back of Store C was a metal cage, secured by heavy padlock and chain. SAM's men were curious. Why the extra security? Welding equipment from the nearby maintenance area soon cut through the chain. The wooden

148

lids were prized open easily. But what was in the pair of long, slim, olive green plastic boxes and two small plastic tubs? It had to be some form of armament, but what? They reasoned that if it was important enough to put inside the cage it was worth taking. They stacked the ten wooden boxes inside the last truck. They said their goodbyes to the rebels, who now seemed more interested in looting military clothing and tinned food, and were driving out of the gates just less than two hours after entering.

For the first hour they drove in close convoy with lights on full as they sped south east down the Gharyan road. For the next hour they spread out along the road and slotted themselves behind and between the container loads and over-laden lorries shuttling backwards and forward to the southern border. By midnight they had changed drivers and were travelling cautiously towards Gadamis. They saw the sunrise but had neither seen nor heard any planes. What they didn't know was that the local rebels, emboldened by the plan to loot the military base, had ambushed the convoy and overrun the soldiers before the convoy had gone eighty kilometres.

Later, when the crates had been relocated to the underground store at the date farm, SAM's team were still unsure what they had looted. Indeed, it was some months later when, at SAM's request, one of his contacts travelled to Gadamis, under the guise of a date buyer, and confirmed they had twenty Chinese Shǎndiàn, or Lightning Strike, missiles.

At the date farm it was a practiced routine that the team had performed a dozen times or more. A large, heavyweight tripod was manoeuvred over the small shipping container.

149

The container was hoisted into the air, the truck reversed into position, and container lowered onto the flat bed lorry. They stacked the ten wooden crates inside the container, in the middle of the floor, and secured them. All that was left was to slide in the previously made wooden partition, like a small wall, and wedge it in place. It left a small end space to fill with boxes of dates. The two rows of boxes of dates, squeezed into place, completely filled the end. The sealed container was still light but would pass a chance inspection. It looked as though the whole container was full of dates. The routine bribe to the supervisor on the dock-side would ensure a smooth transfer through Tripoli.

Within two weeks of being told to transfer items from the date farm to Dar es Salaam a blue twenty foot container, with the name Thalassa Shipping in big white letters on the side, was swinging aboard the *Lee Kwan Fung* and bound for Dar es Salam.

Chapter 20

Consignment ready for shipping

The *Lee Kwan Fung* had been a sound ship, but she was way past her best. The vessel had been commissioned by a Singaporean Group and launched from a Taiwanese dockyard in February 1961 at the start of a massive ship building programme in the Far East. The boom in economic development worldwide, and need to transport materials and finished goods around the world, had outstripped available ships. General purpose freighters were needed urgently and assembled by the hundred. With a length of just over seventy-seven metres, a width of eleven and a half metres and a draft of only four metres she was ideal for small ports. Her two thousand dead weight tonnes gave her the capacity for mixed cargo and the central crane a simple way to handle it.

The first twenty years of her life had been virtually trouble free. Regular return trips between the Far East and Europe, via India and the Middle East, had been profitable. Regular routine maintenance had kept the ship in good condition but general wear and tear began to catch up with her. Just after her twenty-fifth year afloat the accountants in Singapore decided larger bulk carriers and huge container ships were the future and the liabilities of the old ship outweighed her earning potential. The *Lee Kwan Fung* was sold to new Indonesian owners.

The next twenty-five years were not kind to the *Lee Kwan Fung.* Regular routine maintenance was replaced by stop gap repairs to keep the ship working. A succession of inexperienced and low paid crew managed to run her aground three times, be rammed twice whilst manoeuvring in port and generally scrape and mangle the sides and rails of the boat. In an attempt to keep the ship profitable the owners had it refitted for general cargo and containers. The bulkheads were cut back, separate compartments removed with strengthening beams fitted to compensate, and a replacement central hydraulic crane fitted. The changes certainly increased her versatility, but when near empty the ship rolled alarmingly, when fully loaded she was sluggish. The *Lee Kwan Fung* now picked up the cargo and container scraps that weren't profitable enough for the big boys. They specialised in moving small consignments or a handful of containers along their track where cheapness was more important than speed.

Fifty years after her launch the *Lee Kwan Fong* had new owners. The Sacranie Shipping Agency had bought her cheaply and little else changed. The ship still operated on minimum maintenance and shuttled between the UK and India via the Middle East, picking up and dropping off cargo along the route.

The *Lee Kwan Fung* was only partially laden when she docked in Tripoli to drop off nine containers and collect seven. It was mid week, early afternoon and unseasonably hot as they loaded. The battered blue container, which had more rust than paint, and a faded Greek logo denoting some obscure enterprise barely registered with the crew as it was swung from the dockside onto the rear deck and was secured. It could stay there until it was offloaded in Dar es Salam. No one noticed a slim, shabbily dressed man sat on the quayside idly watching the ship load. No one noticed him leave as soon as the pale blue container was secured and the next container was swung aboard. He had a message to send.

For the next few weeks the *Lee Kwan Fung* would meander along the Mediterranean coast, dropping off, and picking up cargo and containers as she made her way to Alexandra and through to Djibuti and Dar es Salam. The final leg across to India would be another long stint for the Pilipino captain and crew, but at least it was steady work. The boat was scheduled for boiler repairs when they reached Mumbai and the crew were already looking forward to three weeks on shore.

Massawa, on the Red Sea, was stinking hot as they chugged past the small mountains of sea salt being piled up by ancient equipment; fed by mahogany stick insects who shovelled the evaporated sea water into piles twelve hours a day. They manoeuvred between other freighters and edged their way to the dockside. With luck they could unload the cargo and containers and be ready to leave on the next tide. The place looked decrepit but the dock workers could turn round ships quicker than most. They were lucky since only one other ship was docked, and that was almost finished unloading; they were next. As hoped, they were turned around at speed and were ready to sail just before high tide.

It was airless and monotonous on the boat as the ship butted through the swell off Djibouti and out into the Gulf of

Aden. Although the threat of pirates, based in Somalia, had diminished the sailing instructions were to sweep around the Horn of Africa and head due south towards the Seychelles. The route would take them south west to Dar es Salam thus giving Somalia a wide berth. They were about three hundred kilometres off the coast, roughly between Kismayo in Southern Somalia and the Seychelles when the navigation officer spotted a small trace on the radar. Whatever it was it was heading towards them at speed. The navigation officer checked their position and marked it on the chart. He and the captain immediately feared the worse and moved to top speed away from whatever was approaching. But even top speed, and fifteen kilometres start, wouldn't be enough to outrun a powerful speed boat, if that is what it was. Ten minutes later, through binoculars, the captain could make out the sleek lines of a speedboat and men on board. He knew there was no way such a small boat should be this far away from the coast, unless it was looking for them. He had an ancient revolver and some ammunition, but hadn't fired the gun in years. He also knew that if the pirates got on deck it was all over. He had heard the stories of Somali pirates throwing the crew overboard and was determined they would fight them off.

The speedboat had looked sleek from a distance. A closer look revealed it was a battered, oil streaked plastic tub that had once been white with red "go faster" stripes along the side. Two huge outboard motors powered it along but threatened to make it stern heavy. There were twin smoke trails streaming out behind the boat as the driver pushed it to the limit. As though to compensate a rough cargo net stretched over the bow and secured yellow drums of fuel.

The captain could make out two men crouched on the bow. One was holding onto the cargo net with one hand and with some sort of rifle or gun in the other. The second man seemed to be holding a ladder with a hook at the end. He could just about make out a third man next to the speedboat driver; there were four of them.

The decision had been made. Four of the crew and the captain would hide under the side of the boat, armed with metal bars, a baseball bat and the World War II revolver. They would wait for the ladder to be hooked over the side and when the boarder tried to climb onboard the captain was going to shoot him dead at point blank range. The other crew were backup in case the gun jammed or he missed.

Chapter 21

Attacked by pirates

The scream of the twin outboards lessened as the speedboat drew alongside mid-ships, where the gunnel was lowest. The captain could feel rather than hear it as the boat bounced against the hull of the *Lee Kwan Fong*. Immediately a steel tubular ladder, with the end welded into a rough curve, hooked over the side. The waiting men could hear shouts as they imagined the two men on the bow struggling to maintain balance and hold onto the cargo net and ladder. The captain could wait no longer. He stood up, brandishing the revolver and leaned forwards to peer over the side; one of the other crew rose and stood beside him. The sound of the gunfire was deafening.

The captain suddenly twisted and dived to the deck; his navy blue captain's hat flew from his head. The Pilipino deck hand, Bala, seemed to spring off his feet as he jumped backwards and landed on his back, spreadeagled on the deck beside his captain. The sound of the gunfire had drowned everything so that when it stopped it seemed quiet. It took a few seconds to register that the twin outboard motors were still screaming and that the captain and Bala wouldn't be getting up. A mass of dark red blood spread across the captain's shoulder and oozed from his chest. A cluster of bubbles erupted and subsided with every one of his breaths. Bala didn't move. He had two red splodges roughly where his nipples must have been. More dark red blood formed a pool beside him. The other deckhands were frozen by the sight. Before they could think what to do next the first pirate was over the side. In the instant they saw him he embodied all their childhood fears of evil. His eyes were wild. He screamed at no one and everyone with lips drawn back over stained teeth. He looked like an Arab with a hooked nose and deeply lined sunburnt face. The neatly folded but stained turban was at odds with the black T-shirt with white Nike logo on his chest.

The next pirate seemed subdued in comparison. A well worn green John Deer baseball cap failed to hide a mass of unruly black hair that sprouted out all around the cap. The worn denim shirt flapped about his body and was almost white in places. Then a third sprang from the top of the ladder. No hat or shirt just scruffy canvas trousers that were several sizes too big; but he also wielded a rifle. They shouted and clubbed the two crew members even though they were cowering on the deck. Nike unleashed a volley of fire into the air that made them squirm on the deck and cover their heads. As John Deer guarded the two crew, the other two ran to the stairs and up to the wheel house. They burst in wielding their rifles.

The navigator had his back turned but glanced over his shoulder as he repeated the Mayday message into the radio handset. Nike didn't hesitate and opened fire, spraying the navigator and the radio with automatic fire. He seemed out of control, running amok. Wide-eyed and screaming he ran back to the main deck, letting off volleys into the air as he ran. He left Baggy Trousers on the bridge and raced back to

157

those on deck. He seemed about to fire on the two remaining crew but a combination of shouts and pushes from John Deer broke the spell.

'Where the crew?' John Deer bellowed into the face of one of the crew members followed by more shouts and prodding of the gun barrel to the side of the head from Nike. The crew cowered on the floor, appealing, saying the only other crew member was the engineer in the engine room. Nike turned and ran towards the back to the ship, looking for the stairs to the engine room. He didn't have to look any further. The engineer, hands above his head, was slowly walking towards him. They had taken the ship in less than five minutes. They needed the engineer but not the crew. Prodded by the barrels of the guns they lifted the captain and Bala to the side of the ship and pushed them over. With more difficulty they manoeuvred the bloody remains of the navigator to the same point and pushed him overboard. All that was left was to tell the two crew members to jump or be shot; they jumped. The pirates didn't even bother to look to check if they had jumped free of the ship or had been drawn into the propellers and chopped into fish food. They had other things to do.

They waved to the driver of the speedboat, signalling that the ship had been taken. They now needed him to radio the mother ship and the team who would sail the ship back to Somalia and into the maze of estuaries south of Kismayo. It was a profitable day. The money Nike and John Deer earned today was more than it would take them to earn in a lifetime on the farm or fishing.

It was the next morning before an old trawler, the mother ship, chugged into sight. They had forced the engineer to run the engine at top speed towards the Somalian coast. They didn't know if the navigator had managed to get a full message off before he had been shot. They didn't want to take the risk of a French destroyer steaming into view with guns blazing. Just over a year ago two of their friends had disappeared in an on board explosion when a French warship had intercepted their speedboat and fired upon it as they had tried to get away.

The trawler matched the speed of the *Lee Kwan Fong* and came alongside. It didn't bother to drop old car tyres over the side to cushion the coming together of the two vessels. As they touched two men hopped over the side, followed by a wizened old man who scrambled rather than hopped. The old man, Umar, had worked on cargo ships for forty years. He was the most experienced sailor in the team and would take the ship up the estuaries and into hiding.

The first thing Umar did was to cut the speed as the engine was over-heating. There was no sense in breaking down mid ocean with no one to call to for help. One of his sons, Santhu, was guarding the engineer. Santhu was a good boy and would ensure the engineer did nothing stupid. Umar also checked the position on the chart and set a course just south of Kismayo. He could now relax, sample the food and drink in the galley and tomorrow negotiate the channel into the estuary.

The mood on the *Lee Kwan Fong* was euphoric. In the last twelve months they had boarded two sailing boats and tried to negotiate million dollar ransoms. They eventually realised that the elderly British couple "sailing around the world in retirement" were not rich. Months of drawn out negotiation had generated US$100,000. When this was shared amongst everyone, and all the costs paid, it wasn't much money for the risk. The young Turkish couple fetched only a little more. But this ship had lots of cargo. They were going to be rich.

The pirates had raided the galley, the store room, the cabins and had helped themselves to whatever they wanted. They had discovered a locked steel cupboard in the galley which when smashed open revealed a case of whisky and half a case of rum. There were other bottles with names they had never heard of and couldn't pronounce. When the initial looting had finished Umar, an elder in the village, started to get them organised. He had found a chicken in the massive refrigerator and fresh vegetables in the store. Within the hour he had a stew bubbling on the stove. As the drama of the day mellowed, evening fell and the smell of the stew wafted through the galley. First one and then another of the pirates helped themselves to the whisky and rum. It was their big mistake.

The pirates were farmers and fishermen; they were not drinkers. The mild brews they drank on special occasions were nothing like the high proof spirits flowing down their throats. Even the serious John Deer was carried along by the mood and eventually gave in and in two gulps drained a whole mug of rum. The effect on John Deer, and the others, was predictable. The sharp tang and burning of the spirit was soon followed by a warm glow and feeling of well being. As the minutes and hours past, and as the bottles were drained, the mood became more and more joyous. The stew and boiled rice was sampled and the men sang and danced. They made impromptu speeches and described how they would spend all the money they had just made. Food,

160

alcohol, the rhythmic sound of the engine and a draining day eventually caught up with all of them. As the singing subsided so did the singers. One by one they slumped onto the deck or on a bench and entered a mindless drunken sleep.

It was past midnight when, tired and hungry, the old man's son, Santhu, prodded the engineer into the galley with the barrel of his gun to get some food. He hadn't heard anything but the engines, but now everyone was asleep. No, everyone was drunk. His father was curled up on a small bench, snoring and dribbling. He tried to wake him, but even when he shook his father by the shoulder there was no more than a murmur.

There was no one on the bridge, it was pitch black outside and the ship was sailing itself. Santhu was suddenly alarmed. What if they ran aground on the Somali shore or rammed another boat? The boat and cargo was only valuable if it was intact, not sunk! He was angry and darted from one of the villagers to another, kicking them awake, shouting into their face, shaking them. His anger increased with his embarrassment as the engineer laughed and started to help himself to the cold stew and rice. The engineer didn't bother with a plate or a spoon but scooped up the now congealed food by hand and ate from his fingers. He even poured some of the liquor into a mug and took a sip.

Some of those slumped on the floor couldn't be roused; they seemed unconscious. He did manage to wake two and by pushing and pulling got them to their feet. He screamed into their faces, 'Get onto the bridge, check where we are, check where we're going'.

In a drunken haze the fishermen stumbled out of the galley and up to the bridge. But they were simple fishermen, not trained navigators. Put them on a fishing boat and they would be able to steer by the stars and guide the boat in the right direction. However, they seldom ventured more than thirty kilometres from shore. The traditional fishing grounds were in shore, not mid ocean. Their job was to seize the ship not to sail it.

Santhu knew one of the villagers carried two pairs of handcuffs in a small canvas shoulder bag. They were old but sturdy and brought along in case they needed to secure any of the prisoners. Santhu couldn't find the villager at first but found him asleep on one of the bunks in a nearby cabin. He tried to wake him, but gave up after a few minutes. He did find the handcuffs and keys in the shoulder bag. He returned to the galley where a fellow pirate was slumped over the sink looking as though he was about to be sick. Santhu didn't wait to find out. He threw a pair of handcuffs at the engineer, who was still eating from the cooking pot, and told him to put them on. Once the handcuffs were on Santhu reached forwards and clicked them a notch tighter. He then told the engineer to return to the engine room and check the engines; he told Tallim to go with him and guard him.

Chapter 22

No one at the helm

For the next few hours Santhu alternated between the bridge, the engine room and the galley. Periodically he tried to wake the others but they were dead to the world. He was on the bridge as a faint light on the horizon gave the first hint of morning. He began to relax a little. Perhaps they wouldn't run aground or ram another boat. He could tell from the ship compass that they were heading towards the coast but wasn't sure where on the coast. If he couldn't wake his father in a few minutes he would throw a bucket of cold water over him. Santhu wasn't an engineer but had looked at all the dials in the engine room. They were all "in the green" or normal. Santhu had threatened the engineer that if anything went wrong with the engine he would follow the captain over the side.

Dawn came quickly. The faint light on the horizon strengthened and then the sun flashed low rays of sunlight across the water. There was little breeze, little current and little movement on the water. Santhu, his anger almost burnt out through tiredness, decided everyone would wake up even if he had to beat them awake. He had just filled a plastic bucket with cold water, and was walking towards where his father lay on the bench, when he was thrown off his feet. The bucket hit the deck and water splashed everywhere. Santhu was slammed against the bulkhead banging his head, jarring his arm and bloodying his nose. The deck tilted beneath him and a deep groan reverberated through the length of the ship. As Santhu tried to rise, the ship tilted even further and seemed to twist, throwing him off balance again. He was wedged between the deck and the bulkhead. Around him men had been suddenly woken from their deep sleep, disorientated. His father was on the deck, groaning and holding his arm that seemed to be an odd shape. What was most alarming was the noise. The thudding engines had stopped.

Santhu sprang to his feet and leapt across fallen comrades as he dashed to the ladder leading down to the engine room. He met Tallim coming up; they both stopped.'What's happened?' he asked Tallim, blocking his way to the deck. 'Why have the engines stopped?'

'Man say we hit rocks, stop engine, check damage.'With that Tallim squeezed past Santhu and disappeared from view.

Santhu scrambled down the last of the stairs to see the engineer struggling with a heavy wrench on a pipe that was spraying water into the air. 'Take these handcuffs off,' he shouted over the background noise of the humming of the engine. 'I can't work without my hands,' and offered his hands to Santhu.

Santhu wriggled his hands in his pockets until he found the key. Fumbling with shaking hands he opened the handcuffs. The engineer said nothing but returned to tightening the joint that had sprung a leak. He dropped his hand to his side. He was weary. He had been working in that engine room for over eighteen hours with little food and water

164

and the knowledge that his captors had killed the captain and all the other crew.

'You've run us aground or rather we have hit submerged rocks,' he announced in an almost bored tone. 'It was a hard strike and I guess there is a lot of damage. I need to check the engine and pumps. You need to check the damage to the hull.'

With that he turned away to check the dials and gauges. Santhu was both shocked and embarrassed. Shocked that they had hit rocks and embarrassed that he didn't know how to check the damage. He retreated up the stairs to tell his father.

There was chaos in the stairwells and in the galley. Men were shouting and moving aimlessly from place to place. Santhu found his father, sat in the galley, clutching his arm. The elbow was either broken or dislocated; his forearm protruded at an obscene angle and he was whimpering in pain.

'The engineer says we hit rocks. He say hard hit and ship damaged … we find out what damage. What do we do?' he shouted into his fathers' face. His father continued to rock on his seat, holding his arm, and whimpering.

'We might be sinking. What do we do?' he screamed into his father's face.

His father's eyes flicked towards him. He let out a long breath. 'Tell engineer keep engine running, no propeller, no want propeller turning,' he explained. 'Tell him check bilges under engine, check pumps.'

Even in pain his father sat straighter. He grabbed the arm of Santhu and went on. 'Space between hull and low deck, bottom … where cargo be. Big metal doors, you get you in.

165

Big locks, you open. Go space between hull and deck, and bulkhead see if water come in.'

Santhu grabbed one and then two of his comrades and explained what they had to do. They set off running, trying to find the way down to the cargo level and the doors that would lead to the space between the hull and the bulkheads. Santhu was making his way downwards, on the starboard side, and noticed it was higher than the port side. The ship was tilting. He saw the metal door with long heavy levers that clamped it shut. He tugged open the locking clips and was surprised how easily it opened and swung towards him. He held it open and peered inside. It stank of stale air and diesel, but he couldn't see anything; it was pitch black. He should have brought a torch. As he struggled to push the heavy door back in place and secure it he thought he heard a noise from beyond the containers bolted to the deck. He ran behind the containers to the other side of the ship. What had been a dry deck was now knee deep in water. He reached the corner and looked along the length of the containers. Tallim was being washed along the deck towards him by a torrent of water; it was boiling out of the hatch.

He waded through the water, grabbed Tallim, and tried to pull him to his feet. Even as he did so he recognised the feeling of a dead weight and the limp uncoordinated way the arms and legs moved. He looked into Tallim's face and was jolted by the sight. The shock caused him to drop Tallim back into the water. There was a massive crease that ran from his hairline, down his forehead, to just above his right eye. The injury distorted his whole face and head. Both his eyes were staring and pale trickles of blood ran down his face. Santhu guessed that as he released the bulkhead door it had burst

166

open and smashed into his head. There was no way he would be able to close that door on his own; he ran back to the engine room.

The engineer wasn't there! Santhu was suddenly alert in case the engineer was hidden by machinery or crouching, preparing to spring on him. Santhu pulled the assault rifle from his shoulder and started to search the area. He soon spotted a small square hatch on the deck; it had been clicked back, a cable ran into it. Santhu moved closer and could see a dull light. The engineer was down in a space with a light; probably checking on something. He called and waited.

A few minutes later the engineer emerged. He moved away from the hatch, winding the long black rubber cable around his palm and forearm. He turned to Santhu. 'The hull near the rear bulkhead is deformed and water is coming in. The rear pumps are struggling to cope with it. I can tell by the list that water is coming in on the port side. I need to check how well those pumps are working and what the damage is.'

With that the engineer simply walked past Santhu and made his way towards the ladder out of the engine room. Santhu didn't know what to do. He decided to return to the galley and check with the others.

His father wasn't in the galley, he was on the bridge. Someone had strapped his arm to his body and he seemed in less pain. His father was bent over the chart table.

'Engineer say water coming under engine room. Say the pumps good. He check other pumps.'

Santhu paused. 'Tallim is dead,' he announced to nobody in particular.

Faces turned to him.

167

'He open metal door, water behind, edge of the door bashed into head. How I tell his wife?' he added with a slump of his shoulders.

The excitement and euphoria of a few hours ago had been replaced with fear and doubt. Santhu's father returned to the chart and spoke out loud. 'We hit "Pinnacles", eighty kilometres off coast, one hundred kilometres estuary, only reef here. Trawler come soon.'

There was a cough at the entrance to the bridge. The engineer was silhouetted against the brightening sun, he still had the black rubber cable draped around his forearm. 'We're sinking and there's nothing I can do to stop it,' he announced. 'From what I can see we have a gash along the port side. It starts just about the for'ard mast and ends just before the engine room. I can't get into the space between the hull and the deck – too much water coming in. Looks like we were stuck on the reef for a moment before we corkscrewed and fell off. The two for'ard port pumps aren't working. Impossible to say if they were damaged when we hit. I will try to get them working but no guarantees.' The engineer paused and ran his fingers through his hair. 'Even if I do get them working I doubt they will cope. The two rear pumps are working but they won't be able to cope when the water works its way round the bulkhead. It's only a matter of time before the water gets into the engine room and the engines stop. The batteries will work for a while, but not for long.'

The engineer paused again and took a deep breath.

'The weather is good, sea calm. I'm not sure how much time we have before she goes down. You need to decide what you're going to do.' With that he turned and retraced his steps to the engine room. The bridge was silent.

Chapter 23

The Lee Kwan Fong was going to sink

Shouts and recriminations flooded the bridge before Umar shouted over them. 'We use crane … lifeboat in water if ship sinks. Trawler coming … three, four hours … back village tonight,' he ended with a forced smile.

Umar had operated dozens of different derricks and cranes over the years. By the time the fishermen had uncovered the lifeboat, checked the engine and fuel, stored water and food he was ready to hoist it into the water. He dropped it over the port side with running lines fore and aft.

Umar had recovered from the initial shock of his injury, to the inevitable loss of the ship and was aware how much depended upon him. He told John Deer to fetch the engineer.

The normally dark, shining face of the Pilipino engineer was now ashen and drawn. It was possible to see the dark smudges under his eyes, his hair and clothes were matted with sweat and filth. He entered the bridge and didn't bother to ask; he just sat on one of the raised chairs before the bridge windows. Umar signalled to one of the villagers to give him a mug of water. The engineer took it, drank half, and rested his chin on bent elbows. He looked at Umar. 'What damage? Pumps OK … ship not sink,' Umar both asked and stated.

'Damage mortal, pumps not OK, ship will sink,' he replied.

The engineer took another swig of water, dropped the mug, and turned to Umar and ignored the others. 'When we hit the reef the hull was ripped open. The gash is about ten or twelve metres long. It starts as a graze and ends in a big hole almost half a metre diameter.' The engineer paused, collecting his thoughts. 'When the ship was refitted they took out two cross bulkheads, replaced them with strengthening beams, and topped it off with a hydraulic crane to handle the containers. What it means is that the small fore and aft compartments are watertight, but the two main ones are not. Auxiliary pumps clear water from the cargo hold but they are not designed to move the massive amounts of water pouring in. Water is flooding the main port side compartments. The damage knocked out the pumps, that wouldn't be able to cope anyway, and water is finding its way around and into other compartments. Once the water is in the main cargo space it will find its way into the main starboard side compartments and the ship will sink. I've taken the two port side pumps apart and reassembled them. They are working but not pumping water. It could be the pipe-work is damaged between the hull and bulkhead. But I can't get to it. I've got nothing on board to make an emergency repair on the hull; it's just too long and too wide. The good news is that the sea is calm and we are not far from land. In a couple of hours, or less, this ship will go down.'

The engineer sighed, stood and walked to the door. In the short time since hitting the reef the boat had started to right itself but was settling lower in the water as the incoming sea flooded through hatches and vents, un-patched holes

171

and ill fitting dividing bulkheads. Since leaning over the side less than an hour ago he reckoned the *Lee Kwan Fong* was down by almost a metre in the water. He wasn't sure how quickly the ship would go down. Would the weight of the containers push it down or keep it afloat? He was too tired to worry. He had even stopped worrying about what they would do with him. He wasn't bothered, and it seemed, neither were they. He strolled to his cabin only to find it had been ransacked. He found his kitbag on the floor and started to fill it as though he were going ashore and on leave. He peeled the photos of his wife and children off the bulkhead wall and slipped them into his pocket. He started to return to the bridge. On the stairwell he could see two of the pirates climbing over the side and making for the lifeboat.

It was clear the *Lee Kwan Fong* was going down. Sea water was almost up to the port side gunnel. Once it swept across the deck and into the cargo hold millions of tons of water would push the ship under. He entered the bridge. Only Umar and his son Santhu were left, and they looked as though they were about to leave. As the engineer entered Santhu turned to him. 'I am sorry for death of your friends,' he said. 'My father say you join us in lifeboat, we take you to shore. You free, go home.'

The three of them made their way down the stairs across the deck and to the side next to the lifeboat. As they approached the lifeboat the engineer smiled at the thought of the old maxim about "stepping up off the sinking boat not down". Santhu stepped across the gap and waited, arm out to steady his father. The engineer steadied the old man as he stepped onto the side of the of the ship, and across to the lifeboat, and then followed. The lifeboat throbbed and gradually it eased away and rounded the stern as they set course for the coast. The mood onboard was subdued. The engineer guessed that part of it was hangover from the excesses the night before, but most because they could see their once in a lifetime chance at wealth slipping away. The engineer kept his eyes on the *Lee Kwan Fong* as they chugged away. He had often cussed at the old girl when bearings ran hot, filters clogged and lines sprang leaks but he had an affection for her. Was it better that she went down whilst still working or torn apart in some salvage yard? She was about to go down. Remarkably the ship was still sitting level in the water. The fore and aft compartments must be holding and keeping her stable. At several hundred metres, and looking into the sun, the ship looked like a submarine slipping under the surface. The curved bridge looked like a conning tower and the forward mast like a periscope as they motored away. He could imagine the water flooding into the cargo area and rushing into any remaining space. He wiped the sweat away from his eyes and when he next looked the *Lee Kwan Fong* was gone.

Chapter 24

Not the job that was expected

Jack wasn't sure how long it took him to recover. It was probably a few seconds before he recalled the carnage of a few hours ago. Were he and the others next?

Jack pushed himself onto his backside and slowly edged his way back to where he had been sat. He felt terrible but had to calm the situation. He rubbed the left side of his face with his hand as he re-made eye contact with the African, and with a confidence that had simply appeared said, 'Sorry, I don't know who you are but if the container you want is to be retrieved we need to plan how it's going to be done.' As he spoke Jack started to stand, lost his balance and then sat back on the gunnel heavily. 'That ship is sitting in forty to fifty metres of water. Have you any idea of what the water pressure is like at that depth?' Looking at his watch he tried to focus but his vision was blurred. He squinted at the watch and continued. 'High tide will be in about two hours and there will be tens of million of litres of water rushing over the hull making it impossible to work, even if you could see anything, which is unlikely.'

Warming to his task Jack stood and took half a step towards the African, still maintaining eye contact. 'There are twenty odd containers on that ship. How do we know which is the one you want?' challenged Jack.

The combination of surprise and confusion was evident in the face of the African as he broke eye contact, looked upwards and grasped both hands in front of himself in a thoughtful-like gesture. Jack wasn't finished, he was just getting started.

'Even suppose we released a container, and I never heard of a diver, without specialist equipment ever doing so, how do we get it to the surface and ...' Jack paused, '... get it on board this piece of shit!'

The demeanour of the African suddenly changed. A broad smile grew over his face and he started to laugh. It was a deep belly laugh that seemed genuine not forced. 'I like you, "whitey",' he said as he wrapped a huge arm around Jack and squeezed. 'You've got balls and I think you and your friends will get me my container, 'Melek', he shouted to one of the group on the dockside, sat on the aluminium gear cases, 'get my young friend a beer.'

'If we are going to retrieve your container my friends and I would prefer water and some food so we can start planning,' replied Jack with a gesture of his free arm to include Sandro, Kev and Penny.

'Melek, Henderson,' he shouted at two of the dockside group. 'Go and get some bottled water, some coke and food for my friends ... and quickly.'

Melek and Henderson didn't need any further encouragement. They had turned and were off towards the town at a quick shuffle. The African turned, stepped off the barge and onto the dockside, and walked towards the aluminium gear cases. Without asking if they had keys he removed a large bone handled knife from his belt and proceeded to lever the locks and hasps off the cases, one by one, and opened them. Jack, Sandro, Kev and Penny gazed on in amazement, unable to do anything to stop him.

'What are you thinking of?' whispered Sandro. 'We're not equipped to retrieve containers at fifty metres, it's madness, we'll get ourselves killed,' he muttered as he shook his head. 'I'd rather be in the water, and buying time, than arguing with gangsters with guns. You saw what they did to the crew of the dive boat without a thought.'

The memory of one of the gangsters nonchalantly turning his gun, one handed, towards Mohammed and Kirru and dowsing them in dozens of bullets came flooding back. The memory was so vivid that Sandro could almost smell the gun smoke and sense the metallic taste in his mouth. He recalled the blood that was splattered around where they had been standing before they were rolled into the water. He struggled to control himself as he felt the bile rising in his throat.

'OK, how do you propose we uncouple a massive container at fifty metres and float it to the surface?' Sandro said almost accusingly.

'I can't do it on my own, but we may be able to do it together,' said Jack with a forced smile. 'Every hour we take increases the chance that people will start looking for us and get us out of here.'

It seemed only minutes, but was obviously much longer, before the two gangsters returned with bottles of Evian water, cans of coke, a cooked chicken, slabs of warm bread and a paper bag filled with some sort of over-cooked vegetable. There was even a jumbo bag of potato crisps! The reaction was unreal. One minute Jack, Sandro, Kev and Penny had been quiet and disconsolate, the next they were laughing as they started to lay out the "picnic" on an old sack they found draped over the side of the barge. Jack suddenly realised how thirsty and hungry he was as he emptied a can of coke in one gulp after another. Penny had water running down the sides of her mouth and down the front of her now ripped and soiled blouse. Sandro had paused with the bottle of Evian in hand as though looking for a glass.

'Just drink out of the bottle,' smiled Kev as he dismembered the skinny chicken and offered pieces around.

Even Penny was drinking out of a bottle and stuffing bread into her mouth whilst smiling. The transformation had been almost instantaneous. A few minutes earlier they had been despondent and out of ideas, now they were energized and full of questions.

Sandro grabbed a second bottle of Evian in one hand and a slab of bread and piece of chicken in the other. He turned to Jack and between gulps of water and swallowing bread said, 'Let's assume the *Lee Kwan Fong* is sat upright on the bottom, intact and the containers are accessible. The chart says the bottom is about fifty metres at that point with a tide of about half a metre. My guess is that visibility would be ten to fifteen metres, but just a guess. With what we have available how do you suggest we raise the container?'

Jack took a final swig of water, turned and sat down where he had been before. He started to share his thinking, picking off the points on his fingers.

'First, the codes of the containers due for off-loading was with all my other stuff on the boat. Without the code we have no idea which container they are after and how much it weighs! If it's a twenty foot container, the smallest, it will weigh about two and a half tons empty. That's assuming it's dry! If filled to capacity the contents could be over twenty

177

tons and thus the whole thing could weigh about twenty-five tons. I haven't looked closely but I doubt this pile of shit is capable of lifting twenty-five tons dead weight out of the ocean. If the one he's after is a forty foot container the weight goes up. It could be thirty to forty tons. Of course, if this guy, SAM, decides there is no way we can salvage his container what does he do with us? He made a snap decision that he didn't need Mohammed and Kirru and look what happened to them.

Second, if it was going to be offloaded in Mombasa it will have been in an accessible position. It's unlikely to be buried at the bottom of the stack. That's a bit of good news, probably the only bit.

Third, I'm not sure how easy it will be to release the clamps holding the container in place, even if we find it. On land the clamp is tightened down onto the container; it's pretty easy to tighten and release it by hand. The thing is, the container is likely to be positively buoyant which will make releasing the clamp so much harder. I'm guessing, but I reckon a metre of metal tubing will offer enough of a lever to release the clamps. The next problem, of course, is that the container is likely to move as one or more clamps are released. It could mean we release two or three clamps only for the container to start to float upwards. This may be sufficient to jam any attempt to release the last one. Then we are really stuffed!

Fourth, if the container is negatively buoyant, or even neutrally buoyant, we can attach air bags to each of the four corners and float it to the surface. It's then a case of rigging lines to hoist it out of the water. But it's my guess that this tub will sink or break apart if it tries to lift twenty or so tons out of

178

the water. It may be better to raise the doors out of the water, remove what's contained, and cut it loose.

Oh, I forgot the fifth. This is all assuming the weather holds.'

'How do you remember all this stuff about the sizes and weights of shipping containers? I'd have to look it all up,' said Sandro as he started to reply. 'The first thing we have to do is check on the kit. I think bullets may have hit one of the crates and there may be damage. Whilst we are doing this we may be able to attract attention and maybe drop a message. The place may be swarming with police or these guys may have sunk the boat when we left. The thing is, without the re-breathers there will be no diving.'

Jack nodded and as though thinking out loud said, 'I've got an idea about a controlled release of the clamps. There must be plenty of cargo webbing and tightening ratchets around the dock. If we got four pairs of them we could hook one end over the top of the container, hook the other on the one underneath it, and ratchet the webbing tight. You can get it pretty tight just using the normal ratchet arm. If we could make up an extension of a metre or so we could get it even tighter. Do you think it would be strong enough to hold the container in place whilst we released the clamp? If we could release the clamps, but stop the container from moving, could we then trip the release or cut free the container?'

'So simple,' replied Sandro sarcastically but with a big smile. 'As to lifting it out of the water – *impossibile,*' he remarked in an exaggerated Italian accent.

'OK, we're agreed. It's risky, but less risky than saying no to this guy. We try to keep safe, watchful and look for a chance of getting all four of us away.' However, how much do we tell, what's his name, SAM?' asked Jack.

'I think you should explain all the points just like you have just done. If this is to work it needs to be planned and we need information about the size of the container. He needs to know that the contents will have to be transferred from an open container at sea.'

At this point SAM finished rummaging through the dive kit boxes and walked towards the barge and looked as though he was about to jump onto the slippy deck. Before he did so Jack laughingly said, 'I suppose I could always ask if he will let us go if we managed to get him his container, but I would find it hard to believe anything he told me.'

'So, "whitey",' SAM said with a smile. 'You see, I am a reasonable man. I give you food and water and will listen to your plan to get my container.'

Chapter 25

Attempted salvage of the container

SAM flicked a hand and shouted a command. In doing so an old guy who had been hidden in the wheelhouse suddenly produced an old, bleached canvas and wooden chair. SAM lowered himself into the chair and it groaned beneath him, but didn't collapse. 'Tell me how you are going to get my container?' he asked as he relaxed into the chair.

Jack handed SAM a business card announcing their *Marine Investigation and Salvage Company.* It seemed bizarre under the circumstances but gave the impression of a professional doing his job. Jack proceeded to list the points that he and Sandro had rehearsed. SAM just sat and listened and gave no reaction. When Jack had finished SAM unbuttoned one of his breast pockets and removed a square of folded paper. He slowly unfolded the paper and searched the contents. Then, in a slow, measured tone he recited:

'My container has a code painted on it, it is TSL U 451107 1. It is a twenty foot container, blue with the name Thalassa Shipping Lines in big white letters painted on the side.' SAM seemed to pause to see what reaction he was getting. 'It says here that the weight of my container is six thousand five hundred and twenty pounds. How much is that?' he asked looking at Jack.

'That's about three tons, which means whatever is in it weighs about half a ton, just over one thousand pounds or about five hundred kilos,' replied Jack. 'It's almost empty and likely to be highly buoyant, assuming it hasn't been damaged and is full of water,' he added. Jack went on. 'If you know what is in the container, can it be removed at sea? Is it one item weighing five hundred kilos or lots of smaller, lighter items?' he asked.

'Ahhhh,' replied SAM. 'There are ten packages in my container. I can lift one in each hand,' and he flexed his forearms and shoulders to give a hint of the muscled body underneath the army camouflage jacket. 'Special container,' said SAM, 'No air out, no water in,' he continued. 'We have the motorboat you were on when we met, with all the bottles of oxygen you need to dive. You can drive it and my men will watch you. We will get the straps you need and tools. What else do you need before we can start?' SAM asked, but the tone was clear … we start tomorrow.

Jack clapped his hands together as though relishing the opportunity to start work on preparing to raise the container. 'We start now,' he answered SAM with a smile. 'I suggest we return to the dive boat with all our equipment so we can check the weather forecast and times of the tide. The charts and tables should be where I left them on the boat so we will know something about the seabed and local currents. We need to check the gear, check there is still a supply of food and water on the boat, get a good night's sleep and be ready to dive the site a couple of hours before slack tide. It's a good two to two and a half hours motoring to get to the site which means we will need to leave around dawn, but we need to confirm the time.'

It was clear that Jack had seized the initiative, that Sandro, Kev and Penny were happy to go along or at least get away from the stinking barge. SAM was providing them with what they needed to retrieve the container but no doubt ensuring his "investment" was well protected. More shouts and more arm waving from SAM produced two old pickups that returned them to the dive boat along with the aluminium kit boxes and several guards. It was when the aluminium crates were being loaded onto the back of the pickup that Sandro noticed the neat bullet holes in one of the crates. Holes where the bullets had entered. He was shocked to see the exit holes or rather huge irregular gashes where the metal had been torn open. He said nothing to Jack but waited until they were at the dive boat.

In an attempt to maintain the shift in control Jack started issuing orders as soon as they got to the boat. 'Kev, can you check the boat is seaworthy and that we have plenty of fuel, water, food and so on? Penny, can you help Kev and decide what we will be eating tonight? Sandro, can you check the weather forecast, time of low tide tomorrow and direction of local currents? Can you also check the re-breathers. SAM, shall we go and get the straps, tools and lines we need?'

It was clear that SAM didn't like taking second place to anyone but it was equally clear that he realised Jack and the group was his only chance of retrieving his container. He grunted and simply said, 'Come,' and walked towards the pickup. They eventually found a pile of old webbing and rusty ratchets behind a dilapidated boat yard along the dock. Jack picked out the least worn straps and the ratchets that looked as though they could be salvaged and with some oil made to work. It was the best they could find. In another backstreet

183

SAM found an antiquated blacksmith complete with forge. It was clear that the blacksmith was aware of who SAM was and quickly donated two lengths of rusty heavy steel tube. He even cut slots in each end with an angle grinder so it could extend the ratchet arm. By the time they returned to the boat the sun was going down.

The first impression, as he stepped onto the dive boat, was that he had gone back in time. Everything seemed to be as it was before the gangsters had arrived that morning, killed Mohammed and Kirru, and thrown a routine shipwreck inspection into a nightmare. Penny was in the galley and was transformed. It looked like she had taken a shower and changed. However, she looked just as much out of place as when he had first seen her. Sandro and Kev were leaning over the map table and chatting. Even in oil stained shorts and polo shirt, and a distinct five o'clock shadow Sandro looked refined; Kev just looked dishevelled. The only thing to break the spell was the sight of the two gunmen, one leaning against the chrome rail on the diving deck, the other in the companion way looking at Penny, leering.

As Jack stepped onto the boat and walked across the dive deck all eyes turned to him. With a smile he held up the straps and ratchets and metal tubes. 'Got all we need, how's it going?' he asked to no one in particular.

'We've got a problem,' announced Sandro. 'When that animal shot Mohammed he also fired bullets through the crate holding the re-breathers, masks and communication equipment. It's damaged beyond repair – it's over US$20,000 of junk.'

Sandro pointed to the open crate and the pile of shattered kit next to it. Jack immediately dropped the tools and webbing and crouched by the crate. He could see at a glance that both face masks were shattered. The precision, Hi-Tech re-breathers were in shreds. There was no way they could be repaired. No way could this kit take them to fifty metres and beyond.

Jack was stunned. All his bravado had been for nothing. If they could not dive then SAM and his gunmen would have no use for them. Jack remained crouched by the crate but his mind was racing. 'We'll have to dive on air,' he announced. 'There's all the kit we need on board: BCDs and regs, masks and tanks. We can use that. We have no choice,' he announced.

There was a moment of silence before Kev spoke. 'Jack, are you crazy?' he said. His voice was so loud that the two guards turned towards them, guns raised. Kev pulled Jack around by the arm to face him. 'At fifty metres you will have maybe five minutes of bottom time. More than that you will have to decompress. You will be hanging under the boat for maybe hours. Even if you did "no decompression dives" you would have to spend hours between dives. The kit is average recreation stuff. It's OK for twenty maybe thirty metres but not for fifty metres. I'd need to confirm with the dive tables but what you are proposing is dangerous stuff. It's verging on suicidal!'

In a tone more belligerent than intended Jack retorted, 'OK, what do you suggest? What do you think SAM will say when you tell him it's too dangerous to dive? ... He'll blow your effing head off without hesitation!'

No one spoke. The tension on the dive deck was palpable.

'Let's check out the feasibility of diving on air,' said Sandro. 'The chart shows the ship at about fifty metres. If it is upright on the seabed the containers may be at, say, forty-five metres or less. A few metres can make a big difference in bottom time. Let's check the dive tables.'

With that the group broke up and moved to the saloon on the main deck. After the sharp exchange a form of truce was adopted. Kev and Sandro soon confirmed that if the containers were at forty-five metres they would have six minutes of bottom time and need at least two hours of surface time between dives. Under such extreme conditions Kev suggested that if Jack and Sandro were determined to go through with it then they should undertake only two dives a day; before and after slack tide.

In the next hour the whole team was brought up to date with what they had worked on. Kev announced that the boat was as they had left it. They were full of fuel and with reserve tanks had enough for two thousand nautical miles, water and food for a month. Sandro confirmed that the *Lee Kwan Fong* was in about fifty metres of water on a sandy bottom with a tidal range of just over half a metre. The current would be fairly mild and pretty much on a NE / SW axis.

'I'm not concerned about the diving conditions,' said Sandro, 'but it will all depend on how she is laying on the bottom. Assuming she is upright, big assumption, and that the container is readily accessible we will be working in about forty-five metres. That means we only have about five or six minutes bottom time if it is to be a no decompression dive. We are going to have to watch the dive time on the dive computer carefully otherwise we will have major problems.

It's likely that we will need to make multiple dives and so we need to make them all no decompression.'

'That's the good news,' said Jack. 'If that container is still watertight it will go up like a cork when it's released; it's virtually empty. It means that the idea of tying down the container with retaining straps is even more critical. The truth is I've no idea about the quality of the straps or ratchets. They could be sound or crap. We can try them out on the dockside bollards but I can't see how we can replicate the force a buoyant container will exert.'

'Let's eat,' suggested Jack, 'It's going to be a long day tomorrow.'

Chapter 26

Day of the attempted salvage

Jack was awake before dawn. He had fallen asleep quickly, because he was so tired, but had been awake for what seemed hours rehearsing the retrieval plan. Just as the sun was rising he made his way forward to the shower, cleaned up, and started to lay out breakfast.

Penny cleared her throat to attract his attention as she stood in the companion way. 'Do you think you can bring the container to the surface?' she asked, looking even paler than he remembered.

'If I were a betting man I'd say the chances are slim; there's so much that can go wrong and we have no backup. However, the alternative of not trying to salvage it, is even slimmer. You saw what they did to Mohammed and Kirru,' replied Jack.

He paused at the memory of it and in an attempt to move on asked, 'Fancy a cup of tea or are you a coffee drinker? Sorry, I didn't mean to sound flippant. I can't get the image on the dockside out of my head.'

'I'm a coffee drinker,' she replied.

Just then Sandro walked into the galley closely followed by Kev and the fateful day had started.

They had finished breakfast and were waiting to cast off when SAM arrived. He was dressed exactly as he was the previous day.

'The barge left last night and will be waiting for us over the ship,' he announced. 'Me and my men will be coming with you. We leave now.'

'Before we leave can I show you the damage to our diving gear?'

Without waiting for a reply Jack led the way to the dive deck, to the bullet ridden crate, and pile of damaged gear. Picking up a broken mask and ripped re-breather Jack explained. 'SAM, when your man shot Mohammed he also fired bullets through this crate and destroyed over US$10,000 worth of specialist diving gear. This isn't ordinary gear you can buy in any shop in Malindi. It's highly specialised, State of the Art stuff. It would have allowed us to dive to fifty metres and to stay at that depth for hours. Sandro and I would be able to talk to each other and to you. That isn't possible until we replace the gear.'

'No excuses,' shouted SAM. 'No excuses, you get my container today or I will be very angry.'

The change in the atmosphere was immediate; SAM glared at them.

'There is an alternative but it is very dangerous and will take time,' explained Jack. Sandro, Kev and Jack outlined the alternative plan based on breathing air with a very short bottom time and long surface interval between dives. At the end Jack invited SAM to contact a dive company in Malindi and to confirm what they had said was true.

SAM glared and as he walked away said. 'I will come back soon. If you are trying to cheat me you will be sorry.'

Within minutes SAM was back on board and said they would leave now and they would use the equipment already onboard.

The ride out to the wreck was tense but surprisingly smooth. Not a *mill pond* but with just a gentle swell and not a cloud in the sky. It would have been a beautiful journey had it not been for the presence of SAM and his men. Jack's only consolation was that neither SAM nor his men were sailors; they looked decidedly unwell. At first it seemed on the cool side with the wind blowing through the open deck. However, as the sun came up so did the temperature. It was going to be a glorious day.

They saw the barge wallowing in the water as it hovered close to the wreck. Despite looking decrepit it must have been carrying some GPS system to get so close to the *Lee Kwan Fong*. Kev manoeuvred the dive boat over the wreck as Jack and Sandro began to sort out the gear. The first thing to go over the side, and lowered to five metres, were four full tanks of air with weights attached. Although they would be performing "no decompression dives" it was good practice to have full tanks at five metres so they could decompress in an emergency.

SAM and his men had started to look a bit better. Perhaps they were getting used to the motion of the boat or felt better seeing another boat. Jack walked over to SAM. 'The *Lee Kwan Fong* should be about fifty metres below us. We are going to enter the water and swim over to the barge. Sandro will take a mooring line and we will attach it to a strong point on the wreck. We are then going to look for the container and see what state it is in. If we find it we will send

190

up a marker buoy. We will not have any bottom time for anything else.'

On the second dive, after the surface interval we need, we will start wrapping the straps over the container and through the retaining lugs on the one below. If we can do that we will be ready to raise the container tomorrow.

SAM merely nodded his agreement. He may have appeared all right but was obviously seasick. But it didn't make him any less dangerous!

Jack and Sandro completed their buddy checks. They looked almost comical in their tailor made, bright orange and bright yellow wetsuits and hoods. It was just one of the numerous safety conscious decisions they had made when setting up the company. You can be seen in the water from one thousand metres if you are in bright orange or yellow. In black you are just a smudge between waves.

Jack slipped on his fins and just before he started to move towards the rear of the boat to enter the water, he beckoned Kev towards him. 'Kev, we'll put up a marker buoy on the container, if we find it, and Sandro is taking a mooring rope from the barge down to a strong point on the deck.'

Jack gave the "OK" hand signal to Sandro, and had it returned, before he moved one hand to hold his regulator and mask in place and the other to hold his dangling gear in a mesh bag, as he stepped off the boat and into the water. No sooner had he hit the water than he kicked his fins to spin and look back at the boat. Sandro was following him into the water. They both signalled to Kev that everything was "OK" and then started to swim over to the barge. The old captain had spliced an eye on the end of the line and threw it to

191

them. Sandro caught it and signalled that he was ready to descend; Jack was ready.

'Give me plenty of slack on the mooring line,' Sandro announced and waited until the captain acknowledged.

Jack and Sandro looked like two brightly coloured Sea-Stars, sharing an umbilical cord, as they splayed their arms and legs and, face down, slowly descended. The visibility was good and at two metres apart Jack could see Sandro smiling behind the mask. It was good to be back in the water. Despite their plight Jack felt relaxed. The rhymic sound of his breathing and seeming weightlessness all helped. He glanced at his dive computer, checking on their descent rate and depth. They were at seventeen metres and the rate of descent was fine with visibility still good, in fact pretty good. They drifted downwards and entered a thermo-cline, the temperature of the water dropping several degrees as they entered that band of water. It was about thirty metres when something caught his eye. Pointing directly towards him was the forward mast. He could see the slender pale finger pointing upwards from the gloom, climbing rungs welded to its side, lights and aerials that wouldn't be working again. He signalled Sandro, but he had already seen it and gave him the 'OK' sign. They both blew a little air into their BCDs to slow their descent and manoeuvred themselves until they were both holding the mast with one hand, the mooring line in the other and their fins perched on the cross piece near the top of the mast. The current was very mild and it took a moment to establish that it was trying to push them away from the wreck.

Jack checked his compass. From this distance he could just about make out the general shape of the Lee Kwan

Fong. She was aligned on a NE / SW axis and in line with the prevailing current. She also looked pretty level on the seabed, canting to port suggesting that she had gone down fairly slowly. He checked the current again and noted it was roughly from the NE.

Jack signalled that they should dive down, dragging the mooring line, and fix it to a strong point. Sandro acknowledged and together they finned down the mast, dragging the long mooring line with them. Jack spotted a heavy shackle secured to the deck about four metres from the base of the mast. He reckoned this had been a strong point to secure the original derrick to the boat. At some time in the past the old box girder derrick had been replaced with a more modern hydraulic crane to lift and position the containers. Jack fed a stainless steel carabineer through the shackle and clipped it back onto the rope. All was secure but Jack was breathing hard.

The water had softened the lines of the ship and she looked almost majestic, sat on the bottom. There was little or no debris around and Jack guessed that the current had flushed away anything that was loose. Jack checked his dive computer. They were at forty-two metres and had six minutes left before they would have to ascend. Jack and Sandro were at the base of the mast and scanning the twin rows of containers with their torches. They started finning against the mild current, along the length of the wreck, above the containers looking for the code or the name THALASSA SHIPPING LINES. Jack was on one side of the line of containers and Sandro on the other as they finned strongly towards the wheelhouse. Underwater, and a couple of metres above the deck the twin rows of containers seemed to stretch into the distance. They finned on scanning the containers and their dive computers. In the distance the wheelhouse emerged from the gloom like a three storey town house that had once been white but which now was grey and streaked in rust. Windows and portholes, like dull dead eyes, looked out across the deck.

Jack checked the dive computer. They had only four minutes left on this dive. They continued their brisk fin over the containers. Under water, and at forty plus metres colours lose their above water vibrancy; they all look like shades of grey. They were approaching the end of the line, and to the end of their dive time, when Sandro rapped his torch against his tank and pointed; Jack glanced across. There it was, THALASSA SHIPPING LINES, grey rather than blue, but no mistaking the code. They had found the right container. Jack checked the dive computer again, they had only two minutes left at this depth. He pulled out his slate again and wrote:

I fix SMB

Join me at forward mast

As soon as Sandro acknowledged Jack finned to the container. He quickly unhooked his Surface Marker Buoy, a fluorescent plastic tube into which he would direct air. He fixed the frame of a reel of woven plastic line to the corner of the container, he grabbed his reserve and squirted a stream of compressed air into the SMB. The flaccid bag suddenly became alive and rocketed towards the surface. The clutch on the reel kept the line taut as metre after metre of line sped out. Jack turned in the water, kicked upwards, and pointed his torch at the dive computer on his wrist. At first he couldn't focus on the read-out as it glowed back at him. It said he had four, no five minutes at this depth! He searched the face of

194

the computer looking for warning symbols, listening for shrill computer alarms. There were none, except several segments were lit on the ascent rate indicator; he was going up too fast. Jack jackknifed downwards and finned with the current, slightly upwards and towards the mast where Sandro would be waiting for him.

A quick glance of the dive computer filled him with relief. By moving to a shallower depth, albeit only metres, his bottom time had increased by four minutes and was clicking up steadily. He could relax and fin slowly to the masthead, buddy up with Sandro, and ascend. They ascended together and within twenty metres of the surface could see the survey boat. They rendezvoused beneath the boat and hung onto the two dangling tanks whilst they completed their three minutes at five metres safety stop.

Chapter 27

Releasing the container

Even as Jack was handing up his fins to Kev, SAM was leaning over the stern. The mixture of excitement and anxiety showing in his face. 'You have found my container,' he demanded. 'Is it damaged? You must go back and collect it for me.' The questions and demands spilled out in a torrent.

Jack gave SAM a big smile and, breathlessly, explained 'Yes, we have found the container, it looks OK and we will go back shortly and start to recover it.'

Jack and Sandro climbed up the rear ladder and started to walk towards the dive benches to take off their kit. Even though Jack was dripping seawater, and still in all his gear, SAM gave him a big hug. 'I knew you wouldn't disappoint me,' he grinned.

Kev helped Sandro and Jack out of their gear and, whilst they were changing empty tanks for full ones and drying off, fetched two steaming cups of tea and a box of biscuits. Jack and Sandro sat on one of the benches on the dive deck with Kev, Penny and SAM gathered round. They were all keen to hear what they had found. In a low key, much understated way, Sandro described how they located the wreck, had nearly been impaled by the forward mast, and eventually found the container. Penny then adopted her official HM Border Force role, asking about the state of the hull, what damage had been inflicted and if the other containers were salvageable.

'Hey, slow down will you,' pleaded Sandro. 'We only had a few minutes down there, that's just enough time to do what we did. The inspections will have to wait until later.' A response aimed more at SAM than Penny even if she didn't seem to appreciate it.

'What's the current like over the wreck at the moment?' asked Kev. 'What's the vis?' It was typical of Kev to ask all the important questions.

'It's approaching slack tide so difficult to say what it will be like in a few hours. However, if the tidal range is only half a metre it shouldn't pose too much of a problem. However, the site looks very clean suggesting the current has washed away any loose stuff. The vis was good, fifteen to twenty metres so, again, not a problem.'

It was clear that SAM was getting agitated. 'You must go now and get my container,' he demanded as he placed his hand on the large bone handled knife strapped to his thigh. 'You can drink tea and talk to your friends when I have my container.'

Jack immediately stood, smiled and moved towards SAM, gently turning him away and stepping away from the group. 'It's one of the problems with deep diving,' Jack started to explain. 'We have been breathing a mixture of oxygen and nitrogen at depth. When you do this the body absorbs nitrogen into the tissue. When you come back to the surface the body starts to get rid of the nitrogen, but it can only do it slowly. If you don't allow the nitrogen to dissipate slowly it forms bubbles in the tissue, which migrates to the bloodstream and either maims or kills you. It's called "The

197

Bends". Sandro and I are keen to go back and retrieve the container but unless we allow the nitrogen to dissipate for a couple of hours or so we will be maimed or die by diving too soon. I'm sorry, I should have explained this to you before,' Jack concluded.

SAM seemed to accept the explanation but in a low whisper confided. 'If you are trying to trick me, "whitey", I will cut your heart out. Do you understand me?' he challenged.

'We will be diving again soon,' Jack announced.

With a line secured to the container it should have been an easy second descent. However, Jack was carrying a spare cylinder and four, three thousand litre air bags. Sandro was carrying the straps, ratchets and two tubular steel bars. Awkwardly they finned gently downwards, brushing a hand against the SMB line as they went. The sight of the *Lee Kwan Fong* still looked impressive as it emerged from the blue-grey depths. Unlike the previous visit there was now a small shoal of fish gathering around the containers, exploring. The vis was so good that they could make out the point where the marker buoy line was attached to the container. The tide had obviously changed and the current was now pushing the line towards the wheelhouse.

They finned steadily to the container and set down their bundles. The straps had been wound up and paired so it was easy to unwind them. Sandro fixed the metal clip at the end of the strap to the container top and the other clip to a strong point on the container beneath. When they had practiced ratcheting up the strap on land it had been remarkably easy. Underwater it was much more difficult. However, the tubular extension worked a treat and in less than a minute the first strap was as tight as a bow-string. The second, third and fourth straps were just as quick. Sandro trimmed off the surplus strap with his diving knife to reduce the chance of entanglement when the container was free. Jack was hovering above the container. He was fitting buoyancy bags to the four corners of the container and dumping enough air into them, from the cylinder under his arm, to inflate them to about one quarter full. They were already straining to be free.

Before the dive Jack and Sandro had agreed how they would release the retaining bolts. Rather than release them side by side they would release opposite corners. They judged that in this way the container was less likely to twist and more likely to stay in position. The downside was that they wouldn't be able to see each other if there was a problem. But they did agree a release sequence.

Jack and Sandro picked up their metal tubes with Jack finning over the container to reach the opposite corner. He rapped the tube on the container twice signalling he was ready to release. Sandro gave a one rap acknowledgement indicating he was ready. Jack slotted the tube over the tommy bar and it turned with little resistance. One turn and it was free. Even though the strap was as tight as they could get it Jack could see and hear some further stretching, but it held firm. Jack swam round the container to check with Sandro. His bolt was free and the container looked stable; they moved to the last two bolts. Jack rapped twice with the steel tube and immediately heard the single rap from Sandro; they were ready. He slipped the tube in place but couldn't even move the tommy bar. A sudden cold flush washed over him. He braced himself against the container, held the end of the tube and heaved. It moved a fraction of a turn. He braced himself again and heaved; another quarter turn. He checked the dive computer. He had only three minutes left at this depth and they would have to abort the dive. Jack manoeuvred himself between the container and the metal tube. With his back against the container he pushed his arms out and it gave another quarter turn.

Suddenly there was a crack and the whole container shivered. Jack finned away from the container as it strained against the retaining straps, encouraged by its own buoyancy and the air bags. The strap made cracking noises as it stretched but it held firm. Jack swam around the container and met Sandro swimming towards him. Jack pulled out his dive knife and simulated cutting the straps; Sandro gave the OK signal and began to swim back.

Jack backed away from the base of the container as he cut the webbing. There was a little movement but nothing dramatic. He finned to the other strap and was about to cut it when the whole container started to tilt towards him. There was a sudden fear that he would be trapped under the shifting container but he kicked out of the way. His heart was pounding in his chest. He could see that the container was starting to rise by its own buoyancy and with the encouragement of the air bags. Everything seemed in slow motion as the far end of the container started to rise but his corner was held down by the webbing. Then it shuddered. Whatever was in the container had shifted. It slid inside the container to the lower end slamming into the wall of steel. With a final screech the ratchet gave way and the container was free.

Jack just hung in the water finning slowly upwards and staring as the events unfolded in front of him. It reminded him of TV footage of the space shuttle blasting off from Cape

200

Kennedy. At first it hardly seemed to be moving, but with each passing second it got quicker and quicker. Despite the air bags at the four corners it wasn't going up level. It seemed to be floating at about sixty degrees and twisted in the water. Although he knew it would happen he was mesmerized by how quickly the air bags were expanding. He knew that when passing through the first ten metres the air inside the inflation bags would double in size. They would double again in the next ten metres and yet again in the next ten metres and so on.

Jack glanced at his dive computer; plenty of air, but time to ascend. Any longer and it would become a dive requiring decompression. He joined Sandro and together they finned slowly upwards. Both were aware that "what goes up can come down".

Chapter 28

Carnage on the surface

Those on the decks of the barge and dive boat were oblivious of what was taking place beneath them. This was until the water underneath the barge started to bubble and then boil. One of the gunmen on the dive boat was the first to notice. He pointed at them and shouted, 'Look!' The other gunmen on the dive boat moved to the edge of the boat for a better look. The two on the barge leaned over the side for a better look. At that precise moment a roar, and then the sound of breaking timbers, broke the silence. The barge reared out of the water and heeled over. It must have shot up by at least a metre and heeled over by twenty degrees. The effect on the barge and the gunmen was dramatic. One minute the two men were leaning over the side in calm water, the next they were flung into the air. The first looked as though he was practicing some diving board routine as he went up smoothly, but came down head first, somewhat less smoothly, entering the water with a splash. The other was less fortunate. As he fell back he hit the solid wooden gunnel, head first, with a resounding crack and tumbled into the water like a broken toy. The barge had seemed suspended in the air for a fraction of a second before its sheer weight, accompanied by the sound of tortured timbers, forced the container back into the water. It seemed to thrash around like some exuberant animal before it settled like a pale blue mini iceberg gently bouncing. It had crashed into the underside of the barge with massive momentum.

After the tremendous noise there was silence until one of the gunmen or the dive boat pointed towards the water and shouted. 'Sonny no swim,' as he moved closer to the edge of the boat and frantically looked around him for help.

Kev realised immediately what Jack and Sandro had done, and what would happen next. He grabbed the chrome rail in the middle of the diving deck, bent his legs, relaxed his stance and shouted, 'Brace.' The turbulence from the container and barge struck the dive boat. Penny and the others really had no time to react before the wave struck. The placid dive boat was transformed in a split second into a bucking bronco. The boat reared and twisted, bounced and spun in a gut wrenching pirouette. Kev had anticipated the movement and coped with it. He heard rather than saw Penny ricochet off walls and tables in the galley. He heard rather than saw the splashes as two gunmen were flung into the water, immediately followed by the cries of alarm of a gunman on deck.

Kev swung from rail to rail as he made his way to the galley. Penny was on the floor nursing a bloody nose and cut chin but otherwise seemed OK. He darted back onto the dive deck and round to the midships. He could see one of the gunmen kneeling by the gunnel reaching out to someone in the water. The gunman turned and looked at Kev. 'He no swim … he no swim,' he shouted as he turned back towards one of the men in the water.

Kev moved forward, towards the raised deck, and unclipped one of the long boat hooks that ran alongside.

Grabbing the boat hook by the shaft he turned towards the kneeling gunman. He had reacted on instinct and was about to move to the gunnel and reach across to the man in the water when he suddenly realised … there was only one gunman on the boat.

The gunman glanced at Kev with the boat hook and then looked back to the man in the water, shouting something. But Kev could hear nothing over the blood rushing through his head and ringing in his ears. The boat hook was good quality. The shaft was ash or beech, well worn, sound and about three metres long. Kev reckoned the hook was cast brass. It was polished smooth in places but in others it was dull and encrusted with green verdigris. He swung it easily in one hand and as it arched through the air grabbed the shaft with both hands and brought it down with tremendous force on the back of the gunman's head. The solid brass casting hit with a solid thud; a sound like an axe burying itself into a tree trunk. The man fell forwards and simply slid over the side like some graceful reptile. Kev dropped the boat hook as though an electric shock had run through it. He turned towards the wheelhouse and suddenly realised that Jack and Sandro were still in the water. He couldn't turn on the engine in case they were underneath, he couldn't motor away without them. He quickly scanned across to the barge; it was mortally hit. Already the stern was lower in the water, being dragged down by the weight of the engine. It lay heeled over to starboard with the blunt bow now higher than before. It may not sink quickly but it wasn't going to sail very far. There was movement on board the barge. SAM and the old captain were scrambling along the tilted deck.

Kev realised that he had to keep the gunmen off the dive boat until he knew what had happened to Jack and Sandro. He shouted for Penny and she staggered towards the wheelhouse. 'Penny, there is only you and me on the boat. The others are in the water and I think I have killed one of them. But I don't know where Jack or Sandro are. We've got to stop any of the gunmen getting back on board. Do you understand?'

Penny gave a bemused nod.

'Take the starboard side and tell me if it looks like any of the gunmen are getting close to us; I'll take the port,' he said.

It was only as he moved to the open deck, and the rushing of blood in his head and ears started to clear, that he heard the screams and thrashing of men in the water. He looked across at the barge. The old captain was coiling a line and was about to throw it to the nearest man in the water. He threw it but it was short; he started to recoil the line for another try. Kev stood helpless. He couldn't prevent the man in the water being rescued and he couldn't leave. The old captain was about to throw the line again when suddenly, the gunman in the water dropped below the surface and seemed to wave goodbye.

Jack and Sandro were ascending alongside their bubbles, and heard, rather than saw, the effect of the runaway container. As they neared the surface between the barge and the dive boat Jack could count the people in the water. Three were motionless and two were a blur of thrashing legs. Jack paused and counted again and tried to identify who was in the water. Not Kev or Penny, not SAM nor the barge captain. It meant all five gunmen were in the

205

water. He turned to Sandro and mimed, *Me, swim to the man in the water, grab legs, pull down*.

He looked into Sandro's eyes and with his right hand made a cut throat gesture. It was clear what he was going to do. He pointed at Sandro and mimed the sequence again. He then pointed at the figures in the water and on his fingers he picked off one, two, three, four and five.

Sandro looked pale behind his mask but nodded and turned towards the drowning man who was furthest away. Jack turned away and started to swim towards the other. He was about two metres below the struggling gunman when he reached for his dump value and pulled it. All the air was dumped from his BCD and he was about to sink to the seabed. He finned strongly upwards and towards the flailing legs and barged into them with his shoulder. The struggling man seemed to pause for a split second before Jack wrapped his arms around the legs and simply hung on for all he was worth. He buried his head behind the man's knees and held on as tightly as he could. The reaction was instantaneous. The man tried to kick away and seemed to shake Jack like a dog might shake a rat, but he hung on. Jack suddenly realised that the pressure in his ears was increasing; he must be going down and he wasn't breathing. He took a gasp of air through the regulator and swallowed; the pressure in his ears immediately disappeared but the man continued to kick and was now thumping Jack's arms with his fists. Then it was all over, a sudden convulsion and the man became still. One or two twitches and he was still, but Jack didn't let go. It had all been over in seconds rather than minutes. Jack opened his eyes and glanced at the dive computer on his wrist. He was at a depth of seventeen metres and going down. He let go of the gunman and kicked away. He couldn't stop himself from looking into the face of the man he had just drowned. The man's eyes were wide open and lips curled back, his broken teeth stained and shirt floating in the water. Jack started to fin towards the surface and reached for his air hose to inject air into his BCD to help arrest the descent and make him neutrally buoyant. He took one last glance to see the body start to turn as the weight from the weapon slipped around his shoulder and pulled him down. Too late Jack realised he should have taken the gun, but it was too late. He glanced at the wrist compass, momentarily disorientated. He started to ascend towards the dive boat and as he did so saw that Sandro was still holding onto the other gunman even though there was no movement coming from him. Jack swam towards them and gave Sandro a double slap on the shoulder. He turned his head, opened his eyes but didn't let go. Jack gave him the universal "it's OK" and "surface" signs and started to ease Sandro's arms from the legs of the gunman. As they drifted apart Jack eased the weapon over the gunman's head and gave it to Sandro with a repeat thumbs up, time to surface. He unbuckled the cartridge belt from around the gunman's waist and wrapped it around his own as he followed Sandro upwards. It was only as they approached the surface that he checked his dive computer. It was good practice to do a safety stop, five metres for three minutes, but we'll skip it today. They finned towards the stern of the dive boat.

One handed Jack removed a fin and tossed it on board. He shouted for Kev as he did so. By the time he had tossed the second fin aboard Kev was leaning over the stern. 'Can you take this?' Jack asked as he handed the ammunition belt to Kev. 'Can you also take the weapon from Sandro; it's pretty heavy.'

Jack climbed out of the water, more exhausted than he had realised. Kev helped him slip out of the BCD and then dumped the kit on the deck; he did the same for Sandro.

'What's happened?' asked Kev, knowing that they had successfully released the container but not sure about the rest.

Both Jack and Sandro simply sat on the bench next to the rail, slouched over, head in hands. Sandro was the first to move. He stood up, walked to the stern and vomited over the back of the boat. He wiped his hand over his mouth. 'We've just drowned two of the gunmen,' Sandro announced as he walked away towards the galley. 'Three of the others are dead. SAM and the barge captain are alive but I'm not sure for how long.'

Jack looked up, 'Kev, are you and Penny OK?' he asked. Kev confirmed that they had the odd bruise but were OK.

'Right,' said Jack. 'Let's get away from here.'

Chapter 29

Tables turned

Jack stooped for the kit and tank and was about to lift it into one of the retaining clips when there was a loud "ping" and the sound of a gunshot as a bullet ricocheted off the metal dive deck. Someone was firing at them. Jack dodged behind the steel plate that formed the side of the super structure; Sandro joined him. Jack peered round it until he could see the barge. SAM was stood, legs braced on the deck of the barge, pointing a gun at them. The stern was at water level and it was clear that the boat was sinking. The bow was even further out of the water and gunnel about to go under.

'I'm going to kill you, "whitey",' SAM shouted and fired another shot at the dive boat.

Jack was now angry. His previous exhaustion miraculously disappeared. He grabbed the gun from the boat deck, hauled it to his shoulder, pointed it at SAM and pulled the trigger, but nothing happened. He looked down at the gun in his hands wondering, why doesn't it work? Water … safety catch?' He looked more closely but his knowledge of guns was solely from TV programmes and films. Another loud ping and bang as SAM fired another bullet at them. But there on the side of the gun, near the trigger, was a lever. He could push it with his thumb. He pushed it, raised the gun again and pulled the trigger.

The sound was deafening in the enclosed space. Jack hadn't put the stock of the weapon firmly into his shoulder and so the gun had kicked back and punched him hard on the bicep. Jack didn't know were the bullets had gone but guessed miles away from the target. But the effect was immediate. SAM dropped behind the gunnel. He didn't know that this was the first time Jack had ever fired a weapon and that he didn't know how to reload it.

'Kev, get us out of here,' Jack shouted as he rubbed his bruised arm. 'The tanks and weights under the boat,' shouted Sandro, 'we need to them on board,' he added. They cut the straps and pulled the heavy tanks on board.

As the dive boat roared into life, and Kev moved them away from the sinking barge, Jack shouted across to SAM, 'We promised to salvage your container, we have. We're off.'

Penny grabbed at Jack's arm. 'You can't leave him there to drown. What sort of man are you?' she asked.

'One that wants to get as far away from that monster as I can,' he replied. 'Do you think for one minute that he would have let us sail away as soon as he had the contents of that container? They would have shot us all, just like Mohammed and Kirru,' Jack replied his face still full of anger.

The anger, like the adrenalin, was short lived. As the barge fell away behind them Jack felt tired and sick. He guessed it was a reaction to the events of the dive and drowning two men. But if they were to get away they needed to think. Kev had the boat on autopilot and had made up a brew. For a moment they sat in silence in the wheelhouse.

'Kev, you said we had plenty of fuel and stores. How far south can we get?' asked Jack.

'More than halfway to Cape Town, but it will depend on the weather. The boat is sound but it's not built for long open water voyages, it's really an inshore craft,' he replied. He went on, 'my suggestion would be to head due south, get out of the range of SAM and his crew, and to contact the authorities for help.'

'Unless SAM stole it when he went through the dive box we have a satellite phone. We could phone Charles. He's the sort of guy who could get us some help,' Sandro volunteered.

'You're right, good thinking, Sandro,' Jack said as he moved towards the aluminium kit boxes and started to retrieve the phone.

Charles picked up his phone on the second ring. He didn't sound surprised or shocked when Jack gave him an abbreviated account of what had happened. He didn't interrupt until Jack paused and said they were currently heading due south with enough fuel and stores to get 'halfway to Cape Town.' He merely asked Jack to confirm they were all OK, the code and name on the container, that it was still intact and the GPS coordinates of the container. He finished by saying, 'One: continue motoring parallel to the coast, twenty-five miles out, outside territorial limits. Two: await a phone call in three hours'; precisely 5.12 p.m. your time. Three: avoid other boat traffic, do not dock, do not go close to shore. Do you understand?'

Jack confirmed the request and Charles rang off.

There was a sudden vacuum on the dive boat. So much intense activity, so much change in their circumstances, so little they could do. Kev broke the spell. 'I've got a suggestion to make. Why don't we get organised and clean up? The boat is on automatic and we should pack all the gear before it

211

gets dark. A shower, shave and clean togs wouldn't be a bad idea either. Penny and I can rustle up a pretty good spaghetti bolognese and I reckon a bottle of red between us would go down well while we wait to hear from Charles. I'm guessing, but reckon it is unlikely we will be diving tomorrow,' he said with a half smile.

There was no disagreement. In fact attending to routine chores seemed to be therapeutic. It was only when Jack spotted a silver streak on the metalwork surrounding the dive deck that he realised how lucky they had been.

The food and glass of wine had been delicious. Jack hadn't realised how hungry he had been as he spooned more sauce onto his plate. Sandro talked everyone through the dive, the damage to the hull of the *Lee Kwan Fong* and what they had glimpsed in the cargo holds. They avoided the subject of the gunmen and what had happened to them. Once everything had been washed up, and put away, conversation seemed to end; they sat in almost silence waiting for the phone to ring.

Jack was reaching for a chart of the area when the satellite phone started to buzz and blink. He unclipped it from its housing.

'Jack?' Charles asked, waiting until Jack acknowledged. 'Is everything still all right?'

Jack told him that they were all fine with everything stowed away. The dive boat was on autopilot running approximately twenty-five miles off the coast on a SW bearing and motoring along at ten knots.

'Jack,' continued Charles in a soft, conspiratorial tone. 'Sir Alistair would like to talk to you; I'll hand the phone to him.'

212

Sir Alistair was business-like. 'Jack, I'm extremely sorry for what has happened over the last few hours and relieved that you and your friends are all safe. I have spoken to some people and I am confident that neither you, nor Sandro, will face any charges over the … er … incidents in the water whilst retrieving the container. It is likely that you will need to speak to the Kenyan authorities but we will worry about that later. I'm afraid you are going to have to trust me over what I say next. The people that I have been speaking to have asked if you could *hove to,* or remain in your current position, and be prepared to receive hourly messages until the incident is resolved.'

Jack was confused. He wanted to get as far away as possible from SAM and the gunmen, not sit around waiting for hourly messages. The tone of Sir Alistair's request seemed to disregard all that had happened. He replied, 'What? Did Charles tell you how the gunmen murdered Mohammed and Kirru? After what we've done that maniac SAM will kill us without a second thought, and you want us to sit around?' Jack exclaimed. Sir Alistair responded. 'Jack, I am going to share some privileged information with you and your colleagues, but you must not share this with any other living person. At some future time you will be asked to sign the Official Secrets Act and if you were to share what I am about to tell you with any other person, between now or after signing the OSA, you will be prosecuted by HM Government. It is that serious. Do you understand?'

Jack was taken aback. What was all this about? Jack said he understood and would stress the need for secrecy with the others. Sir Alistair went on. 'The container you retrieved is now under surveillance by an American military satellite. From observations it appears the man you know as SAM, and a second person believed to be the barge captain, will soon be rescued from the floating wreckage of the barge by persons unknown. The people I have been speaking to are currently trying to discover what is in the container and are making various plans to either secure it or destroy it. You and your friends could play an extremely useful role in these plans. I have also been informed that the British Government would be indebted to you and your colleagues if you were prepared to help. That is all I can say at the present time.'

'I need to talk to Sandro, Kev and Penny. Can you phone me back in five minutes?' asked Jack.

'I will phone back in five minutes,' replied Sir Alistair.

Jack sat on one of the long bench seats, head bowed, took a deep breath and recounted what he had been told. At the end he asked, 'So, do we continue on the current track, heading South West, and away from these characters, or do we stay here and wait for messages from Sir Alistair and his friends? What do you think?'

Kev was the first to volunteer an opinion. 'It sounds as if Sir Alistair has some pretty powerful friends. If they can get American satellite surveillance they will be able to call up all sorts of help. We are about fifty nautical miles away from the container and can make over ten knots if we have to. My vote would be to *hove to* and help.'

Penny agreed, saying that her boss would expect her to offer any assistance she could to another government department. Sandro also agreed to stay and help, hinting that to have the British Government and Lloyd's of London "indebted" could be extremely useful.

Jack made the decision unanimous and as he did so the phone rang.

Chapter 30

A waiting game

Over the next twelve hours the phone would ring and Charles would merely ask them to maintain their current position. Dawn had broken on another glorious day. It promised to be warm and there was barely a ripple on the water as the phone rang again; this time it was Sir Alistair.

'Jack, the French frigate *Nivôse* has been diverted from her patrol off the Somalian coast and is steaming in your direction at top speed. It will take her about ten hours to reach the GPS coordinates you gave us. A fishing trawler left the port of Lammu with five people on board and is now moored next to the container. The barge appears to have sunk. It appears they plan to partly hoist the container out of the water, open it and extract whatever it is inside. We understand that their plan is to then release and sink the container, and take the contents to an unknown fishing port in Tanzania. If it looks as if the contents are going to be landed before the trawler can be intercepted a helicopter from the *Nivôse* will be dispatched to sink it. Do you have any questions?'

Jack had a hundred questions, like how did they know all of this? It wouldn't be possible to learn all this from satellite surveillance – or would it? However, he simply said they didn't have any questions and would await the next phone call.

While they waited for the next phone call Kev busied himself with checks on all the onboard systems, quantities of water and fuel, food supplies and that anything that needed to be secure was secure. Penny pounded away on her laptop presumably writing a graphic account of the incident. Most of it was less than vital but it filled the waiting time. Kev even checked the weapon and ammunition that they had acquired even though he wasn't sure what he was checking. Jack and Sandro rechecked all the diving kit and made sure the log was up to date.

At precisely 6.12 a.m. the phone rang yet again. It was Sir Alistair. 'Jack, there has been a development. The men on the trawler managed to hoist the end of the container clear of the water and have removed several items including ten long wooden crates. From the symbols on the side of the crates my friends believe they have unloaded twenty Chinese Shăndiàn, or Lightning Strike, shoulder launched ground to air missiles.'

Sir Alistair had stopped speaking; Jack had stopped breathing but then let out a long low whistle. This was comic book stuff!

'We estimate that the *Nivôse* will intercept the trawler in about nine hours but are still unsure where the trawler plans to unload its cargo. We need to disable the trawler and, ideally, capture the missiles and the crew. If this is not possible the trawler, and any chance of uncovering the groups behind these missiles, will be lost.

217

My friends have asked if you can think of any way, any safe way, the trawler can be slowed down or disabled? Can I leave that with you and phone back in an hour?'

With that Sir Alistair rang off leaving Jack perplexed. As they were sat around the saloon table Jack explained the challenge they had been posed.

It was Kev who immediately came up with the solution. 'Let's assume there are ordinary fishermen, and also gunmen, on the trawler. Let's also assume they want to keep a low profile and not draw attention to themselves. Finally, let's also assume none of them have seen us or the dive boat. I don't think that is unreasonable. If we position ourselves in their path, let off a flare and fake engine failure, my guess is that they would come and investigate. No trawler captain is going to ignore a distress call. It would be easy to pull one of the electrical leads on the engine adrift, so the engine would be dead.

If Jack and Sandro were in the water when they came alongside the men on the trawler wouldn't see them. We could even have spare tanks slung under the boat. Whilst we are explaining the problem Jack and Sandro could swim under the trawler, wrap one of the lifting straps around the propeller blades and rudder stem, then, hey presto. When they next engage the propeller the straps will tighten and with any luck shear off the propeller, bend the shaft or strip the gearbox. They won't be going anywhere.

We could fit a strap to each of the cleats on either the port or starboard side. As soon as Jack and Sandro hear our engine start they could grab the free end of the strap, haul themselves up and hang on for a couple of minutes. Once we have the engine running all we need to do is ensure we move away as soon as they leave the boat, before they hit trouble. By the time they realise they have a problem we will be a couple of hundred metres away and can haul Jack, Sandro and the tanks on board.'

With that Kev smiled. 'What do you think?'

Sandro let out a sigh. 'If we had two tanks each we could stay submerged for over two hours. I'd be confident that we could wrap the strap around the propeller and rudder in a couple of minutes and back off. I've just got two concerns.' Sandro held up his hand, poked out a finger, and said, 'One, what if they decide to take a particular interest in the boat and what's on her. What if they don't leave and decide to hang around for a couple of hours. Two, I doubt I could haul myself out of the water; certainly not with a couple of tanks on my back. If you roar away there would be the danger of me losing grip and being shredded by the propellers.'

Jack nodded, agreed with Sandro and added, 'If we hung a couple of tanks under the hull, and they were secure, we could attach the weight belts, BCDs and tanks to them using karabiners. It would mean we would be swimming free but it would be much easier to hang onto a strap for a few minutes. Once out of range we could stop and bring everything on board.'

'I've just had a thought,' said Sandro. 'If I were approaching a boat in distress I'd motor all the way around it before I came alongside, to check it out. I'd also come alongside downwind so it would be easier to disengage later. We would have to be directly under the dive boat to ensure we couldn't be seen. These wetsuits are pretty vivid.'

Jack summarized the plan and it was agreed that Kev would suspend tanks and straps from the mid-ship's cleats.

He also found a lead that he would uncouple and which would appear to have vibrated loose thus stopping the engine. They were set.

The phone rang precisely on time; it was Sir Alistair again and Jack explained the plan. Sir Alistair made no comment but said he would phone back in one hour. When he did he was more animated. 'Jack, the trawler is holding a steady course and appears to be heading for a port in Tanzania. If you were to motor to the following coordinates, and position yourself at those coordinates, we estimate you would be in the path of the trawler in less than two hours. Even at its top speed the *Nivôse* cannot be at these coordinates for another six hours. If you can slow down or stop the trawler it's likely that hundreds of lives could be saved and a political crisis averted. But the decision to act must be yours.'

'Can I confirm the coordinates,' said Jack, his voice firm. 'If you can give us updates on the position of the trawler we can position ourselves and make a distress call well before the trawler sees us. They may have radar on the trawler and so we don't want them to see us moving. Oh yes, is there any way you can prevent other ships coming to our aid?'

'All of that is in hand,' said Sir Alistair in a reassuring tone. 'One more thing. Before the *Nivôse* intercepts the trawler you will receive a phone call from the captain of the frigate. You must do everything he tells you to do. A party of armed French Commandos will board your boat and search it along with everyone on board. Tell your friends not to be alarmed. I'm informed it is standard practice.'

There were a few other pleasantries before Sir Alistair rang off. It was now just a case of waiting. The time dragged. Kev suggested an early lunch, which was more for something to do than anyone was hungry. They went through the motions but there was little appetite.

Suddenly the phone rang. Even though they were expecting it the effect was startling. The speaker introduced himself as Captain Henri Lefrere, captain of the frigate *Nivôse.* He spoke in good English, albeit with a strong French accent; Jack replied in fluent French. Captain Lefrere gave Jack the coordinates to which he wanted Jack to sail and an ETA of the trawler at those coordinates. The captain ended the call by saying, 'Phone Sir Alistair immediately after your attempt to delay or stop the trawler. If he does not hear from you one hour, repeat one hour, after the estimated rendezvous he will assume the attempt failed and that you are in difficulty.'

With that the call was disconnected. Jack was initially puzzled by the tone and the language. What does "in difficulty" mean? He guessed that the French Navy didn't want amateurs involved in their operations, no matter how well intentioned. But there was no time to dwell on speculations. Kev had the boat speeding to the rendezvous and Jack and Sandro were assembling spare tanks, wrapping weights around them so they didn't float, and attaching straps so they could be suspended beneath the boat. It didn't take long to reach the coordinates and to check that they were directly in the path of the trawler. It took only minutes to rig the tanks and weights tightly under the boat and to trap spare straps under the webbing so that Jack and Sandro could hang on as, hopefully, the dive boat disengaged from the trawler.

They stood around on the dive deck, Jack and Sandro partly in their wetsuits waiting and looking towards the north

221

east. The phone rang, it was Sir Alistair. 'Jack, the trawler remains on course, ETA one hour and forty minutes. Good luck.'

With that Sir Alistair rang off and Kev moved to the bridge to issue the pan-pan; the distress call signifying that there was an emergency on board but for the time being there is no immediate danger to anyone's life or to the vessel itself. As soon as the three pan-pan calls had been issued he could guess the action on board those craft in the area, and the coastguard. He hoped the trawler had the radio open, heard the call and realised they were close. Almost immediately there was a call on the radio from the Kenyan coastguard, acknowledging the pan-pan and confirming that the boat owner "Alistair Murray" would be informed of the problem. It was clear that Sir Alistair or someone had alerted the coastguard to the ruse.

Every fifteen minutes Kev issued the pan-pan saying they were trying to fix the problem and gave their position. It was Penny who spotted the trawler first. To be fair she was on the upper deck and stood on the table, bracing herself on the frame of the awning. She shouted down to Kev. With binoculars they could make out the shape of a boat and guessed it was them. They waited a few more minutes and then Kev grabbed one of the distress rockets. He ripped off the plastic caps on each end, flicked out the firing pin and aiming it upwards into the path of the trawler, he launched it into the clear blue sky with a whoosh. At night the red parachute flare would have been seen for miles but in the early morning sun it could easily be ignored. After three minutes Kev let off a second red rocket flare and then ran up to the top deck to set off and wave an orange smoke flare.

It was impossible to tell if the men on the trawler had seen them; they just ploughed steadily in their direction. Kev checked with the binoculars. He couldn't make out anyone on the trawler and so it was likely they couldn't see them. Jack and Sandro slid into the water on the side away from the oncoming trawler, deflated their BCDs, and sank below the surface.

Jack and Sandro hung onto the hull straps directly under the boat. Jack had taken a bearing on the trawler before entering the water and so he knew the direction it would be coming from. They heard it before they saw it. There was a dull thump, thump, thump as the old diesel plodded along. Jack could tell it was close but not how close. Then Jack could see the hull as it started to circle the dive boat. It did a complete circle before slowing and coming to rest alongside. The dive boat was rocking violently in the water and both Jack and Sandro had to avoid shoulder wrenching movements as the underwater straps were pulled to and fro. Jack had no idea what was being said but simply waited for the churning propellers to stop. There was no way he would be able to get close to them whilst they were spinning. But the propellers stopped and both he and Sandro finned strongly towards the stern.

It was going to be more difficult than they expected. Even though the trawler was hard up against the side of the dive boat both of them were rocking and pitching, making it difficult to manoeuvre and hold on to each end of the lifting strap. It was obvious that the hull, rudder and propeller hadn't been cleaned in years. All of it was pock marked with a mixture of grey barnacles, other shell fish and was festooned with silky green weed. Sandro pointed to the rear stock of the rudder mounting; the strong point of the whole mechanism. He and Jack threaded the lifting strap between the hull and the rudder, and back on itself; it was a firm anchor. The other end was looped over one of the blades of the propeller several times and locked off in a half hitch. Jack checked the dive computer. It had taken just over two minutes. From the clean sharp leading edge of the propeller blades it was clear to see the direction of the forward thrust. They had left about a metre of the strap hanging in the water. When the propeller was engaged the shaft would spin, the slack would be taken up in fractions of a second, and then brought to a sudden stop. The carbon fibre reinforced material was incredibly strong and Jack had no doubt that the blade, shaft or gear box would come off worst.

Jack signalled that they should strip off their BCD and tank and fix their kit to the strap below the dive boat. They moved to the far side of the dive boat, away from the trawler, and waited for the engine to fire. Jack felt naked in the water. The curve of the hull was such that it was unlikely anyone could see them from the boat. But in just fins, mask and snorkel they couldn't get far; the tanks of air were fixed under the boat. But the die had been cast. Jack and Sandro hung below the boat, a strap firmly around a wrist and holding onto the secured kit with the other hand. What was taking so long? Jack checked his dive computer again. The trawler had been alongside for nearly fifteen minutes. He checked the amount of air but knew he would still have plenty. He couldn't hear anything and just hoped all was going well.

Then something caught his eye; there was movement in the water off to his left. Jack turned his head. A large green turtle was slowly finning along and had come to investigate.

The green and yellow markings on the head and shell were vivid. It was good to see. But before Jack could continue his musing the dive boat engine kicked into life. Had they done it? Jack and Sandro spat out the regulator and pulled themselves along the two straps to the surface. However, it seemed like an eternity before the dive boat eased away from the trawler, slowly at first and then faster. Jack and Sandro were being pulled along in the water; slowly at first and then faster.

It was then that they heard it. There was a quickening of the dull thumps as the engine revs were increased, then an odd straining noise, a sharp crack, and then the release of a high pitched scream as the engine raced. Jack knew that the trawler was going nowhere. The engine raced for a few more seconds before it was cut back. However, the elation was short lived because Jack was also having problems.

He had never been dragged behind a boat before but soon realised it wasn't a comfortable experience. Jack sank his teeth onto the snorkel mouthpiece, clamped one hand onto his mask to stop it being ripped off and simply hung on. By controlling his breathing he could breathe through the snorkel, spitting sea water out of it between breaths. But he was being tossed around like a rat on a string. He had no control. As an automatic reaction he flicked onto his back, hooked his free arm around the strap and flared his legs. He could now almost aquaplane as the boat picked up speed. But he was bouncing off the side of the hull with each dipping of the bow. It felt like his arm was being ripped off. Jack buried his face into his arms, protecting his mask, as he hung on with both hands. It seemed like a long time, but it must have been only minutes, before the noise of the engine dropped and the boat immediately slowed.

Kev was at the side, peering over and shouting, 'Jack, Sandro … are you OK? We did it.'

Jack had lost sight of Sandro, but there he was grinning through his mask.

'Hang on and I will bring us to a stop. We can then get you and the kit on board,' shouted Kev.

Jack was so preoccupied by releasing the tanks and BCDs, straps and weights, and hauling them to the back of the boat, that he forgot about the trawler. The kit was stowed and Penny had mugs of hot tea and biscuits laid out in the saloon. As Jack dried his hair he picked up the phone and dialled Sir Alistair. Jack doubted that the phone had actually rung before he was connected.

Chapter 31

Mission accomplished

'Jack, give me an update.' It was Sir Alistair.

'The trawler is disabled; it's dead in the water. My guess is that the gearbox has been damaged beyond repair, the propeller ripped off or drive shaft seized. Looking at the state of the boat I doubt they have the spares to effect a repair. They are about eight hundred metres away and we have them under surveillance.'

Jack laughed. 'God, after acting like a US SEAL I'm starting to sound like the military!'

'Congratulations,' said Sir Alistair. 'I suggest you have a cup of tea and wait for the French Navy. Oh, and by the way, when you're next in London please do call in.'

Kev took the helm and circled the crippled fishing boat. He picked up the binoculars and scanned the scene but there was no activity. At this distance the lines of the boat were pleasing; tall blunt bow tapering to a low waist and then blunt stern. Almost all of the main deck was taken up by the fish hold with the bridge relegated to a squat box perched near the stern. The two sturdy masts, fore and aft, would be the anchor points for the nets. Kev had remarked that the stench of fish had been almost overpowering when the boat had come alongside. It was clear it had been well used over the years. Repair patches dotted the mottled hull and constant hauling of nets over the side had worn always the once thick rails. There was clutter and frayed ropes, plastic tubs and floats strewn around. Kev felt quite sorry for the skipper. He had done the right thing by coming to their assistance and in doing so had condemned himself and all on board.

Although the grizzled skipper of the trawler was unfamiliar with the dive boat engine it had only taken the old man a few minutes to trace the wiring and find the loose connection. He had beamed at Kev when the engine kicked into life.

Kev realised they should have got underway as soon as possible but felt, in the role, he would have offered food and drink to his rescuers or something for their help. In the end the skipper had accepted a cold beer and a couple of six packs for the rest of the crew. Kev thought of what was hidden in the hold; no one would ever suspect. But in a few more hours the *Nivôse* was expected.

The phone rang. To Jack's surprise it was the captain of the *Nivôse.* In a very brusque tone he instructed Jack to take up a position one thousand metres due east of the fishing boat and to disengage the engine. That was all. A few minutes later they spotted the shape of a ship on the horizon, coming straight towards them. It grew bigger every minute. Even at a distance the bow wave was clear. The outline appeared to be bristling with antennae and was menacing. Jack realised he was relaxing now that the French Navy was on the scene. The spectre of SAM and his huge knife, his gunmen and the bodies on the pier at Lammu, were starting to fade a little. But Jack was jolted back to the present by a weird whistling sound that started low and increased rapidly. It was like an express train from nowhere that was screaming past a platform. A tower of water leapt from the sea about one hundred metres ahead of the fishing boat. Just as the spray was falling back Jack heard the distant crump of what he guessed had been the frigate's gun. Then another shell screamed overhead and into the water with the distant sound of the gun firing. It seemed to be out of synchronisation. The sound of the gun didn't seem to match the strike of the shell. Jack lost count of how many shells had been fired and just stood there mesmerized as the fishing boat rocked and the water churned.

The frigate was close and appeared to be changing course to sail between the dive boat and the fishing boat. It was slowing and as it started to pass between the two vessels they could hear a loud drumming as other armament poured hundreds of bullets into the water off the stern of the boat. Jack ducked as a series of amplified commands split the air. The crew of the fishing boat were being told in French, English and then in some other language, that the crew must surrender and stand on deck with their arms raised. As the frigate curled around the fishing boat first one, and then the others, stood with arms raised. Jack counted them; they were all there. The frigate slowed further but instructions continued to pour from the ship. 'Armed men are about to board your vessel. Any resistance will be met by deadly force.'

The message was repeated constantly as a zodiac, loaded with heavily armed men, bobbed towards the fishing boat. The frigate had circled the fishing boat slowly and now seemed to be stationary in the water; between the fishing boat and the dive boat. Apart from the annoying repetitive loud commands from the frigate they couldn't see anything.

229

The excitement was over. Kev even suggested a cup of tea to celebrate, but the celebration was short lived.

Jack guessed that by now the fishermen and gunmen would be held on board the frigate and whatever was stowed in the hold would be taken on board the *Nivôse*. He was suddenly confused when the commands from the *Nivôse* changed and were directed at the MV *Karwe*. They were instructed to gather on the rear deck with their hands raised. The commands were in French and English and accompanied with the threat of deadly force should they resist!

Somewhat bewildered they assembled on the dive deck, hands in the air, as the black zodiac buzzed towards them and nestled against the stern. Even before the zodiac came alongside guns were pointed at them and a loud instruction from the frigate told them to 'Stand still – do not move.' There must have been ten or a dozen heavily armed men on the zodiac. They were dressed in black military uniform with matching steel helmets, balaclavas and associated pouches that seemed stuffed with equipment. Everything was black, he could see no insignia, no other colour, no bright metal – they were even wearing black gloves – and it was almost thirty degrees! The men moved quickly. They fanned out across the boat deck as two men pointed menacing looking weapons at them. Unlike Jack's pathetic attempt to fire the gun he was sure these guys knew what they were doing. What was unsettling was the balaclavas – there was no facial expression – just squinting eyes.

One of the French soldiers shouted at them aggressively in French and English. 'Keep your hands raised. Step towards the bulkhead. Face it,' he demanded.

Jack glanced at Kev, shrugged, and the four of them shuffled forwards, tense.

'We are going to search you,' the soldier shouted. 'Do not move, hold your hands up, look forwards.'

One of the soldiers stepped forwards and began a thorough body search whilst the other positioned himself so that he could see, and obviously shoot, any of them. Palms and fingers moved from wrist to armpit, ankle to groin … and everywhere in between! When it was Jack's turn he was both embarrassed and impressed by the thoroughness. He suspected that Penny wouldn't be too happy.

They stood in silence for what seemed a long time, increasingly confused, and wondering what was going on. Why were they being treated and held like this? 'We're the good guys,' thought Jack. After what seemed a long time, but was probably fifteen to twenty minutes, one of the soldiers approached them, and in perfect English, said, 'Lady and gentlemen, please lower your hands and relax. I apologise for the last few minutes but we have to follow a … protocol. There can be no exceptions. You are Jack Collier,' the soldier announced as he offered Jack a clumsy looking military phone. 'The captain of the *Nivôse* wishes to speak to you.' He offered the phone to Jack.

Jack took the phone gingerly and noted the previously glowering eyes had been replaced by smiling ones. 'Jack Collier here – what's going on?' he asked.

'Mister Collier,' replied the captain in a business-like tone. 'Please accept my apologies for our actions over the last few minutes. We are required to follow certain procedures in these circumstances and there can be no exceptions.'

The captain paused as though deciding how much more to say, how much to reveal. Then, in a rather formal manner, went on. 'On behalf of myself and the French Government I would like to thank you and your colleagues for your help in disabling the fishing boat. It was a brave act. I understand you are aware of the cargo we have removed from the boat. If that cargo had fallen into the wrong hands many people may have died. We had to confirm there were no other persons on board your boat, no devices had been hidden, nothing that would endanger you or others. I'm happy to say your boat is clear and you are free to proceed. Good sailing and thank you.'

With that the phone line was disconnected and Jack handed it back to the soldier. It was then that he noticed the men in black were climbing over the rear rail and into the zodiac; the final soldier followed them. One minute they had been held at gunpoint; the next they were free to go. It was an anticlimax after all that had happened.

'So, what next?' asked Kev. 'Do we head for Cape Town or Mombasa – or back to finish the job?'

'I reckon we get clarification from Charles about any statement we need to make to the Kenyan authorities. The *Lee Kwan Fong* isn't going anywhere.'

Chapter 32

Completing the job

It was agreed that they would return to the *Lee Kwan Fong* and complete the survey. Somehow Charles even arranged for two armed Kenyan police to be waiting at the Lammu jetty and to stay with them until the survey was complete. Jack had ordered replacement re-breathers and all the kit that had been damaged. He'd worry about an insurance claim later. The police would eventually accompany them to Mombasa, and to the police headquarters, to provide written statements. Charles reassured them that a decision had already been taken by the Kenyan authorities not to take any action against them.

The weather was glorious, and visibility good, as Jack and Sandro drifted down the mooring line and towards the deck of the *Lee Kwan Fong*. In contrast to their previous dive on the wreck this was a joy. The full face masks gave unrestricted vision, there was no sound of air being drawn in and air blowing out as bubbles; it was silent. Jack and Sandro could speak to each other and coordinate the survey task. Over a series of dives they checked the hull for any other damage, measured and photographed the long gash caused by running onto the Pinnacles and assessed the integrity of the containers in terms of possible salvage. They also completed, with some difficulty, a survey of the engine room. The last task was to inspect the covered hold containing the general cargo and check off items on the manifest. Jack and Sandro finned to the for'ard starboard corner of the cargo hold and with a dive knife cut a large entry flap through the thick plastic sheeting that was stretched across the top of the hold. Jack shone a torch inside. The manifest had listed agricultural machinery and agricultural spares. Sandro fixed a guide line to a cleat and led the way into the hold. The torch picked out the track ahead of him. The strong yellow cord, that now looked like grey thread when the torch wasn't on it, paid out behind him as he swam downwards.

The hold was pitch black with just a patch of grey behind them where Sandro had cut through the tarpaulin. They finned slowly to avoid stirring up any of the muck and debris that had settled on the hold floor. A coil of rope was suspended in their path and a wooden pallet had floated upwards and was nestled against the underside of the tarpaulin. The scene was similar to other cargo wrecks Jack had dived upon, but this one was pristine rather than coated in algae and sediment. The torch beam immediately picked out one of the three large tractors that were on the manifest. Jack guessed it was painted yellow or orange but at this depth it appeared grey until the torch beam hit it. They continued on their simple grid as they inspected the hold. It took less than fifteen minutes to confirm the three tractors were in place; chained to the deck. Next to them were three large wheeled trailers into which were secured what looked like tractor attachments, and numerous large wooden cases. Sandro photographed each of the main items including the vehicle identification numbers on the tractors. The plates, easy to see, were fixed to the rear of the tractors. They could be cross checked against the manifest later.

Back on board Jack and Sandro were happy with the inspection. The combination of measurements, notes and photos would be more than enough to assemble their report. Jack had already mentally drafted the main conclusion. The *Lee Kwan Fong* was beyond economic salvage. He doubted the modified hull, coupled with the damage from the reef, would survive any attempt to raise it. The cost was likely to be more than the scrap value of the ship. The good news was that all the containers were intact, did not appear to be leaking, and could be readily salvaged. Similarly the tractors, trailers and goods in the cargo hold. Jack had only a vague idea of the cost of a tractor but guessed the three of them, plus trailers, could be worth US$300,000; well worth salvaging.

Kev and Penny were happy with the news that the job was done and they could return to Mombasa. The two Kenyan policemen were more than happy; they were delighted. It was clear that they preferred the land to the rocking and rolling of the boat. A few days sailing south west and they were docking in Mombasa. A representative from the boat company was waiting to meet them and take back responsibility for the boat. No mention was made of Mohammed and Kirru.

Within an hour of docking their luggage was going one way, to the hotel, and they were being driven to the police headquarters in Mombasa. It was a bureaucratic paper chase and took hours. Separate statements were taken from the four of them. Then they were typed up, checked and eventually signed. Jack guessed that some senior officer was making sure everything was covered before they were allowed to leave. When they did leave Jack was surprised that it was dark outside and he suddenly felt weary. But the good news was a good night's sleep lay ahead and more time to sleep on the long haul back to London and Manchester.

Jack and Sandro had made their farewells to Kev and Penny the previous night in Mombasa. On arrival in London they briefly exchanged goodbyes and went their separate ways.

The Inspection Report was completed within three days of returning to the UK. It marked an anticlimax. The job was done, there was the prospect of a large cheque that made the company secure for a couple of years, but Jack felt flat. He struggled to motivate himself to start searching the websites for potential jobs.

Section 3

The Sacranie Shipping Agency

Chapter 33

From law-abiding to criminal

The perfectly legal and routine handling of shipping containers in and out of Liverpool, other European, Middle Eastern and Indian ports maintained the façade of a small shipping company doing well. The "acquiring", a euphemism for stealing, of all the agricultural equipment they needed to transform peasant farms in Haryana State in India, into profitable concerns, was funding their retirement fund. Similarly, stealing almost new cars from the driveways of unsuspecting owners in the UK, and shipping these to the Middle East at huge profit was adding to the fund. It was one that was growing steadily. As such a request to transport a single container of dates from Tripoli to Dar es Salaam hardly raised an eyebrow; even if the request was from a completely new customer. Indeed, neither Aashi, Amir nor Abdul Sacranie were directly involved in the day-to-day orders – they merely had an overview of the work of staff they now employed. The UK Foreign Office website indicated that the main port in Tripoli was working as normal. There were no restrictions on businesses working with Libya and so no reason not to negotiate the contract.

It was only when Aashi received a phone call from the office manager, about the failure of the *Lee Kwan Fong* to make routine location calls, that the apprehension started.

Nothing had been heard from the vessel for more than twenty-four hours. A few questions to the office manager, and inspection of the Passage Plan, confirmed that at or about the time the first missed call was due the ship would be about three hundred kilometres off the East African coast, roughly between Southern Somalia and the Seychelles. The route skirted around the zone where Somali pirates had previously operated. In the last eight months French and US warships had intercepted and destroyed several high speed launches that refused to stop. However, despite the lack of any attempt to hijack ships in the area for months Aashi immediately thought the worse. She phoned both Amir and Abdul to alert them to a potential problem. They met hastily in Aashi's apartment – away from any other ears.

'No need to worry,' Amir said. 'We hope for the best but I've already planned for the worse.' He followed up by saying, 'You might remember I briefly explained how I was covering our tracks in relation to the transportation of agricultural machinery to the farms. I've set up dummy corporations to supply the kit and made it impossible for anyone to trace the equipment back to us. All of that is still in place. I'm sure everything is tight but I'll confirm all the documents are in order.'

Aashi was reassured. She had every confidence in Amir's IT skills and knew the amount of time he had spent on their systems. She speculated, 'It's possible that it is a simple communication breakdown. On the other hand the ship could have been taken by pirates … or even sunk. The office manager checked the weather in the area and it's good.'

In a confident tone and relaxed manner Amir announced, 'I will double check the manifest, all the cargo, and ensure

239

that there is no paper trail linking us to any of the stolen goods and that we acted in good faith. I'd previously set up the farm equipment as being supplied by two fictitious companies. From an inspection it will look like we purchased the second-hand equipment legally. It will only become clear that these are dummy companies if authorities start to check. As long as we maintain the position of the duped party we have nothing to fear.'

It was over a day later that the office manager, on a poor quality phone call from the chief engineer of the *Lee Kwan Fong,* confirmed that the ship had indeed been captured by pirates off the Somali coast. The vessel had subsequently hit a submerged reef some forty kilometres off the coast and sunk. The chief was the only survivor of the attack and was currently in a police station in Mombasa. The police had allowed him to make the phone call. Apparently he had been taken off the sinking ship by the pirates and, inexplicably, set free once reaching the shore in Somalia. He had made his way to the nearest town and caught a bus to, and across, the Kenyan border and notified the police as soon as he could. He was now in Mombasa and wondering what to do next. Some urgent emailing and telephoning had him booked into a hotel awaiting further instructions.

More phone calls to the insurers, Lloyd's of London, confirmed the story. Sacranie Shipping Agents were told a news story would break within hours and suggested they made no comment at this time. Aashi was in the office when the phone call came through from Lloyd's. She immediately phoned Amir and Abdul and hastily arranged another meeting in her apartment.

Amir had taken responsibility for the security of the businesses. As the three of them sat around the dining room table he explained. 'I've phoned our cousin in Mumbai. By this evening he and his wife will have cleared out every piece of equipment and every scrap of paper from the Mumbai office; it will be completely empty. They will also wash the place down to ensure there is nothing left for anyone to find; no scrap paper, no fingerprints, no nothing. They will put all of the office in storage as previously planned. There is no way either they or us can be traced to our front company, OK Osman Bros.

There was nothing else in transit other than the cargo in the ship, so no leads for anyone to follow. I've told them to plan for a month long holiday and I will contact them when we want to set up the office again in another part of the city. We have thirteen cars in the warehouse and more expected in the next few weeks. There's no link between Sacranie Shipping Agents and the warehouse. My suggestion is that we simply carry on as normal in both enterprises; but make less trips to the warehouse until we know what is happening. To move the cars now is a bigger risk than leaving them where they are.

The *Lee Kwan Fong* was insured but not against *force majeure*. The ship will be a total loss. The tractors and other equipment were insured through OK Osman Bros. but they will not be making a claim. I've double checked everything. All the accounts are in perfect order and as long as we sit tight there is no problem,' he concluded. 'It's work as normal.' He smiled.

'Work as normal,' repeated Aashi. She sighed and went on. 'We've come so far since those scary days when Dad was taken ill and we rescued the Agency.'

Chapter 34

Back from the brink

Aashi thought back to how her legal career had changed abruptly into a criminal one. Farouk Sacranie, her father, had worked for the British Merchant Navy in Liverpool during the 1970s. Farouk had been part of a team that coordinated cargos in and out of Liverpool. For the team it wasn't just a case of allocating a mixture of cargos to suitable ships but ensuring a similar mixture of cargos on the next leg and so on until the ship eventually returned to its home port. Farouk was meticulous, loved his job, took pride in it and was good at it.

However, as the British Merchant Marine shrank so did the need for his coordination and planning skills. It was at this time that a series of events changed his life for ever. In the space of two months Farouk was made redundant from the Merchant Navy, married to Neelam, through an arranged marriage by his parents, and out of work. It was then that a fluke encounter with a ship owner changed his life. Walter Bailey was a ship owner, well off, well connected and smart. He had inherited three ten thousand tonne freighters which were still good for another million nautical miles. He had the ships, knew that there was massive demand for transporting goods around the world, he had contacts but didn't have the skill to coordinate it.

Walter had dealt with Farouk regularly for years and was certain he was the man to coordinate the cargos of his three ships. So, over a meal at the Adelphi Hotel in Liverpool, costing more than a week of groceries for Farouk and Neelam, and with the encouragement of Walter Bailey, Sacranie Shipping Agents was born. At first Farouk worked out of a spare bedroom, and later from a small office near Albert Dock. Farouk coordinated the manifests of the three ships, liaised with other agents, with suppliers, agreed delivery and pick up dates and within months saw the three ships working close to maximum efficiency. It became a challenge to Farouk for a ship not to sail until fully loaded, to spend the minimum time in port and not to retrace its track. As the shipping business prospered so did Farouk. A daughter and two sons arrived in quick succession, as expected by the two sets of parents. Walter introduced him to other owners and he had more than enough work for him and his wife to handle. Life was good.

Farouk and Neelam were agreed. Each of their children would get the best education they could afford, including their daughter, even if it meant going without themselves. They paid for extra tuition for Aashi, Amir and Abdul, gave them every encouragement. They sought to identify their strengths and made it clear that each of them was expected go to university and get a degree.

Aashi was the first. She went to the University of Liverpool and got a Law degree, Amir went to John Moores University, also in Liverpool and got a degree in Information Technology, Abdul went to Manchester Metropolitan and came out with a degree in Accountancy. It also contributed to Farouk and Neelam's vision of their children taking over the business and taking it into the future. But it had been at a cost. Farouk wasn't wealthy. He had invested in his children rather than the business. He had a mortgage on two dilapidated warehouses near the docks, a modest three bedroom semi and old car, and declining health. His smoking habit had finally caught up with him; a diagnosis of lung cancer and a prognosis of three to six months to live.

At twenty-six years of age Aashi was still a junior member of the Liverpool law firm Goodrich & Child. She was part of a small team handling a large portfolio of clients who needed advice and assistance in navigating the increasingly complex world of company law, insurance liability as well as import and export tariffs. It had been her father, Farouk, who had guided her along this path and his contacts that had secured the post at Goodrich & Child. In doing so Farouk had a dream that one day his daughter and sons would take over Sacranie Shipping Agents and make it the most respected in Liverpool. Indeed, Aashi saw her work at Goodrich & Child as a valuable apprenticeship and was happy to wait for her father's invitation to join the family firm. Amir and Abdul were obediently following similar paths. Amir was working for the Manchester Chamber of Commerce, advising small and medium enterprises on computer systems. Abdul was working as an accountant within a car hypermarket on the outskirts of Manchester. Still in their early twenties all three children had left home, bought small apartments in Liverpool and Manchester and were busy working up their career ladders, or so they thought.

Sunday lunch with their parents had become one of the regular features of the week and seldom broken. Occasional holidays, the need to travel on Sunday to distant Monday morning meetings and the odd cold or sore throat had caused one or more of them to cancel. However, they knew how much their mum and dad enjoyed having them at home and hearing their news, albeit for only a few hours. It had become only "a few hours" that Farouk could hide how increasingly unwell he felt during these Sunday lunches.

When the phone rang that Sunday morning Aashi was still asleep, savouring the extra couple of hours in bed before getting up, ready and driving around for lunch at home. She enjoyed her independence, although the monthly mortgage payments on the small apartment took a major part of her salary. She also enjoyed being home for a few hours and catching up on all the news and how her brothers were doing. She wasn't expecting the devastating news from her mother that her father had collapsed that morning, had been taken to the Royal Liverpool Hospital and was in intensive care. Frantic phone calls to her brothers had got them converging on the hospital and to learn for the first time that their father had lung cancer and was very ill. It was their mother, Neelam, who explained that they had known for some time that Farouk was unwell but that they had not wanted to worry them. That morning Farouk had got up as usual, was running the vacuum cleaner over the carpets as his wife started preparing the Sunday lunch. It was only when he seemed to be taking a long time to finish vacuuming the lounge that she went in and found him collapsed on the floor.

The drive to the hospital, parking and finding the Intensive Care Unit had been a blur. Aashi couldn't even remember where she had parked. It had taken her and her brothers almost an hour to console their mother, to tell her they were all here and praying for their father, that everything would be all right. Even though they all knew it would not be all right. Hours later it was the arrival of a tired looking doctor that confirmed their worse fears; that their father was dangerously ill. It appeared that the lung cancer was advanced, may have spread to other organs, and that further tests were needed to confirm the initial diagnosis. It would take a few days to confirm the cancer and its spread, but it was clear that they would have to take over and run Sacranie Shipping Agents. There was no one else.

It only took a few hours on Monday morning for Aashi, Amir and Abdul to get compassionate leave approved, to handover their ongoing jobs, and for them to meet in the small rectangular office that had been constructed high above the floor of the main warehouse; an office that gave a view over the whole inside of the building. As children they had all looked out and seen men busily loading and unloading the contents of containers with forklift trucks, stacking and sliding the crates and boxes. Farouk had likened it to a chess game; getting all the right pieces in place as smoothly as possible if they wanted to win – to make a profit.

Today their first impression was one of bewilderment. What had happened? As long as they could remember their father had always been neat and tidy; obsessively so. Working with the Merchant Navy had reinforced his need to have everything "ship shape and Bristol fashion". It was a phrase they all remembered. But this place - it was a mess. The place wasn't just dusty it was dirty. The floor hadn't been swept in months let alone vacuumed. Aashi remembered, as a young girl, the huge pin-board that covered almost all of the rear wall from knee height to ceiling opposite the window. A pin-board covered in vivid green baize with dozens of typed manifests arranged squarely on it. They were all colour coded and moved around the board like chess pieces as cargo moved from one stage to another in the transport process. She remembered helping her father fit the three metal light shades that she had found. They had been thrown out of an old military office along the dock. They were typical government trumpet type issue – dark green backs with white enamel insides about thirty centimetres in diameter. This afternoon only two of the lights worked making the office look even more gloomy. She remembered the tall grey filing cabinets lined up like soldiers and the pot-bellied stove on the far wall that had glowed dull red on winter afternoons as they stoked it with coal. There were so many memories of the place humming with activity with everything in its place. Today it looked derelict.

There were only a handful of manifests pinned haphazardly onto the dull green baize; one was on the floor along with numerous drawing pins. Two of the filing cabinets had drawers half open and files lay strewn across the old mahogany desk. Nobody had cleaned the windows in months. Dust, old spiders' webs and fly droppings made the glass appear dull; it all looked seedy. Years ago Amir had persuaded his father to computerize the operation and a red dot glowed near the base of an old tower computer. Another red light blinked on the answerphone and Aashi remembered they should check the mailbox and go to the post office and collect any other mail. They stood there in silence, depressed. Aashi tried to remember when she was last here and realised it was over four years ago.

It was Abdul who broke the silence. 'Where is everybody? We know Dad is in the Royal but we haven't phoned anybody else. Why aren't the men here working?'

'Perhaps they phoned home and Mum told them not to come in today,' said Amir.

'She wouldn't do that,' mumbled Aashi, more to herself than the others.

'We need to sort this lot out,' said Abdul. 'Find out what needs to be done immediately, what's coming up soon and what we can leave for a bit. I'm happy to start wading through the accounts and contacting the bank. Where do you want to start?'

Amir said he would start on the manifests on the wall and find out what shipments were due in and out this week and what was due after that. He would also make a list of people to contact about containers in and out.

Aashi said she would start on the working files and check emails and went on, 'Let's give ourselves the rest of the afternoon … until five or six, share what we have found by then and decide what we do tomorrow, OK?'

The brothers agreed and set to their tasks.

They worked in virtual silence for the first few hours as they began the process of mapping the state of the business. It was mid afternoon when Abdul blurted out. "Shit".

Aashi and Amir stopped what they were doing, turned their heads and in unison asked, 'What's wrong?'

'The place is bankrupt,' cried Abdul. 'The business account is overdrawn, Dad sacked the last workman months ago and it looks as if more is going out each month than coming in. It's a fucking disaster. What was he doing?'

'OK, it looks like Dad had a problem. Let's see if we can find out what it is and what we need to do about it.' Why don't we continue until six o'clock, lock up, go for a meal and decide what to do tomorrow,' said Aashi.

For the next few hours they delved deeper and deeper into the files and began cross checking the information. Just before six o'clock Amir said to no one in particular, 'I think I've found out what pushed Dad over the edge. He signed a contract with *TransOceanic* almost two years ago. The Agency was to handle their containers in and out of Liverpool. At first glance it looks like quite a good deal. There would be a steady flow of containers; until you read the small print! It looks like Dad agreed to pay a whole list of administrative costs and charges. This cut his margin to the bone. *TransOceanic* also included a penalty clause for every twelve hour block of time containers were late in delivery, based on time of first unloading. Just looking at the invoices it seems as if *TransOceanic* were getting Dad to work for free. I'll cross check the income and outgoings but I'm pretty sure this is what was draining the accounts. What a group of bastards! I don't need to see any more today, let's go eat and talk about it.'

Aashi, Amir and Abdul stood up, surveyed the debris around them and just walked to the door, switched off the light and plodded down the steep wooden staircase to the warehouse floor. The light coming through the skylights in the roof was just enough for them to find their way to the door and out onto the street. It had been a long day.

Aashi knew the area well and quickly found an Indian restaurant she had eaten in lots of times, first as a student and later when she was too tired to go home and cook. They sat around a small table in the back corner of the room. Amir and Abdul each sipped a Cobra beer and Aashi a coke as they recounted what they had discovered. A grim picture was beginning to form.

Over the last two years the number of clients had dropped steadily as complaints about delayed and missed schedules increased. Income had dropped steadily and Farouk had sacked first one and eventually all the men working in the warehouse and delivering the containers around the country. He had cut his profit margin to the bone in an attempt to maintain the business. He had hired temporary drivers and casual labour, but inexperienced staff only added to the problem of missed shipments and delays. It was a downward spiral.

Unknown to his wife and children Farouk had re-mortgaged the house and warehouses just over a year ago in an attempt to raise some cash. This had given short term relief. Sacranie Shipping Agents was haemorrhaging money at a steady rate and little was coming in. There were unpaid bills for truck repairs with one of the trucks off the road with a gearbox problem. There were outstanding bills for diesel, the last three months of mortgage repayments on the two warehouses and the house were overdue with a request from the bank for a meeting to discuss the outstanding sum. The company bank account, and personal accounts, were almost zero. On top of this there were containers to deliver and transport that would cost more to handle than the company would be paid! However, perhaps the most serious was an outstanding tax demand from HM Inspector of Taxes. It wasn't for a lot of money but there simply wasn't any money

251

or assets to sell – apart from the three trucks and flatbeds that were well past their best.

Sacranie Shipping Agents was bankrupt and Neelam was about to lose the house. This was a disaster that had been coming for months. Sat around the table they suddenly realised the toll that the lung cancer had taken and the pressure that Dad had been under. No wonder he just collapsed under the mountain of debt and disappointment. But what to do?

Before heading to their respective apartments they agreed to spend the next day in the warehouse office, to complete their review of the company and devise an action plan. Aashi agreed to phone Mum, but not to tell her the bad news, but rather to say they were still checking arrivals and deliveries.

Chapter 35

Surveying the damage

The next day didn't reveal much more, just more detail and precise figures about the amount of monies owed. Amir had discovered that twelve containers packed with electrical goods were due to arrive from Taiwan via Rotterdam in the next four days and that it would be merely a case of clearing them and transporting them to a distribution centre somewhere between the A5 and M6 motorway. It was a *TransOceanic* shipment and it was touch and go whether they would make a profit on the handling. There were no other containers in-bound and only two currently in the other warehouse, waiting for delivery to Ireland. There was an appointment with a potential customer in The Midland Hotel in Manchester planned for tomorrow but Amir said he would phone and cancel it. The only odd discovery was a second manifest, but for a different shipping agent in Liverpool. *TransOceanic* had attached it to the back of the Taiwan consignment. It was for twelve containers of electrical goods from Japan: fridges and washing machines, TVs and air conditioning units! Amir had no idea where it had come from. He could find no other reference to it either in the papers or computer files. It appeared to have nothing to do with Sacranie Shipping Agents. It was as though it had been accidently attached to the back of the Taiwanese manifest.

Abdul had reviewed the company finances; it was a sorry state of affairs. The outstanding mortgages on the two warehouses and house, including outstanding payments, were just over £340,000. The tax bill was another £36,000 and total assets, the trucks and flatbeds, were less than £12,000, maybe a little bit more. All bad news.

Aashi announced that direct debits from the bank meant that the utilities were up to date and that the telephone and broadband contract had another eight months to run. It was going to be touch and go whether the money in the combined accounts would even cover these charges! They just sat for a few minutes before Aashi said, 'Let's go and see Dad. Mum will be there and the nurse said we could call in whenever we wanted. Better than sitting here and it will give us time to think. But let's put a brave face on it. Let's not make Mum feel any worse.'

They drove separately to the Royal Liverpool hospital, parked and walked together to the Intensive Care Unit. They smoothly negotiated the stairs and corridors of the hospital and paused at the nurse station just inside the entrance to the ICU. 'Is it OK to go in?' asked Aashi.

'Sure,' replied the small, slim nurse in pristine uniform.

After hours in the grimy office and grubby files Aashi felt dirty. She was used to clean desk tops, freshly printed memos and vacuumed carpets. The contrast with the ICU and nurse was marked. She smiled and together with Amir and Abdul walked through to where her mother sat by her husband's bedside. Farouk was awake, looked like a shell of his old self, but raised a weak smile.

'Hi, Dad,' the three of them said almost in unison. 'How are you doing?'

After the initial greetings and superficial comments the next few minutes were awkward as their mother wanted to know how they had got on at the Agency, was everything under control, did the workmen know what to do? You could see the apprehension in Farouk's eyes as he wondered what would be revealed.

'It's all under control, Mum,' said Aashi. 'It's all "ship shape and Bristol fashion".'

'You know, Mum,' said Amir with a forced smile, 'quality management is what happens when you are not around.'

You could see the relief spread through Farouk as he realised his children would be keeping his secret for a little longer. He seemed to sink into the bed and almost disappear.

'Dad, are you happy for us to do what we think is best for the business? I see there is a meeting with a possible client tonight at The Midland. I'm planning to go along and chat to him,' said Amir.

'Do what you think is best,' said Farouk. 'Whatever decisions you make will be the right ones,' he concluded.

Just then the door swung open and the nurse returned. 'I think that's about long enough for tonight,' she said. 'Your father needs to rest. Why not come back tomorrow?' she said with a smile.

It seemed they had only been in the room for minutes, but it was an opportunity for Aashi, Amir and Abdul to leave and reassess the situation. They said their goodbyes and retraced their steps to the car park. 'We are starting to dig ourselves into a deep hole,' muttered Abdul. 'We can keep up this charade for a week or so but I do not see a way out of this. The company is bankrupt and if we don't find a magical solution the bank will be knocking at the door next week.'

'You're right,' said Amir with a nod. 'Let's sleep on it and meet up tomorrow morning at nine. I'll go home via The Midland and meet the client,' he said. 'I think I should tell him that we don't want the consignment at this time. We need breathing space not more loss making jobs,' he added.

The three of them agreed, embraced each other with firm pats on the back, before drifting off to their cars and off to their apartments. Amir breathed deeply and set off on the drive to central Manchester. Fortunately the rush hour traffic was over and he had a pretty smooth drive along the M62 motorway. He negotiated the interconnecting roads and came into the city close to the Mancunian Way, that raised dual carriageway, built on stilts, that cut across the edge of the city. Amir decided to park in the NCP car park next to The Midland. He wanted the short walk, time to think and rehearse what he was going to say. In the event the meeting with the client was a formality. The receptionist had phoned the room, Daniel Greenaway had come down and been directed to Amir who sat hunched in an over padded leather chair. In less than a minute Amir had explained his father's illness and the need to pause on future contracts. Greenaway simply said, 'Thanks, another time perhaps,' and returned to his room. Amir immediately thought Greenaway had other agents lined up, but was looking for the cheapest. From what Amir had seen, Sacranie Shipping Agents was likely to be the cheapest. He rose and without looking around made his way towards the door, looking down not around.

'Hey, Amir, what are you doing here?' a voice from across the room cut through the *piped musak* and background buzz.

Amir turned towards the voice he recognised. A broad smile transformed his face as he stepped towards the tall, elegantly dressed young man with well groomed hair, short black beard and moustache, olive skin and brilliant white teeth. Amir grabbed the outstretched hand with both hands and then pulled the man to him, wrapping his arms around the man and swaying. He broke away, 'Hussein, what are you doing here? I live here but you should be in Dubai.'

'Arrrr, work, work and more work,' sighed Hussein with a mock grimace and a slouching of his shoulders. 'I'm in the UK for a couple of weeks sourcing items for a project and not getting very far,' he confided.

'Come, have a seat,' said Amir. 'What have you been doing since I last saw you? How's the business in Dubai? Are you still with Shahlia? How is your father and mother? How long are you in Manchester …?'

Question followed question without giving Hussein any chance to reply. Hussein held his hands up in surrender and a weak smile formed across his face. 'Mum and Dad are fine. Mum is about to have a hip replacement in Dubai. She has been putting it off but eventually the pain and discomfort has told in the end. It should transform her life as she and Dad start their retirement. They are going to be based in Dubai but travel to all the places they wanted to, but never had time.

Dad has made me CEO of the company and I'm now realising how much work he used to put in every day and how many plates he managed to keep spinning!

Ahhhhhhhh, afraid Shahlia wanted a lifestyle that I couldn't offer. Last time I heard she was sailing between islands in the Caribbean on a yacht with some American, but what about you and your brother and sister …?'

Amir filled the pause with the names of Aashi and Abdul. It then started as a trickle, with a summary of what he and the others had been doing in recent years. Then it became a flood as Amir recounted the last couple of days and the dire straits of the Sacranie Shipping Agency.

Hussein sat in sombre silence, moving his hand onto the shoulder of his old friend in compassion. When Amir had finished he felt spent, not tearful, not resentful just spent.

'Have you got some time now?' asked Hussein, 'because I've got a problem that may help us both. I've got a room here … have you eaten? I can order room service so we can be alone and I can tell you the story.'

Amir felt drained. He didn't have the energy to resist or object and was happy to have a bite to eat with an old friend and to forget Sacranie Shipping Agency for a few hours. In a daze he followed Hussein out of the lounge, into the lift and up to Hussein's room. He vaguely heard Hussein ordering food and drinks on the phone as he sank back into the armchair next to the window overlooking the bright lights of Manchester city centre. He closed his eyes and felt so tired.

'I've got a big problem,' announced Hussein. 'Let me tell you about it and see if we can help each other.'

At first Amir wasn't really interested, he feigned interest, but wasn't concentrating; he felt totally drained. However, he was soon awake and concentrating. It seemed that just before announcing his retirement Hussein's father had obtained massive finance for a large reclaimed waterfront block in Dubai. He had plans approved for a luxury serviced apartment block, three hundred apartments and linked marina. It was multimillion dollar stuff. Hussein had taken over responsibility for the whole project, with everything from negotiating approvals and construction, to apartment design and fitting out, from utilities and services to even sub-letting of floors for offices and agencies that would service the apartments. It was a massive undertaking. Hussein confided that he now realised that he was out of his depth. He had delegated tasks to heads of section and tried to retain overall supervision and oversight of the budget. However, he soon realised that his father had shielded him from the corruption that was endemic in Dubai. The "favours" that were called in at all levels, the generous gifts, the bribes, that had to be paid if the supply of concrete was to be maintained, if the scores of official approvals were to be signed, if the electricians and plumbers were to stay on schedule and their supplies were not to disappear. It went on and on as expenditure didn't match completion targets. He was simply running out of money.

As they picked at the sandwiches and fruit, and sipped bitter, reheated coffee, Hussein explained that he had avoided trying to raise more money in Dubai to complete the project. If the business community smelled any "blood in the water" he would be devoured in weeks. Suppliers would want cash on delivery, goodwill would disappear, tradesmen would drift away. He had tried to raise money in London, visiting one merchant bank after another. Although they told him his request would be fully considered he knew by the tone and body language that the answer would be no. They couldn't wait to get him out of the office. He explained to Amir that with the budget available he could finish the structure and final fix of the apartment block and marina. However, he wouldn't have enough money to decorate and equip the public rooms, restaurants and apartments to the design specification. The budget for vehicles and service boats alone was estimated at over US$1 million.

It was then that Hussein floated the idea he had been building up to and that Amir had already guessed. Could Amir "procure" the pickups and minibuses, outboard motors and dinghies, TVs and washing machines, cups and saucers, sheets and towels at massive discounts and deliver them to Dubai?

Amir was ahead of him, and had been for some time. His mind raced between thoughts of the debts that Sacranie Shipping Agents had amassed, the manifest of electrical and white goods from Japan stapled to the back of the Taiwan Manifest, and what would have to be done to 'procure' the twelve containers and deliver them to Dubai. It was possible but he couldn't do it on his own, and what was the cost of being found out?

'Can you give me a list of everything you need to fit out the apartments and marina? Every washing machine and wine glass, every minibus and cooking pot, every outboard and bed?' asked Amir with a tone that surprised Hussein, 'and the date you need them.' If Sacranie Shipping Agents can procure some, or all, of these items and deliver to Dubai what percentage of the estimated cost would we receive?' demanded Amir with a calmness and resolve that was like a drowning man being thrown a lifebuoy.

'I've got the lists in my briefcase,' volunteered Hussein as he rose from the heavily upholstered chair and moved across the room. 'If I'm going to keep to schedule everything needs to be delivered in the next three to four months. I can give you a copy of the spreadsheets that link items and dates needed,' replied Hussein with an urgency that had suddenly entered his voice. 'If people in Dubai see the containers arriving, and the rooms being fitted out, and if I host a series of "Open Days" to prospective letting agents, it will generate confidence and allow me to raise some additional money.'

Hussein paused, a sheaf of paper in his hand, and turned to Amir. 'What about a quarter of the estimated cost? I save a couple of million dollars and you make a couple of million. What do you say?'

'One-third of the estimated cost for every item delivered,' stated Amir with a firmness that surprised him. 'But one more thing before we go any further. What we are talking about here isn't about procurement it is about theft on an industrial scale. If we are found out we all go to prison. I may be able to obtain the items you need but I doubt I will be able to change serial numbers on electrical items, chassis numbers on cars and so on. It means that if anything goes wrong with these things you will not be able to return the goods or take them for repair; there can be no warranty. Do you understand?' challenged Amir.

'If I don't take this gamble I'm dead,' confided Hussein. 'This gives me a chance and I know the risks. We would be in it together,' concluded Hussein.

'I will need to speak to Aashi and Abdul and draw up some initial plans,' announced Amir. 'Can we meet here, in this room, tomorrow night; let's say at seven p.m.?' asked Amir with weariness suddenly overtaking him.

Hussein agreed and seemed elated. He was grinning and shaking Amir's hand so enthusiastically it was almost uncomfortable, saying how grateful he was to Amir and how he was sure they could pull it off, how he would be eternally grateful. In contrast Amir was simply tired and just wanted to get home, to flop on his bed and worry about what he had agreed to do tomorrow.

Chapter 36

An audacious plan

Despite his tiredness Amir didn't sleep well. He had been restless all night with a confusing kaleidoscope of images of shipping containers swinging over awaiting ships, Customs officers suddenly confronting him, his mother weeping as she was evicted from her home … and the condemnation of friends and family who lined the street as he walked past flanked by faceless lawyers.

He left for the meeting with Aashi and Abdul early. On his way to the shipping office Amir stopped off to buy a jar of instant coffee, carton of milk and bag of sugar. He knew Abdul liked his coffee sweet and the stuff in the office looked as if it had been around for months. On the spur of the moment he also bought a pack of six jam doughnuts. Why? He didn't particularly like doughnuts; perhaps he was thinking of "sweetening the pill" he was going to ask Aashi and Abdul to swallow.

The warehouse area was quiet with just the odd car and cyclist around. It would be busier in an hour or so. In the cool light of day Amir could see just how run down and seedy the entire area had become. His memories had been through rose tinted glasses, but this morning he could see the graffiti and litter, the sagging fences and unpainted boards; he already felt depressed.

He switched on the light and cursed himself for forgetting to remember to bring a new light bulb. The office was just as they had left it yesterday with papers and files strewn across the central table. He quickly found the rogue manifest and started to read through; it ran to several pages. When he had scanned it yesterday he had only looked at the manifest heading and first few items. Once he realised it wasn't connected to Sacranie Shipping Agents he had discarded it. Now he realised the extent of the possibility it offered. The first three containers held five hundred Sony TVs; the next the same number of Sony CD / DVD players and radios. The next two consignments held one thousand Hitachi air conditioning units whilst the next six contained *white goods* - LG washing machines, fridges and freezers – the list went on and on.

Amir stood and walked to the computer printer in the far corner of the office. Almost absent-mindedly he advanced a sheet, held it taut as he flicked the perforated join to tear the paper, and ripped off a sheet. He strolled back to the table and began making a list of the value of the contents of the twelve containers against the list Hussein had given him. He scribbled down the figures. Almost an hour later he sat back in his chair. It looked as though the total consignment of twelve containers was worth about £2.1 million; one third of this would extricate Sacranie Shipping Agents from the mire.

He was still musing when he heard the small door rattle and a shout from Abdul. 'Up here,' shouted Amir. 'The kettle is on,' he added.

Aashi and Abdul shuffled into the office. It was clear that they also had sleepless nights with tiredness etched onto their faces. Amir poured hot water into the mugs and opened the pack of doughnuts. 'I've got a suggestion,' announced Amir; a high risk suggestion. Both Aashi and Abdul turned towards him and sat down at the old dark table pushing away the folders scattered across it. 'I bumped into Hussein al Waffre in The Midland last night. You remember Hussein: tall, suave, in my seminar group at Liverpool, father a big developer in Dubai, loads of money.'

Aashi and Abdul murmured that they vaguely remembered him, but so what.

'He's now CEO of his father's company. He's taken over a massive luxury apartment and marina development on a waterfront site in Dubai. The complex is up, at first fix stage, but he doesn't have enough money to complete it to the design spec nor to fit out all the rooms and offices, purchase vehicles and white goods and so on. He's prepared to pay us one-third of the cost of any items we can land in Dubai. No questions asked.'

The office was suddenly totally silent as the enormity of what Amir was saying hit them. The coffee mugs sat steaming on the table, the doughnuts untouched.

'Yesterday I found two manifests and collection orders stapled together. One of ours and one from *TransOceanic*. The *TransOceanic* manifest is for twelve containers of TVs and videos, air conditioning units and washing machines, radios and fridges. There are even vacuum cleaners and microwave ovens. Everything in those containers is on Hussein's list, and is worth over £2 million. Our share would be over £600,000. That's enough to save the company at a stroke.'

The room remained silent. Only the expressions of Aashi and Abdul gave any indication of what was being suggested.

'The containers arrive in four days,' continued Amir. 'Since we have the manifests and collection orders it is a pretty good guess that *TransOceanic* do not. They know the containers are on the way but not that their arrival is imminent. We have flatbeds that we can use to collect the containers and we can use the old brass templates that Dad used to number containers. I'm sure we will be able to find them. This morning I found the file where Dad recorded all the discontinued containers; the ones that were damaged or scrapped over the years. I reckon we could collect the twelve containers, bring them here and re-number them, and immediately ship them to Dubai without *TransOceanic* even being aware they are in port. It would take weeks for anyone to realise the containers were missing by which time they would be in Dubai. The containers would simply disappear.'

'You're crazy,' exclaimed Aashi. 'You're bound to get caught and you'll end up in prison. What are you thinking of?' she said as she shook her head in disbelief.

'OK, what's the alternative?' asked Amir. 'You've seen the files, the Agency is bankrupt. There are no assets and I doubt anyone will be remotely interested in giving us a loan. Even if they did how would we repay it? It's just a matter of months before Mum loses the house. Perhaps she can move in with you; your apartment is bigger than mine,' said Amir with a smile that seemed odd in the circumstances.

'We have three flatbeds and only two cabs,' said Abdul. 'We know how to drive the cabs and handle the containers under the gantry. The paperwork is pretty simple and straightforward and Dad has contacts in Dubai that could clear the containers at that end. The entire switch could be done in twenty-four hours,' remarked Abdul in a quiet, dispassionate voice.

'You're going along with this madness are you?' blurted Aashi. 'I don't believe what I'm hearing. Yesterday you two were law-abiding members of the public and today you are talking about theft on a massive scale. You'd never get away with it,' exclaimed Aashi.

'OK,' said Abdul, picking up a doughnut in one hand and his coffee in the other. 'Before the coffee gets cold, and the doughnuts get stale, why don't we indulge ourselves for a few minutes and map out what we would have to do if, repeat if, we decided to go down the grand theft route. What would be the critical points that could lead to disaster?' he asked.

For the next hour they discussed the various aspects of the outline plan that Amir had proposed. At first every time an issue was raised Aashi would begin to list the problems, how they were insurmountable or the enormity of the risks involved. On each occasion Abdul or Amir countered with practical ways that the problem could be overcome. For example, Amir could clone paperwork for an actual transport company and Abdul could make up number plates for cabs that actually existed. They all had HGV licences and knew how to drive the cabs. They could simply remove the painted numbers on containers with paint stripper and re-spray new numbers that resurrected containers owned by Sacranie Shipping Agency. The overhead cranes that ran from the hard stand area into the warehouse would allow them to work on the containers in secrecy. They could easily create the paperwork that would send the renumbered containers to a fellow agent in Dubai. It could work. As the minutes passed Aashi became less critical and more constructive. She

267

quizzed Abdul as to how this "fantasy two-thirds of a million" could be transferred to Sacranie Shipping Agents without attracting the notice of the authorities. How they could stall the bank and tax man?

It was mid morning before the pace of the exchanges slowed and they realised that they were facing a massive decision; should they think seriously about stealing the containers or work on an alternative plan. It was Amir that broke the spell. 'OK,' he said. 'Thanks for indulging me for the last hour or so. Why don't we put the Dubai solution on one side and think of an alternative way to save the company. Any ideas?' he asked.

No one spoke for a few seconds. It was Aashi who broke the silence. 'I spent most of last night thinking about "legal" ways we might save the company. This ranged from inviting a takeover by a local company to financing it ourselves. None of them is likely to work. The problem is the massive debt that exists and the demands we already have from the bank and the Inland Revenue. The only way we can get any breathing space is to convince them that we have a business plan that will repay the outstanding sums in the next six months and return the Agency to profit in the next two years or so.'

Aashi paused, she appeared to be deciding what to say next. 'Amir, do you think Hussein would sign a contract making Sacranie Shipping Agency the sole agency for handling their imports into Dubai? Do you think he would canvass two or three other major players in Dubai to sign similar contracts?'

'I reckon Hussein would sign any contract we ask him to sign; he's up shit creek and he knows it,' said Amir ' ... but why?'

'In the short term we need official documents, documents that will bear scrutiny, that we have secured deals in Dubai that will allow us to pay off the overdrafts in months and in the longer term return to profit. It doesn't matter if we never actually handle goods for these other companies. In fact we can always create shell companies and use these to front transactions that will allow funds to enter accounts in Dubai and eventually ours in Liverpool.'

'So you think we can do it,' said Amir.

'Yes, I think we can. I can't think of an alternative. But if we fail ...' Aashi paused as if leaving the rest unspoken. She then took a deep breath and made eye contact with first one and then her other brother. 'If we're caught we're finished as a family. Mum will lose Dad in the next month or so and will then lose the house. With no family and no money I don't see how she would cope. If we are caught it will probably kill her.'

Aashi breathed out heavily through her nose and gazed down at the floor. 'As a first offence, and with a good barrister, I reckon we would get three to five years; maybe out in just over two. However, I'll never be allowed to practice law again and all three of us will struggle to get a job, any job. Are we sure we want to do this?'

Abdul and Amir turned their heads towards each other. Amir spoke first. 'I've tried to think of another way and can't think of one; and the clock is ticking. The containers are due in four days and I doubt there will be another opportunity like the one that has presented itself. I suggest we plan to steal the containers and redirect them to Dubai. Once all our

269

planning is done I then suggest we review it and decide to go ahead or drop the entire idea and accept the bankruptcy. We then have to think how we can soften it for Mum.'

'I agree,' said Abdul with a sound of resignation. 'Let's get to it.'

Chapter 37

Theft on an industrial scale

By mid morning they had allocated most of the main tasks between themselves and started to elaborate the outline plans. Amir showed why he had done so well in his IT degree at John Moores University. Before lunch he had driven back to his apartment, collected originals, and then had created fake HGV licences. With sweaty hands and a bit of dust from the floor he made them look ten years old. He'd found a haulage company in Blackburn, north of Liverpool, and copied both their name, logo, phone and fax numbers in the form of an electronic file so that he could print it out on a thin sheet of plastic and stick to the side of the cabs. They could transform their anonymous cabs into clones of Robertson & Sons of Blackburn.

After almost an hour Abdul found the brass templates that they could use to renumber the containers. He made a note to buy some paint stripper that evening and cans of quick drying spray paint. He also arranged to return to his office at the Auto Hypermarket just before it closed on the pretext of urgent work he needed to complete that evening. No one would be around when he strolled into the garage area and made up three sets of false plates. It was all coming together. Aashi drew up several copies of a Memorandum of Understanding that she wanted Hussein and his friends to sign and then completed the paperwork for shipping the renumbered containers to Dubai. Just after lunch they had completed all they could. One problem remained; they only had two roadworthy cabs, where could they get another?

They agreed that Amir would go to meet Hussein at The Midland Hotel in Manchester, get the MOU signed and stress how important it was to get other signatures to bolster their case with the bank and Inland Revenue. Abdul would take a drive to Blackburn, locate the base for Robertson & Son, and see if he could get the number plates of three cabs. Once he had the plate numbers he could return to the car hypermarket and hopefully make up the number plates they would need. Aashi would go to visit Dad, confirm the sequence of events by which documents are used to collect containers and see if he had any contacts that would loan him a cab for a few days or where they could hire one.

Abdul had no problem locating Robertson & Son. It was on a corner plot of an old industrial estate. There were small businesses and storage depots and a double glazing / conservatory centre opposite. Just as Abdul arrived a cab carrying a container was turning into the broad drive but he couldn't get the number. After a few minutes he realised that he needed to position the car so he was as inconspicuous as possible and could read number plates more easily. He cursed himself for not bringing a paper or a book to disguise his wait but he did have his briefcase in the boot. He could simply lay out various papers and give the impression he was killing time prior to a meeting. He sat for over an hour before two cabs and flatbeds slowly exited the compound and turned in the direction of the M6 motorway. He'd no sooner written down the numbers when another cab arrived with another container on board. He had the numbers he needed. The only problem was that the cabs were fairly new and the ones owned by the Sacranie Shipping Agency were fairly old. He decided to wait a little longer in case an older model of cab came through. Just as he was about to leave he was rewarded by an old Volvo; a similar vintage to the one in the warehouse. He made a note of the number plate and started his journey back to Liverpool. He even had time to stop off for a quick snack before turning up at the office before they closed.

Abdul arrived just as they were closing the office, just as he had planned. Those colleagues he bumped into were full of kind wishes for his father and hoped he would be well soon. Abdul just couldn't tell them he was dying and had only a couple of months to live; he simply thanked them and drifted towards his office. Mandy, one of the typists brought him a cup of coffee as she made her way to the door and then to the nearby bus stop, and told him not to work too late. 'Can't you get someone else to do it?' she enquired as she headed for the door.

It seemed to take ages for the garage to clear. At first it was easy, he could hack through the stack of mail that had accumulated over a couple of days and scribble notes or draft replies. He became so engrossed that it was a surprise when he looked up and realised it was past seven p.m. It was time to get going. An elderly security man normally locked the offices and set the alarms just after six o'clock or as the last one left. Abdul caught him just as he was about to set the alarms – telling him he had to work late but he would tell him when he was leaving. A few more minutes in the office and then it was just a short stroll through to the garage to the bench where the apprentice made up the plates for new cars. He had seen the jigs used a few times; it didn't seem particularly difficult. But as he reached for the back-plate a sudden sickening feeling enveloped him; are the plates square or rectangular on the cabs and flatbacks? For a moment he couldn't think and he was horror struck. Think, he told himself. What do they look like? Are they the same or different? It took Abdul a couple of minutes to calm down and visualise each of the three cabs in turn. He had last driven one probably two or three years ago. It had been the old maroon Volvo. Yes, he remembered. All the numbers on the front were rectangular and on the back of the cab and flatbacks they were square. Abdul took out the slip of paper listing the false number plate numbers. His heart was racing and his head seemed to be buzzing as he arranged the letters and numbers on the back-plate and marked the drilling points. It took him over forty minutes to make up the nine plates but he was happy with the result. They were too new, but he knew how he could make them look old. He'd do that back in the warehouse. With his heart still beating he retraced his steps to the office, closed down his computer and set off to find the security guard. Phase one was done.

In The Midland Hotel Amir was sipping a cool beer in Hussein's hotel room. He was surprised how relaxed and exhilarated he felt, sitting back in the large easy chair, knees crossed and smiling. He had surprised Hussein by telling him that the first twelve containers would be delivered in Dubai within a month. He handed over a list of the contents with "discounted" costs summarized at the end of each of the products. Amir's initial estimate had been pretty good. The final cost of the contents of the containers was £2.2 million.

He confirmed that Sacranie Shipping Agency expected to be paid on landing but details of payment would follow. He also explained the need to create the impression of a business link between the Sacranie Shipping Agency and clients in Dubai. As such they would be setting up an office in Dubai and perhaps Hussein could suggest where they could set up such an office in the city. Hussein couldn't thank Amir enough, nor sign the memorandum fast enough, nor promise that he would persuade several colleagues to sign and get the original documents delivered by courier service within the week. It was as though Hussein had seen the abyss and been dragged away from it.

Aashi was not enjoying herself. She found it hard to come to terms with the massive deterioration in her father's health, the way in which the business had sunk into bankruptcy, the apparent complicity in which she was engaged. She suddenly felt sick at the thought. As she walked into the ICU she saw her mother sitting by a bedside but the bed seemed empty. There was a flutter of apprehension until she saw her father's head buried in a pillow. She hadn't realised how her father's body had shrunk; he formed barely a ripple beneath the pale green airtex bed cover. The first few minutes by his bedside seemed so false. She did want to know how her father was feeling, if there was any further news of treatment, any further tests that could be conducted, would he be moving out of intensive care in the near future and so on. She also wanted to talk about the business and the information they needed if the plans were to have any chance of success. There was a lull in the conversation, enough for Aashi to change the direction of the conversation.

'Dad, I need to talk to you about the business and a contract we are thinking of taking. Do you feel strong enough to talk about it for a few minutes?' she asked.

It was as though her mum knew this was awkward because immediately she made an excuse to go and talk to the ICU Sister and get them all a cup of tea. She hadn't done this since Dad had been admitted but it was the opportunity Aashi needed.

'Dad, we have the chance to collect and ship a dozen containers. It could be very profitable for the business, but we only have two serviceable cabs. Do you know anyone who would loan us a cab for a day or so, or where we could hire one?' asked Aashi. 'I also need to know the practicalities how we go about collecting containers from the docks, what documents we need, what notice we have to give prior to collection, what security we need to satisfy and so on. I've never collected a container and I don't know what to do. I can work out how to prepare the export documents but again, I don't know the procedure involved in delivering them to the docks.'

Farouk paused for a few seconds, as though he was collecting his thoughts or about to ask if Aashi knew the state of the business. There was no money to hire cabs and it would have to be very profitable to even meet the immediate cashflow demands. Farouk suddenly changed. He seemed to be jolted into life, the slack expression being replaced by a determined look. 'You will need to take some notes because it's a lot to remember,' croaked Farouk.

They didn't notice when Neelam returned with two paper cups of tea. Farouk's eyes were open but he seemed to be staring into the past as he listed the documents Aashi would

276

need and where she could find the blanks. He described the gate numbers and directions to loading and unloading bays, the documents to present, the ones to sign, the ones just to carry. Aashi was engrossed in recording everything accurately as her mind raced to other details that could ensure a smooth pick-up and delivery.

'There's one last thing,' muttered Farouk as he took a deep breath, as if the effort of the last few minutes had drained him. 'Go and see Jonny Spate in Boundary Road, near the old car transport jetty. The company is called Williams Haulage & Co but old Walter Williams has been dead for years. Jonny and I have always done each other favours over the years. If anyone can help you then Jonny can. Tell him you're my daughter and that he can phone me here if he needs confirmation.' With that Farouk just seemed to sink back into his pillow and to breathe heavily with his eyes closed; he seemed exhausted.

'Is everything all right?' asked Neelam. 'I know Dad has been worrying about the business but he wouldn't tell me anything.'

'Everything is fine,' smiled Aashi, 'but it looks as if I've tired Dad out. I'll go now and come back tomorrow.'

The next morning Aashi and Abdul sat around the old wooden table, coffee mugs in one hand, a doughnut in the other. Amir was standing on the edge of the old wooden table and reaching up to change the blown bulb for a new one. As it clicked in place the room suddenly brightened, as did his smile.

It was Aashi who broke the spell as she announced, 'I spoke with Dad last night at the hospital. I know which documents are needed to collect and deliver the containers. I know which gates to use, documents to carry, which to sign, what to do and what not to do and so on. Dad also gave me the name of his old friend, Jonny Spate at Williams Haulage & Co. Dad says if anyone can lend us a cab he can. With the original documents we have, the ones we can prepare on behalf of the Sacranie Shipping Agency, and the ones Amir can create for us I reckon we have all the paperwork that we need.'

Aashi glanced at Abdul who took this as his cue. 'I've made up three sets of number plates for the cabs,' said Abdul. 'They are not false plates but the same as three cabs from Robertson & Sons of Blackburn. The only snag is that two of the sets of plates are for more modern cabs than ours and different makes.'

Abdul and Aashi turned to Amir. 'How have you got on' they asked.

'I've created a computer file that will allow me to print off thin transparent plastic sheets, carrying the names, telephone number and fax number of Robertson & Sons. You simply wet these sheets and squeegee them onto the cab doors. In an instant you have a company cab that looks just like the real thing,' he smiled. I've also got fake HGV licences,' he added.

'What else do we need?' asked Aashi.

Around the table there was silence as they each rehearsed the phases of the container switch they were planning.

'I reckon we can switch the containers,' said Abdul. 'Getting the money from Dubai into our account will be protracted, but that's the easy part,' he smiled.

It was Aashi who posed the key question. 'So, is it go or no go?' she asked looking first at Amir.

'It's a go,' said Amir as both he and Aashi turned to Abdul.

'It's a go,' as he stood to embrace Aashi and Amir. The die was cast.

Chapter 38

Performing the switch

For the rest of the morning it was Aashi who rehearsed the pick up and drop off routine with Amir and Abdul until they were all confident. Before lunch the three of them had agreed who would do what and when, and when they would meet up again.

Aashi phoned Jonny Spate at Williams Haulage & Co and arranged to meet him that afternoon. Abdul drove off towards Liverpool to buy the masking tape, cans of paint stripper, scrapers and spray paint; all the stuff he thought he would need to re-number the containers. Amir set himself the goal of finding out as much as he could about *TransOceanic* and the container ship that was due in a few days.

Aashi found Williams Haulage & Co easily, parked in one of the slots marked "visitors" and walked the few yards to a two storey brick building emblazoned with the name of the company and a sign, only a little smaller, that said "Reception". Jonny stepped out of the doorway as Aashi approached. He had been expecting Aashi to be on time, like her father would have been, there was also something about her that looked like her father.

'Hi, good to see you,' smiled Jonny with an outstretched hand. He shook Aashi's hand firmly and pulled her gently into the reception area. As he did so he turned to her, and in a voice that sounded like rough gravel confided, 'Sorry to hear about Farouk, I only heard yesterday. Is he in the Royal? Any chance I could get to visit? Anything I can do to help?'

Relief flooded over Aashi, so much so that tears welled up in her eyes and a lump came to her throat; she brushed away the tears. It was obvious that Jonny thought this sudden show of emotion was due to her father's illness, not the realisation that she was likely to get her hands on a cab. Aashi recovered quickly and mumbled a brief summary of what the doctor had told them at the hospital. Jonny was sympathetic, making all the right noises at the right times. Aashi also gave him a brief account of the way the business had run down in recent years but not the level of debt. She also explained how they had the chance to halt the decline with the promise of work from a friend in Dubai. Aashi had already decided there was no point trying to hide the fact that the Sacranie Shipping Agency was in trouble. In the small world of haulage companies in Liverpool they all had a pretty good idea of what was happening. The men Farouk had laid off would be going round all the other haulage contractors looking for work; it would all be common knowledge.

'Yes, I did pick up that your dad was having a bit of trouble and had to lay off some men. When I last saw him he didn't look well and we didn't have a chance to chat. What can I do to help?' offered Jonny.

'I need to beg, borrow or steal a cab for a few days; at least a couple of days, a week at most. Truth is I can't afford to hire one,' said Aashi.

Jonny pursed his lips and looked to the side for a few seconds. He breathed deeply and then asked if Aashi, or the driver of the cab, had a clean HGV licence. Aashi confirmed that if a cab was available she would be driving it, and she did have a clean licence. She didn't tell Jonny that it had probably been two years since she had driven a cab!

'I've got a DAF as a backup cab until the end of the month. I can put you on the insurance and you can have it until the end of the month. The only thing is that if one of my working cabs has a problem you'll have to return the DAF straight away. I can't afford to let the schedule slip. Will that help?' he asked.

Aashi grabbed his hand. 'That would be fantastic,' she gushed, as she pumped Jonny's hand up and down, beamed all over him, and then gave him a hug. 'It could really help us out of a deep hole. 'I owe you a favour,' promised Aashi.

'I'll tell you what,' suggested Jonny. 'There is a favour you can do me immediately. About four years ago your dad and I bought a second hand car transporter - five up. We thought there was money in transporting cars from the port to dealers and from the factories to the port. At first we did steady business but I don't think your dad has used it in over a year, neither have I. The problem is that the car makers tend to use their own transporters and so do the dealers. There's not enough work for it and I need the space more than the transporter. If we could store the transporter at your dad's place I reckon the favour is repaid. What do you say?' said Jonny, his tanned face breaking into a grin.

'Done,' said Aashi. 'I've got my licence here and if it's OK I'll collect the DAF cab tomorrow morning, hitch up and take the car transporter away.'

A few miles away Abdul had found a pile of old, blue, boiler suits in the corner of a large open sided wooden shed inside the warehouse. It looked as if the workers had used it as a place to hang up wet clothes, to sit and have a break. At one end there was a battered cream, oil filled radiator below a drying rack. At the opposite end of the shed stood half a dozen tall metal lockers with doors hanging open. It looked like the workers stored their ordinary clothes in the lockers after changing into working clothes, but all that remained was rubbish. An oil stained electric kettle sat forlorn on a small formica table, now stained with countless tea bags and coffee rings. There were well used wooden clipboards scattered over the table top plus scraps of paper, an assortment of stained mugs sat on an old rickety table, flanked by two equally rickety wooden benches. Overlooking the scene a young, bare breasted woman, Miss December, grinned from last year's calendar. She was advertising truck tyres. Someone had drawn a bullseye over her right nipple; it all looked sordid.

Abdul picked out the best three boiler suits. He would put them through the washing machine tonight since they would need them soon. He then turned his attention to an empty container stacked to the side of the main warehouse bay. The rust on the corners and along the sides of the container blended into the red / orange paint of the huge steel box. Abdul looked around until he found what he was looking for; a wooden ladder that would let him work on the top sides and ends of the container. But as soon as he had placed the ladder against the side of the container he stopped. He realised he could practise on any part of the container and when he felt confident could have a go at the numbers.

Abdul soon realised the secret to paint stripping. It was making sure the area around the paint to be removed was protected, masking tape well stuck down, before daubing thick layers of paint stripper onto the paint and giving it time to work. There was no point trying to rush it. If the masking tape wasn't firmly in place the stripper leaked underneath it. Once the paint was totally blistered it came off in one firm scrape. To be sure he timed himself on taping up, applying the paint stripper gel and removing the paint from one of the numbers on the old container. He could do it in ten minutes. Whilst he waited for the stripper to work he could be preparing the next one and so on.

He then practised spraying new numbers using the old brass templates. Within a few minutes he was getting good results. A sheet of newspaper stuck over the edge of the template avoided paint being accidently sprayed onto the container. Cutting a rectangle out of an old tarpaulin was even better. The only problem was that the numbers looked too new, too white. Another trip to a local DIY shop provided a selection of grey sprays. When two shades of grey were used, lightly, and dust from the roof of the wooden shed blown onto the drying paint, it looked as if the numbers had been painted twenty years ago. Abdul was pleased. He reckoned that if they worked together they could re-number three containers inside ninety minutes; two hours at the most.

Amir grew increasingly impressed as he searched for information about *TransOceanic*; it was a massive Singapore based operation. They had several large container ships plying the major trade routes between the Far East, North and South America, Europe and the Indian subcontinent. It was easy to trace the progress of *TransOceanic II,* the ship carrying their twelve containers as it made its way from major port to major port. It was dropping off and collecting containers on route before making a similar return trip. The

TransOceanic II was due in Rotterdam late tomorrow and into Liverpool two days later. A thought suddenly struck Amir, what else was she carrying that they could redirect to Dubai? Could he access the Liverpool Port Authority computer and locate the manifest of the *TransOceanic II*? He recalled that one of his friends at John Moores University had been part of a small group who would break into commercial computer games. This wasn't to steal anything, or to be a nuisance, but just for the challenge and to see how the game was constructed. He now remembered that he had been given a copy of their software, the system they used to break into the game. But where was it? It was years ago; think. Amir had downloaded all his university files onto an external drive during his last few weeks at university. He wasn't sure how much of it he would ever use but there were some very clever routines and patches from which he could devise others.

As he climbed down the stairs he called to Abdul. 'Hey, I'm going home to try and find some software that might be useful to us. Anything you want?' he asked. There wasn't. Abdul seemed engrossed in wafting spray paint lightly across a fold in an old green tarpaulin and admiring his handiwork.

It took Amir over an hour to get back to his apartment, dig out the external drive and confirm that the software was on it. Soon afterwards he was sat at the computer above the warehouse. Farouk, like all others working with the Port Authority, had a link so that he could check on the arrival of ships, collection and dispatch of containers. What he didn't have was computer clearance to inspect the actual manifest; only the controller or administrator could do that. What the clever piece of software, that his former friend and fellow

285

students had created, was to derive the ID and password currently being used so that he could inspect all the manifests from every container arriving or departing; it was the key to a goldmine. It was a goldmine that would stand open for a few days until they discovered that containers had gone astray and worked back to discover when and how they disappeared. If they could intercept, say, half a dozen containers in a couple of days, and remove any link to the Sacranie Shipping Agency it could set the Agency up for years. He started work reviewing the content of the manifests for *TransOceanic II*.

By late afternoon Aashi had returned. Amir was cleaning the brass templates and wiping his hands with a paraffin rag and Amir was still bent over the computer. 'Fancy a break,' called Aashi as she strolled across the office to switch on the kettle. 'How about we have an update on what we have been doing and what we do next,' she suggested.

Abdul moved to the table and sat down, throwing the paraffin rag towards the waste paper bin and missing. Amir was staring at the computer screen, making notes on a pad and holding the pencil between his teeth. 'Give me two minutes and I'll be with you,' he muttered without stopping.

Amir stood, stretched, and walked towards the draining board collecting a mug, spooning in coffee, pouring in the hot water and splashing in some milk. He sat at the large table and stretched his legs. There was something in his manner that attracted the attention of Aashi before she spoke. 'We have a cab for the third flatbed, we can have it for ten days unless one of their cabs breaks down and we have to return it. Jonny says we can have it for no charge,' smiled Aashi. 'We have the transport to pull this off,' she added.

'I reckon that in under two hours we can strip off the container numbers and renumber them so that they look twenty years old,' added Abdul.

'We have all the paperwork we need to switch the twelve containers. It will take me a couple of weeks but I can set up half a dozen companies and accounts in Dubai and transfer money into and out of these accounts to anywhere in the world,' said Amir. 'I also have another suggestion,' he added.

Chapter 39

Plan into action

Amir paused as he organised his thoughts and glanced at the notes he had been making. 'The *TransOceanic II* is due to unload hundreds of containers in two days time. I've just spent the last couple of hours scanning hundreds of manifests. I'll explain how I've managed to do this later. Guess what. There's everything from Italian glassware to Japanese cutlery, Indian cotton sheets and towels to Bokara rugs on that ship. I need to cross reference to the list that Hussein gave us but I reckon we could switch another dozen or so containers before we close down the operation.

In the next twenty-four hours several haulage companies will be setting off to collect these containers; routine stuff. However, if we were to contact them, ostensibly from the Port Authority, and say there was a ... crane problem ... and it would be forty-eight hours before they could collect their containers, it would leave a window in time that we could exploit. We could switch these containers and route them to Dubai.

Amir went on, 'I'm not sure if Dad had scrapped that many containers over the years but it will take a few minutes to check. If we are going to do this we need to get cracking and create the paperwork. We can leave the Robertson & Son containers for a couple of days, phoning the Authority to say we have a scheduling problem and will collect in a few days. What do you think?' he concluded.

For the next hour or so they argued back and forth over the prospect of playing safe with the twelve containers due to be collected by Robertson & Son as against the risk and rewards of attempting to steal nine others. In the end it was the fact that the containers that Amir had identified were all from *TransOceanic II* that tipped the balance.

'What's that phrase?' asked Aashi. 'It's something like "revenge is a dish best served cold". Those bastards at *TransOceanic* killed off this Agency and in the process have killed Dad. I reckon it is payback time.'

The two brothers agreed. It would be a totally committed throw of the dice to steal all twenty-one containers.

The next twenty-four hours were a blur of activity. Aashi drafted all the export documents needed to ship the containers to Dubai. Amir secured all the information he needed from the Port Authority to create container collection documents before closing the system down and obliterating any trace back to the Sacranie Shipping Agency. Abdul dug out old container numbers and began the process of creating several companies in Dubai with corresponding bank accounts.

On the morning of the switch Aashi, Amir and Abdul stood at the foot of the stairs in the warehouse. They were dressed in worn blue boiler suits. The Everton FC baseball cap and heavy sunglasses transformed Aashi into an anonymous worker. They were all nervous and excited; any stumble could result in everything being destroyed. But it went like a dream. The sequence of events, that Farouk had described, were followed precisely and it went like clockwork.

The security guys on the gates, and those handling the documents, hardly blinked as the cabs were waved through. The system that Abdul had practised to strip off and replace container numbers proved a success, they even reduced the turnaround time to ninety minutes. In three days they had switched the numbers on twenty-one containers and returned them to the port for export to Dubai. They had "procured" goods with an estimated value of over £3.5 million. When Amir phoned Hussein in Dubai, and told him to expect twenty-one containers in a couple of weeks, Hussein was delighted. Amir also said he would travel to Dubai so as to be present when the containers were delivered.

The following week the three of them even managed to switch a consignment of top of the range Ribs and Yamaha outboard motors from Felixstowe to Rotterdam and on to Dubai. However, the icing on the cake was procuring the vehicles. Five brand new, top of the range, silver grey Toyota Land Cruisers were collected from a storage facility outside London. A day later five Toyota people carriers, of the same colour, that were due for export from Southampton docks, were also switched. It then became a challenge to find five Toyota Hilux pickups that would match the colour of the other vehicles that had been stolen. Amir tracked them down in a storage compound on the outskirts of Glasgow. A phone call, false documents, an anonymous car transporter with fake number plates and the Toyota pickups were gone. In just over a month they had diverted over £5 million in goods to Dubai. They knew they had been riding their luck and as soon as the last pickup was dropped off at Liverpool docks Amir made sure he had obliterated all traces of their involvement and closed down their computer system.

A week after switching the last consignment, and confirming that everything was en route, the three of them set off in the early hours of the morning for London's Heathrow Airport. They took the Monday morning BA flight to Dubai. That evening was one of celebration – but the rest of the week was work – planning for the future.

Two weeks after the visit to Dubai Farouk died. He simply failed to wake on that dull Thursday morning. The night before Aashi, Amir and Abdul had told him and Neelam of the Dubai contracts, how they had restructured the business and were confident of significant profits in the tax year. They announced to both their parents that they were so confident in the business that they had resigned from their posts with immediate effect. Farouk and Neelam were delighted.

The excuse, that they had decided to join the family business, was true. It was also true that they saw huge financial benefits in transporting goods to the Middle East. There was mild protest at their respective companies, but not too much, new staff could be appointed at a lesser salary.

Whilst in Dubai Abdul had arranged a series of long term monthly transfers of money from an account controlled by Hussein into five separate accounts in Dubai. Hussein was delighted to go along with the plan for monthly payments rather than pay for the contents of the twenty-one containers in one go. It gave him funds in reserve and avoided unnecessary questions.

One of the transfers that Abdul arranged was to a bank in Liverpool. Over a period of fourteen months the overdraft and mortgages on Neelam's house and the warehouses were paid off; there was even a modest credit. With money from the other accounts they set about resurrecting the Sacranie

291

Shipping Agency. They needed a legitimate front for what they had decided to do. What they decided was to continue to ship containers but to "procure" quality, nearly-new cars, and ship them to Dubai. They had realised there was a massive market in the region and it was very, very profitable. A single transporter load could be worth £250,000.

Two more trips to Dubai succeeded in renting a car showroom with an attached garage and getting it refurbished. They subsequently hired extended family members, cousins and nephews, and four months after signing the rental lease the *Deutsch Auto Centre* was opened. Over the next year they created a system that procured quality German saloon cars and 4 x 4s: Audi, BMW, Mercedes, VW and shipped these to Dubai via the smaller of their two warehouses. They simply divided the business in two. The legitimate container handling was based at the main warehouse, complete with new drivers, office staff and labourers. The car export business, involving the extended family, at the second.

Abdul had arranged for one of his contacts in the trade to install a heavy duty electric winch and detachable ramps to a conventional covered trailer. Two relatives, Deepak and Sanjay, proved to be adept at spotting desirable cars and in the early hours winching these off a drive, up the ramp and inside the trailer. They could move a car in under five minutes. The five car transporter, that Jonny Spate judged to be superfluous to requirements, was in regular use as these were delivered to the docks for transportation to Dubai. When the scheme was running as they wanted they were dispatching consignments of about fifty vehicles every three months. Even selling them for half the original purchase price in the UK the sale netted about £500,000 per trip; about £2

million a year. The skill was to balance demand with
availability and to be aware of the old maxim "if a deal looks
too good to be true … it probably is".' They soon judged the
market price for the cars, sweetening the deal by offering
three years' free warranty on each of the cars sold, if the car
was maintained by *Deutsch Auto Centre*. In this way they
generated regular servicing for the garage and avoided the
chance of the fake identification numbers on the cars being
checked by anyone else.

Chapter 40

Creating the retirement fund

Three years on the Sacranie Shipping Agency was doing well – but not so well as to raise eyebrows, and to be able to submit a tax return that was never queried. The three of them had previously agreed that they would do nothing to draw attention to themselves. They still lived in their original apartments and paid their monthly mortgages. They still drove non-descript cars and avoided expensive holidays. They replaced the old cabs, but not with new ones. They bought Volvos that were a couple of years old. The warehouses were made secure, but nothing that drew one's attention. However, a problem was looming. They had growing amounts of cash that had been transferred from accounts in Dubai to an account in Zürich; significant amounts of cash were building up.

It was Neelam who, by chance, solved their problem and decided their next direction. The three of them had resumed their Sunday lunch ritual. However, rather than just turning up to eat they spent the morning with their mother helping her prepare and cook the food. It was after the meal, whilst they were sat chatting, that Neelam announced that she was thinking of taking a holiday to India. She wanted to return to her home State of Haryana, to see the farm where she was born, and meet childhood friends.

'When are you thinking of going?' asked Aashi who remembered all the stories her mother had told her of India but which she had never visited.

'I'm thinking of going this November. It's always so cold, wet and miserable in Liverpool in November, but it is beautiful in Haryana. The days are always warm and evenings cool. The grass will be high and flowers will be in full bloom. Ah, I remember the smell in the afternoons as I walked home from school,' said Neelam with a sentimental smile. 'Could you check the bank account for me? I'm sure Farouk would have put aside more than enough to cover the cost,' she added.

Aashi quickly glanced at her brothers and with a broad smile announced, 'I reckon it should be our treat. In fact, why don't we all go,' she added as she re-scanned the faces of her brothers.

Abdul and Amir immediately caught the mood that Neelam and Aashi had created. They joined in the fun of starting to plan a trip; deciding when they could get away and for how long, how they would travel, where they would stay and so on. They could see that their mother was thrilled at the idea of returning to her home village and showing off her children.

In the days following it was clear that it would be impossible for all of them to be away at the same time. There were too many sensitive issues, collections and deliveries to attend to that couldn't be delegated. However, the solution was easy. Aashi would accompany her mother to India whilst Abdul and Amir took care of the business. In turn they would travel out to India, replacing the one who was there, thus ensuring two of them were in Liverpool almost all of the time.

As November loomed they were busy, not only with the day to day movement of containers in and out of Liverpool but handling the consignments of cars to Dubai. In addition they were putting in place the arrangements that would need to be undertaken whilst they were away.

On the 7th November Amir and Abdul drove Aashi and Neelam to Liverpool John Lennon airport to catch the shuttle to London Heathrow and then the direct Air India flight to New Delhi. Even the grey skies and drizzle couldn't dampen their enthusiasm. Amir parked in the drop off zone adjacent to the entrance to departures. Abdul ran off to find a trolley even though they had only a short walk to the entrance. Aashi had booked them on Business Class and so didn't expect much of a queue. Despite the weather Neelam was wearing a buttercup yellow sari, trimmed with gold thread and Aashi was in a dark blue business suit; they looked prosperous and just what Neelam secretly wanted. She had left her village, the eldest daughter of a poor farmer, and wanted to impress those she had left behind.

Haryana is in the north west of India. It is bordered by Punjab to the north, Rajasthan to the south west and Uttar Pradesh to the south east. Neelam's village was a two day drive from New Delhi. The early excitement of the check-in, business class lounge, boarding the plane and take-off faded during the seven hour flight. However, it was renewed as both Neelam and Aashi marvelled at the marble, granite and glass of the huge Indira Gandhi International Airport and the mass of people jostling to queue for emigration and the baggage reclaim. If they thought this was busy they were mistaken. As they followed a porter with their bags, into the arrivals area, it was like stepping into another world. They

296

both squinted at the bright sunlight after the tinted windows of the airport, they basked in the warmth that flooded over them and into the melee of greeting friends, relatives and taxi drivers.

It would be a long drive from Delhi to the village and after a long, tiring flight Aashi didn't want her mother to arrive exhausted. Instead she had arranged an overnight stay at probably the best hotel in New Delhi, the Imperial Hotel on Janpath. One of the partners in Goodrich & Child had made several business trips to New Delhi and had raved about the hotel. A few minutes looking at the website confirmed its opulence but hadn't captured the grandeur of the brilliant white building, the polished marble floors that looked as though they were covered with a thin layer of water, the polished brass glowing and the quality that seemed to ooze from every direction. Her mother was entranced. She had never been in such a luxurious hotel and never dreamed of staying at such a place in India, but she glowed with satisfaction and Aashi loved it.

Aashi had arranged a car and driver to take them to the village the next day. After a massive breakfast that must have been reminiscent of those at the time of the Raj, they stepped out of the air conditioned hotel and into the warm sunshine before climbing into the white, air conditioned, Mercedes. Aashi had decided that with an early start they could afford an hour or so to see some of the sights of New Delhi. It would be just a short detour. Aashi and her mother just sat back as a kaleidoscope of colour swept past the car windows.

They entered the city and cruised past India Gate and Parliament, the light brown stone glowing in the early

297

morning sunshine. They swept around Connaught Place, the Victorian columns and facades daubed with advertising banners and signs. They threaded their way down narrow crowded lanes to be confronted by Jami Masjid, the ancient mosque in New Delhi. They paused for a moment, to stretch their legs before a long drive, outside the massive Red Fort with streams of visitors and hawkers swirling around the entrance. But soon the sophistication of New Delhi, with broad tree lined boulevards and streams of small cars soon gave way to narrower roads, colourful overloaded trucks, bullock carts and cyclists as they made their way west.

At first the roadside scenes were captivating. There were water buffalo in the fields, women in drab saris hoeing, children running around. There were cowpats struck to mud walls – drying, ready for burning – and trucks being repaired by the roadside. After a few hours the suspension of the Mercedes was being tested as the roads deteriorated.

They stopped early evening in a small town that boasted the only three star hotel in the area. It was nothing like the Imperial Hotel but after a long day in the car, and the prospect of arriving in the village tomorrow, it was ideal.

They started driving again in the early morning. It was overcast and cool as they got in the car. No air conditioning was needed. It was late afternoon by the time they entered the village with Neelam at first confused by the way it had changed. The landmarks in her memory had been demolished or extended, replaced or position changed by the not so new road through the village. However, it seemed there were "lookouts" everywhere. Small boys waved the car down and directed them to where a welcoming party was waiting. It was clear that Neelam's relatives had spent not hours but days preparing the rooms, the food and decorations. As her mother launched into greeting everyone, accepting thimbles of tea, tiny morsels of food of every colour and shape Aashi was happy to take a back seat. By early evening Aashi was weary after a long day, countless introductions and ceremonies of welcome.

By late evening she was beginning to wonder how long she could survive the visit. She had quickly realised she was a British city girl, not an Indian villager, and felt slightly awkward. However, just as her eyelids were about to close she was suddenly wide awake. One of her mother's oldest friends was explaining that the local landowner had announced that he was selling off all his farms in the valley. The young men and women were leaving the land and seeking their fortune in Delhi and Mumbai, those remaining simply got older. There was no one to farm the land in the traditional way and he couldn't afford the cost of machinery to improve production. It was the same picture across the entire State, even though demand for grains and vegetables, timber and milk were high. There was simply not enough workers.

Aashi knew not to interrupt with questions, it wouldn't be polite, but she would follow this up at the first opportunity. That opportunity was early the next morning at breakfast. They had the car and driver for a month and her mother's friend was only too keen to take a ride in the air conditioned car and take them on a tour of the valley. They bumped and bounced over dirt tracks, got out to look over the vista of fields, rivers and woodland, stopped at the ruins of old schools and churches and had countless cups of tea with distant relatives and friends. But over the morning a picture emerged. There were over forty small to medium sized

299

farms, covering about two thousand hectares, leased from the one landowner. They were growing a mixture of cereals, seeds and vegetables. Her mother's friend knew that the landowner had other farms further up the valley but wasn't sure how many and the price they would be sold at. She knew the price of wheat, millet and linseed were good, but there weren't enough field workers to plant, tend and harvest the crops.

In the back seat of the Mercedes a plan started to take shape. Aashi guessed that they probably had more than enough money to buy the farms – even though she had no idea what the asking price would be. What she did know was that the Sacranie Shipping Agency could "acquire" all the farming machinery and trucks they would need and bring it to the valley. They could get advice on how to make the farms more productive, and even had relatives in the area who could help organise the work. The Indian market was booming and the farms would be an ideal way to redirect the piles of cash that were being accumulated.

That afternoon she left Neelam to rest with her old friends and asked the driver to take her to the nearest town where she could send an email. She had already composed the email to Amir and Abdul but would not contact the landowner, if at all, until they replied.

It was the next afternoon, when Aashi returned to the small and hot cyber café with the blaring music, that she read the reply from her brothers. They both thought it was a great idea and Abdul would bring detailed questions in a week or so. They asked Aashi to make preliminary enquiries about the asking price of the land to help them decide if the idea was indeed viable.

Looking back the three of them were amazed at the chance events that had brought them to the Valley and to the mountain of work they had naively undertaken. It was certain that without almost limitless access to cash, the ability to acquire everything from tractors to backhoes, covered trucks to ploughs, seed drillers to harrows they couldn't have pulled it off, but they had. Without the buffer of cash, before crops were harvested and sold, they would have struggled to fund the necessary irrigation work, the building of storage sheds, the training of local men as tractor drivers and so on. They had also decided to buy an old freighter that they could use to transfer the agricultural machinery from the UK to India under the guise of mixed cargo plying between Europe and the Far East via India. It really didn't matter if the ship made money, it saved them money and made transporting "procured" equipment so much easier. The ship they eventually bought, the *Lee Kwan Fong*, was reaching the end of its life, but would only be needed for a few years. By then Sacranie Farms would be a legitimate and very profitable concern.

They had agreed a fair, but not generous price for a collection of farms. Over the next three years they had transformed the crude, labour-intensive, disparate farming practices into a coordinated, mechanised and highly efficient business. State grants supplemented their investment and contracts with Indian and multinational companies started to show a handsome return on the investment. A spin-off, that they hadn't initially expected, was that the efficiency of their farms put neighbourhood farms under increasing pressure. They simply were not cost effective and soon spiralled into decline. It seemed hardly a month went by without a

301

landowner asking if Sacranie Farms wished to invest in other farms or buy them out. Sacranie Farms grew steadily in size and influence in the State.

Chapter 41

Collision course

SAM was smouldering with anger, humiliation and frustration. He was angry because of the loss of his twenty Chinese missiles and the US$3 million that he nearly had in his hands. He had already decided that with that amount of money he could disappear. He could retire to the Nyika Plateau in Malawi, buy an impressive farm, stock and a couple of wives. A few dozen workers could attend to the farm allowing him to relax and enjoy his retirement. But "whitey" had ruined everything.

SAM felt humiliated because his remaining men knew he had been defeated by a couple of young men and a woman. He had lost five useful men; men he would have to replace. He had to run from Kenya like a child, driving through the bush to avoid police and army patrols. On the first night, camped in the bush, he had raged against whitey vowing, in front of his men, to find him and cut his heart out. It was then expected that SAM would carry out his vow.

SAM was also frustrated and cold as he sat, wedged, in the corner of a graffiti and sticker covered bus stop in Manchester, England. It smelled of urine and he had already glowered at a man, who looked homeless, seeking shelter from the fine rain that drifted out of the sky. The man had moved on quickly. Bus passengers came and went regularly.

When SAM had returned to Dar es Salaam, and unpacked his bag, he realised he still had the business card that whitey had given him on the barge in Lammu. He had an address and a phone number in Manchester and rapidly formed a plan. Over the years SAM had used a Hawala agent in Dar es Salaam. Hawala is the ancient system of transferring money and goods or acquiring goods, across borders, without anything actually being transferred. It is a secret system, based on trust, and whatever the temptation not worth breaching. The same amount of money and similar goods, less a percentage or small fee, will be waiting for him anywhere in the world. SAM simply deposited two brand new Russian automatic handguns with the agent; similar guns would be waiting for him and Mohammed in London. He also requested a Fed Ex uniform and cap, medium size, for Mohammed. If SAM returned the guns his own weapons, would be returned for a small fee. The cost of the uniform seemed expensive but SAM didn't quibble and that would not be returned. It was easy.

Just over a month after returning to Dar es Salaam SAM had flown to London to find whitey. On his first full day in London he bought warm clothes in a department store for both himself and Mohammed; he hadn't expected it to be so cold! He then strolled around the shops in Covent Garden and savoured his purchase of a vicious looking, and expensive, filleting knife in a cook shop. He liked the way the gleaming blade flexed between his fingers. Then, with Mohammed, he travelled by train to Manchester and booked into the ageing Britannia Hotel in the city centre. SAM could afford one of their better rooms. Mohammed booked in separately, in a cheaper room.

It had been easy to find the apartment block in which whitey lived. A simple phone call to the office of the *Marine Salvage & Investigation Company* had confirmed that Mr Collier was expected in the office mid afternoon. It was merely a case of identifying two vantage points from which he and Mohammed could watch for him. Despite the cold and damp SAM had a rage burning inside him. His plan was simple. He would give whitey five minutes after entering the apartment block. Mohammed would then throw off his heavy padded coat and, in brown Fed Ex overall and peak cap, would ring his apartment bell and announce he had a parcel to deliver. As whitey accepted the parcel, and his attention was focused on signing for it, Mohammed would threaten him with the gun and force him back into the entrance hall of the apartment block, immediately followed by SAM. Together they would force him inside his own apartment where SAM would "cut his heart out". SAM knew it was a risk. Other people may be in the apartment block foyer. If so they would end up dead like whitey. There could be people passing by, but in the rain SAM judged it was worth the risk. SAM didn't expect any trouble from whitey. When people see an ugly gun pointing at them they suddenly lose any thought of fighting. He didn't think whitey was a brave man.

SAM had been sat in the bus stop shelter for over two hours when his mobile phone rang. It was the signal from Mohammed that whitey had been spotted. SAM turned his head first one way and then the other. Then he saw him, walking briskly down the street carrying some sort of slim briefcase. There was someone with him and SAM smiled. It was "Pretty Boy", he had both of them. He smiled broadly, moving one hand to his jacket pocket to feel the shape of the

305

knife, the other the solid bulk of the revolver. It was a short barrelled 0.38 and was perfect for what he wanted; it was black, solid and looked menacing. 'Not long now, whitey,' SAM whispered to himself.

Jack was in a good mood. Life was good and getting better; Jack smiled to himself. He and Sandro hadn't expected the invitation to Lloyd's of London and to meet up with Charles and Sir Alistair again. However, the comment from Charles, that "we have something to give you" was intriguing. They had caught the Manchester Pullman train and had been in Lloyd's offices after the morning rush hour. In truth both Jack and Sandro had been preoccupied with the future rather than the past and had not been thinking about the *Rockingham Castle* and the salvage operation that was underway. It was only when Sir Alistair announced that *NorSav* had recovered the eight containers that held items constituting the *Italian Masters* Exhibition, that he realised what the meeting was all about.

'Thank you for coming this morning, at short notice, but I wanted to share good news with you as soon as possible,' announced Sir Alistair once they had the obligatory tea in their hands.

'Earlier this year the British Museum and the V&A collaborated with various museums in America to mount an exhibition of *Italian Masters* – paintings by Canaletto and Rubins, Caravaggio and … er … others. These were all sent to America by air cargo. However, sculptures by Benini and Donatello, Michaelangelo and … er … others were shipped in containers. You see why we were so keen to locate and salvage the cargo. The eight containers that *NorSalv* salvaged last month were transferred to another container ship, and returned to their respective museums. They subsequently confirmed no damage was sustained to any item. It was a very satisfactory outcome. The Board met on Monday and it was approved that a further one percent of the insured value of the cargo should be paid to you, with our thanks. Today was the earliest I could get our finance people to issue a banker's draft.'

With that Sir Alistair rose from his chair, turned to his desk and retrieved a slip of paper. With a smile and a flourish he handed the draft, of almost £250,000, to Jack. Jack couldn't stop smiling as he first shook the hand of Sir Alistair, then Charles and finally hugged Sandro.

As the congratulations subsided Sir Alistair coughed and continued. 'Gentlemen, I suspect that your company is now financially secure, in the short term, but what of the future? If you intend to extend your operations into deep sea salvage you need to gain an insight into such work and experience of it. If you are interested I could have a word with Jurgen at *NovSalv*. I'm sure he would be prepared to take you on for, say, six months or a couple of projects. Such experience could prove to be … how should I say … extremely instructive. If you are planning to make a career in marine inspection and salvage there are no better teachers than *NorSalv*. But I leave that to you.'

Others had been busy since returning from Kenya; Penny in particular. She gave out a weary sigh, stretched and rubbed her eyes. She had been wading through scrolls of figures all morning. Penny had been told that she would be working with Ellie and Bob, two Forensic Accountants within HM Border Force. What this really meant was that she would be doing the hack work that they asked her to do. This was

307

mainly checking for trends and inconsistencies amongst the mountain of paperwork associated with the Sacranie Shipping Agency.

This was a far cry from the first few days back in England; those days had been exciting. Her colleagues were keen to hear about her adventure and seemed genuinely concerned about her. Her line manager had agreed that she should finish her report and then transfer to the Fraud Team. They were already checking out the cargo of the *Lee Kwan Fong.* She would have transferred to a new section in a few weeks anyway. At first Penny thought she would crack the case in days. The vehicle identification numbers that Jack had taken from the three John Deer tractors were false. Penny found it difficult to describe the thrill upon discovering this. With the help of Ellie she also traced three John Deer tractors, of the same model, that had been reported as stolen from a sales compound in Gainsborough, in the north of England, several months earlier. This was simply too much of a coincidence. She knew they would have to confirm the real VIN numbers once the cargo was salvaged, but it looked like agricultural machinery was being stolen in the UK and shipped to India. With Bob's help she identified the shipping agent in Mumbai, OK Osman Bros who were handling the tractors and who would be arranging subsequent delivery. Further checks revealed that a lot of agricultural machinery was handled by them. Penny had also cross matched the list of imported machinery to lists of stolen equipment in the UK. It looked as though they could roll up an entire illegal operation.

However, it had taken over a week of frenetic activity, piles of paperwork and numerous conversations with colleagues in India, to set up the raid on OK Osman Bros. The deflation, upon hearing that the office of the shipping agent in Mumbai had been abandoned and everything, including light bulbs, had been removed, was a blow. It seems that the single room office, above a small, local restaurant, had been active for several years. Then, a week or so ago, everything was cleared out of the office and they disappeared! The Indian Police were trying to trace OK Osman Bros but Penny wasn't confident they would be successful.

Since the Sacranie Shipping Agency were handling the export of the tractors, and they were being transferred in their own ship, they became the centre of attention. Ellie and Bob, with Penny as skivvy, were also wading through the accounts. It had taken almost a week and the conclusion seemed to be that the business was doing well, but not abnormally well. The daughter and two sons had brought the Shipping Agency back from the brink. There was a sound, but not huge profit, at the end of each financial year. The daughter and sons each had modest apartments in Liverpool and Manchester, all paying mortgages. They each drove modest cars, dressed conservatively … had modest amounts of cash in bank accounts, nothing seemed out of the ordinary.

As Penny returned to the computer printout she noticed, within the columns of expenses, several return flights to Dubai. This was nothing particularly strange. The Sacranie Shipping Agents did a lot of work with companies in Dubai. Indeed, the contracts agreed with several companies had essentially rescued them from bankruptcy. It was then that Penny had a thought: "All work and no play". She had seen files listing holidays and holiday pay for the workers in the office and yard, but no reference to holidays taken by the daughter and two sons! It all looked too perfect, too sanitised.

She stopped work and strolled over to where Ellie was working. 'Ellie, have you come across any reference to holidays taken by Aashi, Amir and Abdul Sacranie?' asked Penny.

Ellie stopped what she was doing and looked up, thinking. Penny continued. 'Have you also noticed that it all looks too neat, too orderly, too ordinary? There's nothing out of place. It all looks too good to be true.'

'Emmmm. Now I think about it you are right. No hiccups, no problems,' said Ellie. 'Let's check and see if our friends have been travelling recently.'

Ellie switched to another database. She typed in her ID and password and a few minutes later pushed her chair back from the desk, put her hands behind her head, and in a loud voice announced 'very interesting. Listen to this guys' said Ellie. 'Aashi, Amir, Abdul and their mother make regular return flights to New Delhi … in Business Class! They have been doing this for several years. Mother Sacranie spends several months in India before returning. It seems the daughter and sons take it in turns to visit, typically a week or so. As one returns to the UK another one goes out.' Penny butted in and with a smile said, 'If they are paying for business class seats, regularly, my guess would be that they are not catching a bus into the city; they will be hiring a car or a taxi. The Indian police will be able to check and, hopefully, we can trace their movements. At the moment we don't know where they go, but we can find out. We can also check if everything inside the Sacranie Shipping Agency is as ordinary as it seems.' Penny started to move away, back to her desk, when she added, 'Oh yes, I'll also check out the business links in Dubai. That all sounds too neat, too convenient.'

Chapter 42

Wheels of Justice

Mohammed stood with his back towards the rain as it fell more heavily. He held the clipboard and a small package against his chest, as though protecting it, as he reached out and pressed the brass doorbell against the name of Collier. The rain was good luck. It kept people off the streets; there was no one around. Mohammed could feel the bulk of the revolver tucked inside his shirt and trouser band. He stood still and merely looked down at his feet. He didn't bother to look around since he knew SAM would be only a few metres away; just out of sight.

'Romeo, GO, GO, GO! Golf, GO, GO, GO!' shouted the officer into his microphone as he stared at the two TV monitors in front of him.

Commander Jim Jardin couldn't see the reaction of the two armed teams, code named Romeo and Golf, as they burst from plain coloured, panelled vans, but he knew precisely what they would be doing. They would use overwhelming force to subdue both men and use firearms if they were about to be fired upon.

The police Anti Terrorist Unit, headed by Jim Jardin, had been following Soloman Abraham Mbano (SAM) and his accomplice within moments of them stepping off the aircraft at Heathrow Airport just outside London. High level cooperation between the British, French, Kenyan and Tanzanian authorities, especially when sophisticated weapons were involved, had ensured the rapid exchange of information. The Tanzanians had been extremely cooperative and responsive. They provided photographs and descriptions of the two men and confirmed that both were under investigation for numerous crimes. They were actively monitoring known associates of the two men, related businesses, and were preparing for numerous, simultaneous arrests. The Tanzanians had concluded their report by saying that both men should be considered extremely violent and were travelling on forged South African passports. They could be arrested at any time and it was hoped they would eventually be returned to Tanzania for trial.

The surveillance teams had followed SAM and Mohammed on their shopping trip in Covent Garden. The warm clothing could be expected but at first they were confused at the purchase of the kitchen knife. However, checks in Tanzania revealed its likely use! It seemed that SAM had a liking for sharp knives and using them. The teams also followed SAM to an African craft shop in Islington, an inner London borough. Soon after speaking to the owner SAM had disappeared through a rear curtain, only to emerge minutes later. It was Jardin's guess that he had picked something up – something he shouldn't have. Shortly after SAM's departure a search of the premises, and several hours of forceful questioning, revealed that SAM had acquired two .38 revolvers and of ammunition. It wasn't the only firearm on the premises! The craft shop closed early that afternoon; a note on the door said the owner had gone on holiday, but he wouldn't be going very far.

313

The Anti Terrorist Unit had quickly deduced the likely target for the attack. It was Jack Collier, the man who had prevented SAM from delivering the missiles to his base in Dar es Saalam. However, the case against SAM and his accomplice would be much stronger if they were caught in the process of committing the attack. What was the phrase, 'Terrorists need to be lucky only once, security services need to get it right every time.'

'Romeo to control. Romeo to control. We have both men in custody. Transferring to secure vehicle now, over.'

Moments later a flurry of messages were exchanged between London, Paris, Nairobi and Dar es Saalam as the arrests were confirmed and others initiated. It would be a long drive down the M6 and M1 motorways to London's Paddington Green Police Station; the most secure police station in the UK. The Unit could then hand over their prisoners to faceless men in grey suits and their job would be done. It may take weeks or months to untangle the various parts of the illegal operation in Tanzania and elsewhere, but it was underway.

Penny sat around the small conference table with Ellie, Bob, five other seconded members to the Fraud Team, and the Acting Deputy Director of HM Border Force. Ellie thanked everyone for attending the meeting and distributed slim folders around the table. Opening the folder she directed everyone to Document 1: a single page summary. She briefly identified the case in question and the persons of interest to them; the Sacranie family and the Sacranie Shipping Agency. In Document 2 Ellie provided a chronology of recent events and flagged the main elements of the investigation. An attached diagram illustrated how everything pointed to the

Sacranie family being involved in illegal activity, but there was no concrete evidence. After a short pause Ellie continued saying that Penny had been reviewing financial information, checking the contents of containers and contracts. Penny had assembled a plausible scenario to account for what was known and had a suggestion for the way forward. Ellie invited Penny to continue.

'The file provides information on two linked investigations we have been conducting with overseas colleagues; one in Dubai and one in New Delhi. Could I direct you to Document 3 and appendices 3a to 3d.' said Penny. 'A review of the finances of the Sacranie Shipping Agency revealed it to be bankrupt at the time Farouk Sacranie died. The Agency had debts of just over £340,000 and no significant assets. Yet, within months the Agency had secured several contracts in Dubai, had a business plan approved by their creditors, and within two years had not only cleared their debt but made a small profit. Over recent years the Sacranie Shipping Agency has made good, but not outstanding profits. We also suspect that large sums of money are being invested in farms in India, but we aren't sure where the money is coming from.

Firstly, Dubai: with the help of colleagues in Dubai we have confirmed that at the time Aashi, Amir and Abdul Sacranie took over the Shipping Agency, the most active contracts were with a Dubai-based property development company headed by Hussein al Waffre. In particular, a luxury apartment complex and marina that was under construction. We have established that Hussein al Waffre had a meeting with Amir, in The Midland Hotel, Manchester, at the time Farouk Sacranie was in hospital. Farouk Sacranie died shortly after he was admitted. We know that al Waffre was in the UK trying to arrange extra funding for the apartment and marina complex. It seems the project was facing disaster unless he could obtain funding to furnish and equip both the apartments and marina. The bankers we have spoken to recalled that the original budget had been grossly exceeded and the whole project was high risk – much too high. Hussein al Waffre left the UK without securing any funds. However, within a month of his return to Dubai shipping containers started to arrive with goods that equipped the apartments and marina. If you look at appendix 3a you will see the most complete list of items that arrived at the Development.

At our request, colleagues in Dubai have just completed a routine Health and Safety inspection of the apartments and marina. It was merely a cover that would allow them unrestricted access. They checked the electrical wiring, plumbing, air conditioning and so on. They even checked floor coverings. If you look at appendix 3b you will see that much of what was used to equip the apartments and the marina were in shipping containers stolen from Liverpool docks several years ago. The original serial numbers on fridges and freezers, TVs and air conditioning units all match the items that were stolen. Similarly, identification numbers on vehicles and outboard motors also revealed them to be stolen. It wasn't possible to check items that didn't have serial numbers but we believe the contents of the stolen containers all found their way to Hussein al Waffre. We further believe the containers were stolen and redirected by the Sacranie Shipping Agency.

Other checks have failed to find evidence of tangible transactions between the Shipping Agency and other companies in Dubai that were part of the business plan and who each signed a Memorandum of Understanding. We believe these are merely paper trails that will eventually reveal that no transactions actually took place.

We are also in the process of examining the bank records of the Shipping Agency in Dubai; these are listed in appendix 3c. Unfortunately these are incomplete at the present time. However, it does reveal large sums of money were transferred from al Waffre to the Sacranies through a network of accounts. Only a fraction of these transactions appeared in the tax returns of the Shipping Agency. We believe the sums involved represent a pay-off for the containers that were stolen.

Secondly, India: when the freighter, the *Lee Kwan Fong,* sank off the coast of Kenya it was carrying tractors and trailers on a Sacranie owned vessel to Sacranie owned farms. We have established that the tractors and trailers were stolen. We have also established that there are dozens of items of agricultural equipment that have been exported from the UK to these farms. These are listed in appendix 3d. To date the Indian authorities have only been able to check on one tractor vehicle identification number; it is false. We have calculated the cost to the Shipping Agency of purchasing the farms and estimated the cost of the agricultural equipment. I've listed these in Appendix 3d. The figures cannot be reconciled with the published accounts of the Sacranie Shipping Company nor funds transferred from al Waffre. Funds have been transferred from banks in Dubai to banks in India but we can find no link to al Waffre; the money comes from somewhere else.

We have presented the accumulated evidence to our legal advisors who tell us that at the moment the case against Hussein al Waffre is extremely strong; against the Sacranies it is extremely weak. There would be difficult questions for the Sacranies to answer … but they may be able to offer plausible answers. The problem is that we know only part of the story. We need concrete evidence to link the Shipping Agency to the thefts bound for both Dubai and India. We also need to discover where the money is coming from to fund Sacranie Farms.'

Penny paused, and with growing confidence, looked to the head of the table and at the Acting Deputy Director General. 'We have a proposed strategy and would welcome your comments.'

Hussein al Waffre glanced out of the side window of the car as he was driven, from home, along the coast road towards the Central Business District in Dubai. The raw morning brightness was muted by the tinted windows. He could see the heat haze on the ground and the flickering distortion it caused. Inside his newly acquired Mercedes E350 it was pleasantly cool and comfortable. He smiled and savoured the quality of the gift from Amir Sacranie; the precise leather stitching and attention to detail. It was the perfect car for Dubai. It was luxurious but similar to hundreds of other cars; it blended into the background. The car slowed as the driver indicated and turned off the major road towards the office block where Hussein worked. Minutes later the driver indicated again as he swept down a ramp, triggered the electronic garage doors, and entered the air conditioned underground car park. He stopped by the elevator and allowed Hussein to get out before he drove away.

Hussein stabbed the call button and thought ahead to the items on his list for the day. He preferred early starts to the day; a chance to work uninterrupted for a few hours. A dull chime signalled the arrival of the elevator but he was surprised when three police officers, in uniform, stepped through the doors. The one in the middle held up one hand, palm outwards, signalling him to halt. In the other raised hand he held an official looking ID. The other policemen moved and stood either side of him.

'Hussein al Waffre,' announced the officer. 'I would like you to volunteer to accompany us to the Central Police Station to help us with our enquiries. If you do not volunteer I will arrest you for receiving stolen property. Do you volunteer?'

As Hussein began to mumble a confused reply, a police car slowed to a halt beside them and one of the policemen opened the rear door, ushering Hussein into the car. It had taken fifteen seconds from start to finish. Hussein, cramped between two officers, took less than fifteen seconds to regain his composure and to demand an explanation, but no one in the car spoke as it manoeuvred its way to the police station and to a discreet rear entrance. As they climbed out of the car the officer invited Hussein to follow him through a maze of dusty corridors with plain concrete floors and bland, painted walls. It took two elevator rides, and more corridors, before he was seated in a plain room with just a plain table and four upright chairs in it. He was left alone. Hussein didn't know whether he was above ground or below; there were no windows to the outside. He couldn't tell if it was hot or cold in the room but he could feel the sweat on his body and the churning of his stomach. What was it the policeman had said? 'If you do not volunteer I will arrest you for receiving stolen property,' Hussein immediately knew what he was talking about.

Hussein's brain was in a whirl. How much did they know? How had they found out? How could he get out of this? Who could he contact? He glanced at his wristwatch; it was still early, his secretary wouldn't be arriving for another couple of hours. He heard a noise outside the door. It opened and in walked two men; a police officer and a well groomed man in a western suit. They were followed by another officer carrying a tray of tea. The first two men sat at the table, the tray was placed on the table, and the third officer left the room.

The man in the suit touched his forehead and greeted Hussein. *'As-salamu alaykum,* peace be upon you. Thank you for volunteering to help us with our enquiries. Please, join me in having some tea,' he said in a pleasant, friendly tone.

Hussein started to protest and demanded to know why he had been brought to this place, but a gentle smile and a raised hand was enough for Hussein to stop speaking.

'My name is Asif and I want you to listen very carefully. If you agree to help us with our enquiries you will be rewarded. If you decide not to help us I will arrest you for being an accessory to theft, the receipt of stolen property, false accounting, the procurement of Chinese missiles and accessory to murder; these are serious crimes.'

Hussein's immediate reaction was to protest, but the smile and raised hand from Asif quickly stopped the bluster.

'Please listen carefully and then decide what you wish to do,' said Asif. Without any notes, or pause, Asif proceeded to recount what had happened years ago. He gave dates of the unsuccessful attempts to raise money with merchant bankers in London, the meeting with Amir in Manchester and the arrival of containers in Dubai to furnish and equip his first project – the new apartment and marina complex. Asif had held out a hand to his colleague who provided lists of stolen property and their serial numbers, property currently within the apartments and marina. Other lists provided records of monies transferred from his Development Company via Dubai banks to the Sacranie Shipping Agency. Asif's colleague produced another sheet of paper that highlighted inconsistencies between published accounts and other transfers of money.

'We know Amir, his brother and sister make regular visits to Dubai, the last one a few months ago. I believe it was during one of these visits that you agreed to procure Chinese missiles. Missiles that were transported on a Sacranie owned vessel and eventually intercepted by the French Navy.'

Hussein was stunned. Asif handed him a collection of photographs showing the partly submerged container in the sea, photographs of the fishing trawler, the French frigate and a display of the weapons.

'Several innocent men were killed in the theft and transfer of these weapons. Some of those involved are already under arrest. The question is do you join them?'

With that Asif again held up his hand to stop any response. 'If you agree to help us with our enquiries, and to build a case against Amir, Abdul and Aashi Sacranie, you will be immune from prosecution. The two conditions are that you tell us everything you know, and are prepared to testify to whatever you tell us, in court. The second is that you make reparation to the insurance companies for what was stolen.

Please, drink your tea and consider what you want to do. Oh yes, whatever you decide I think it would be in your interest to have a lawyer present in all our future discussions. I will be outside.'

Hussein was no longer bewildered and no longer belligerent; he was calm and calculating. He came to a decision quickly. There was no way the police would fabricate the information he had just been given unless they had already verified it; he knew it to be true. He had no idea what the penalty would be for receiving stolen property and false accounting, but it would be possible to find out quickly. Initially he had been alarmed at the prospect of being charged for procuring Chinese missiles and an accomplice to murder. However, he now believed this was a scare tactic to get him to cooperate. It didn't matter, he was going to cooperate and to do so fully. He was a rich man and although repaying the value of the containers would drain his personal funds he would still have the Development Company and escape prison. It was clearly Amir, Abdul and Aashi that they wanted – not him.

Hussein reached for the glass of tea and took a sip; it was cold but delicious. The sick feeling in his stomach had disappeared. He drew the attention of the policeman who stood next to the only door in the room, and said he would like to speak to his colleague, Asif.

It took over three hours, and several phone calls, to contact one of the best criminal lawyers in the Gulf. His company lawyer was excellent in his field, but not in criminal law. It was thus almost midday when Hussein, his lawyer and Asif sat down together.

322

The pleasantries continued for a few minutes before Asif addressed Hussein's lawyer. 'Sir, let there be no confusion. If your client cooperates fully, I repeat fully, with our investigations all the charges I have mentioned will be dropped. He will receive complete immunity.'

Asif handed the lawyer several sheets of paper that listed the charges that had been assembled. He then handed over an official document granting Hussein immunity for his cooperation.

'Please take your time to read the documents,' said Asif. 'You will note that the offer of immunity is signed by the Ruler of Dubai and his signature was witnessed by the Director-General of His Highness the Ruler's Court. This is an indication of the seriousness of the charges against your client. However, also note, if evidence comes to light that your client has not fully cooperated, or has failed to disclose important information, the offer will be revoked.

'One more thing,' said Asif. 'Several people have been killed in stealing and transporting the Chinese missiles listed in the charges. For the safety of your client we would like him to remain our guest until all our questions, and verification of the answers given, is complete. I will leave you to confer.'

Asif and the two police officers in the room left. Moments later Asif entered an adjacent room and greeted Penny and Ellie as they looked at the monitor displaying Hussein and his lawyer. It was vision only; no sound. 'He is going to cooperate,' announced Asif.

Before lunch Hussein made a phone call to his personal secretary explaining he had a series of unexpected meetings, would be out of the office for a few days, and didn't want to

323

be disturbed. The secretary was told to contact him by email with anything judged to be important.

The first series of interviews started that afternoon, extended into early evening, and followed a pattern. Broad questions were posed, which set the context, then very specific questions followed. After about half an hour Asif would suspend the interview and leave. He explained that he needed to brief others to verify what was said. This was partially true. Asif was also discussing what had been said with Penny and Ellie who were listening to the interview via headphones. They were also formulating questions to elicit further information.

It took most of the next day to exhaust all possible avenues associated with the theft and transportation of the containers. The questioning served to consolidate the case against both Hussein and the Sacranies. It was solid information and being refined all the time. The afternoon switched focus to the actual payment to the Sacranie Shipping Agency, the banks and account numbers, the dates and sums involved. It was clear they needed Hussein's records, but these were held in a safe in his apartment. That evening they were collected. Later, as Hussein enjoyed the modest comforts of a VIP cell, Asif, Ellie and Penny scrolled through the paperwork, checking every line.

By mid afternoon on the second full day Asif, Ellie and Penny came to the conclusion that although Hussein had been complicit in the theft of the shipping containers, and transfer of funds, he knew nothing about the Chinese missiles nor the farms in India. It was clear that despite being drained he was desperate to cooperate yet nothing linked him to the missiles or the farms. During a break, around mid afternoon, Asif, Ellie and Penny brainstormed a final list of general, open-ended questions. These were wide ranging, spin-offs from previous questions or designed to focus upon anything previously overlooked. Asif, Ellie and Penny knew the questioning was coming to an end. Over lunch Hussein's lawyer had asked how much longer the questioning would continue since his client was visibly tiring and had cooperated fully.

It had been Penny who had framed an innocuous question, asking if Hussein knew of any other investments, or business ventures, in which the Sacranies were involved. Hussein glazed into space for a long time as though searching his memory. He then gave an ironic smile and replied, 'A few years ago I attended a charity dinner.' As though talking to himself he asked, 'Where was it? When was it? Who was that man?'

Hussein continued, 'It was at least two to three years ago. It was held at the Palace Hotel in the city ... it was to raise money for local children ... but I can't remember the actual charity. It was one of those events where you change tables between courses; to mix and meet others at the dinner.'

Hussein paused as if trying to recollect the event and order his comments. 'During the meal I moved to a different table and sat next to a banker. He had his name, and that of the bank, on a name tag like me and so I knew what he did. I remember him vaguely because he thanked me for introducing the Sacranies to his bank, but I never introduced them! We used four banks and his wasn't one of them. He mentioned something about a garage development but I wasn't really interested. I probably moved to another table as soon as I could to get away from him.'

Hussein paused again and then said, 'I probably have his business card; it will be in my card box in my office. I never throw them away because you are never sure when a contact will be useful. I will only have a few cards from bankers so we can trace him – if he is still around.'

Within the hour Penny had collected the slim wooden card box from Hussein's secretary. Back at the police station the three of them were sifting through the cards looking for those from bankers. They found seven, but it took Hussein only seconds to identify the one from the banker. A simple phone call to the bank located the banker and set up an urgent meeting. A police request for help in connection with money laundering got an immediate response! Although cooperative it did take some time for the bank to provide the information Asif wanted. The Sacranies had indeed invested in a site in Dubai and developed the *Deutsch Auto Centre,* due east of the CBD, the Commercial Business District, in Al Warqa, just off the E44 road. The banker had explained that once the required written requests were provided the bank would release detailed information about the various financial transactions. He did reveal that the profits from the car sales were significant. Asif was given both the showroom address and the UK address of the principal investor. It was Abdul Sacranie.

Asif told Hussein about the *Deutsch Auto Centre* and asked if the Sacranies had ever mentioned it. Hussein forced a smile, and snorted air through his nose as though in displeasure, as he sat back in his chair. 'It's an impressive place. They specialise in high quality, almost new, German cars. On his last visit Abdul gave me a Mercedes E350 as a birthday gift. I didn't know that he owned the place.'

Asif instructed Hussein to phone his driver and to have the car driven to the Mercedes main agent in the city where he should deliver the car to the manager. He then suspended the interview. As Asif walked into the observation room, next to the interview room, he was beaming with both fists clenched.

'I think we've got them,' he said through clenched teeth. 'I need to phone one of my colleagues so he can be at the garage and check the car. I think we will find the Mercedes was stolen in Europe and shipped to Dubai by the Sacranie Shipping Agency. I think they are selling stolen cars and using the money to fund the farms in India.'

The car was indeed stolen and the confirmation prompted another flurry of activity as Asif coordinated the paperwork for the simultaneous arrests of garage and showroom staff. At the same time Ellie contacted the Acting Deputy Director of HM Border Force in the UK to arrange the simultaneous arrests of the Sacranie family and their staff in Liverpool and India. The list of arrests to be made grew and it was past midnight, as Hussein slept in his cell, that Ellie and Penny started to relax. They believed they had cracked a major criminal enterprise and it felt good.

Postscript

Soloman Abraham Mbano and Mohammed Kihva Nampaya were deported from the UK to Tanzania. They were arrested immediately on arrival in Dar es Saalam. They await trial, with accomplices, upon a number of charges including the supply of illegal arms, attempted murder and murder. Information received by the Tanzania authorities have enabled other associates, in Libya, to be detained and an arsenal of weapons to be secured.

Aashi, Abdul and Amir Sacranie were arrested in Liverpool and were remanded in custody. They continue to help the police and HM Border Force with their enquiries. Charges against Neelam Sacranie were dropped. Indian authorities arrested several farm managers who are awaiting trial. Unfortunately the whereabouts of the staff of OK Osman Bros, Mumbai, is currently unknown.

Penny Pendleton-Price continues her year of training as an HM Border Force Officer.

Jack Collier and Sandro Marcus Calovarlo decided to take a holiday together and, at leisure, decide the future direction of their company. They agreed to join Kev Donnelly on a liveaboard in the Celebes Sea off the northern coast of Indonesia. They planned to spend a quiet two weeks mapping underwater routes for recreational divers.

To date there is no information on the person, or persons, who sought to procure the Chinese missiles. The investigation is ongoing.